Margaret Hilliard,

a daughter of the rich, kept a tryst with Death in a lonely park at night—

But who killed her, and why?

THE STREETS OF SHADOW

By Leslie McFarlane

First Fiction House Press Edition March 2018

First published in *Munsey's Magazine* in 1929

ISBN 978-1947964327

www.FictionHousePress.com

CHAPTER I
THE DARK CAVALIER

LOUDS drifted across the moon. The park was sinister with shadow. Trees creaked, dead leaves skittered, clumps of dry brush rustled in the wind. Mount Royal loomed black and gigantic against the sky, and at its base, in the deserted gloom of grassy slopes, the little green benches were forlorn.

Constable Gervais looked up at the gigantic cross that blazes its electric benediction upon Montreal from the summit of the mountain. He felt the little tingle of awe that he always experienced when he saw the immense symbol that appeared suspended between heaven and earth, stark and terrible against the sky. It was odd, he reflected, that, although the cross was usually comforting and friendly, on autumn evenings such as this it seemed forbidding and austere.

He shrugged. It was all in the weather.

The park was dismal these nights, and the mountain was a dreary place. No wonder the blazing cross lacked its customary warmth. Gervais was a devout

The image of this girl was stamped indelibly on Brent's memory

man, and as his heavy boots resounded *clop-clop* on the pavement he mused on his chances of a glorious resurrection and toyed gloomily with thoughts of the death that comes like a blighting wind to leaves and men alike.

That was the effect the cross had on him now. He wasn't quite as cheerful as usual. The park is at its worst in autumn. In spring and summer there are the strolling couples, the whispering lovers, and up on the mountain driveway the carriages and clattering horses; in winter there are the snowshoes, the sleighs with jangling bells, the tobogganists away over on the slide; but on the chilly nights of fall the pathways are deserted.

For this reason Gervais was interested when a girl, who had been walking quickly down the street toward him, left the pavement and went up one of the rustling, shadowy paths. There was a light just at that point, and in its radiance he could see her quite clearly. She wore a neat little red hat and a fawn-colored coat; he had a distinct impression that she was young and very pretty.

Then she went into the gloom of the path under the trees, dead leaves brushed aside by her twinkling little shoes.

It was not very late, but he took particular notice of the girl because few people came to the park these evenings, and seldom a young girl alone. He reasoned, however, that she was doubtless going to meet her lover, and he would have put the matter from his mind had it not been for the appearance of a man who turned swiftly around a clump of bushes that obscured a bend in the street.

The newcomer moved into the light with a certain deadly grace, as lithe and silent as some beast of prey, and it was not until he caught sight of Gervais that he slackened his speed. Then, with an obvious effort at nonchalance, he slowed down to an idle stroll.

A subtle aura of evil clung to the dark figure as he passed Gervais. The man's keen, pallid face, the smooth silence of his gait, aroused the constable's instinctive hostility.

Psychiatrists may differ on the existence of a definite criminal type, but in the mind of Constable Gervais there was no doubt. He always maintained that the habitual criminal could be distinguished at a glance. Intelligent police officers, he firmly believed, develop a sort of sixth sense in this respect; he considered himself intelligent, and his sixth sense told him that this man was of the enemy.

They eyed one another warily. In the pallid man's sidelong glance there was a lurking defiance, as though he had said aloud: "You may think what you like. You have nothing against me."

And by the same subtle language, in which no word was spoken, Gervais told the stranger: "Be very careful, my friend. I have my eye on you."

The constable strode ponderously ahead. He vanished beyond the clump of trees at the bend. There, however, he halted. He stepped off the pavement into the dry turf, returned toward the bushes. Sheltered by the mass of branches, he watched the man.

The fellow had stopped. He was looking back. He seemed to be deciding something. Then, as though he had made up his mind, he turned and sped swiftly toward the entrance of the path.

The gloom engulfed him as it had engulfed the girl.

It was never the policy of Gervais to interfere with lovers, but he was quite convinced that this was not a rendezvous. In the first place, the girl was obviously of a class remote in the social scale from that of the man. One could tell that at a glance. And, in the second case, he had been following her with a predatory intensity that could not be mistaken.

Gervais went back to the path.

To his surprise he found that the girl had not ventured far into the depths of the park. He could just distinguish the vague blur of the fawn-colored coat. The man was approaching her.

The constable's feet crunched in the gravel as he strode up the path.

As he drew near, he saw that the girl was frightened. She was twisting and untwisting her gloves in her hands, and even in the gloom he saw the expression of panic on her face.

The man watched him sullenly.

"Well?" growled Gervais.

The man shuffled uneasily.

"What's the matter?" he demanded in a metallic voice.

"That's what I want to know." Gervais turned to the girl. " Is this fellow annoyin' you, miss?"

"I didn't say nothin'," whined the man. "I never said a word to her."

The moon emerged from behind a cloud just then, cold silver beyond the tracery of branches, and in its pallid glow the head and shoulders of the fellow were revealed. His face was gray and tense.

"He followed me in here," said the girl, hesitantly. She had a low, musical voice.

"I gotta right to walk on the path. I didn't say nothin'."

"You got no right to annoy girls. Was he botherin' you, miss? Say the word, and I'll run him in."

She seemed nervous and agitated.

"No. Please don't do that. I don't want any trouble. I was just—it doesn't matter. He didn't speak to me."

The man appeared relieved. Evidently he had been expecting the worst.

"You see!" he said impudently. "She says herself that I wasn't annoyin' her."

Gervais was disconcerted.

"None of your lip, or I'll run you in as a vag."

The man thrust his hand into a side pocket and produced a few silver coins which he jingled mockingly.

"There's my visible means of support. You've got me all wrong, cop. All wrong. The park is free. I got a right to walk here if I want to."

"Well, then—walk!"

"Sure. I'll keep right on the way I was goin'. That all right with you?"

"Beat it!"

The man wheeled about and strode jauntily up the path. With a puzzled glance at the distressed face of the girl, Constable Gervais turned back toward the street.

“Thank you very much, officer,” she said.

“That’s all right, miss.” Gervais was annoyed because she had made no complaint against the man. He felt that he had blundered.

“I was really frightened. But I didn’t want to cause any trouble, as long as you drove him away. After all, he didn’t actually speak to me, although I think he was going to. I’ll be all right now.”

She made no move to go away. She was standing close by one of the park benches, in front of a dense mass of bushes.

“All right, miss.”

Gervais touched his helmet and departed. There was something strange about the whole business, but it was evidently none of his affair. He went back to the pavement. Once he looked behind. The girl was standing where he had left her, in the somber shadow of the trees.

He wondered if she really knew the pallid-faced man after all, and if the fellow would return. Well, he had given her the chance to make a complaint if she wished.

The incident had been the only break in the tedious routine of his patrol that evening, and he pondered idly on it. Some strange things happen in the city. Thousands and thousands of people, their lives touching and mingling in the oddest ways—it is really tremendous, when you come to think of it.

You have no idea of the enormity of the city unless you go up on the driveway, to the Lookout, beneath the cross. There you can look down on the great, glowing ocean of lights, twinkling and shimmering away off to east and west, with a black gap where the St. Lawrence flows darkly, and then little clusters of lights on the distant shore, far, far, right to the black horizon where they can scarcely be distinguished from the stars.

That girl, now. She was one of the million down there, and she had come to this park, no doubt, to meet a man, another of the million, and they both thought it was vastly important. Constable Gervais, who was somewhat of a philosopher, wagged his head. And at that moment he heard a scream!

It rose high and sharp, vibrant with sheer terror, and it ended abruptly, blotted out by the explosive report of a shot.

Gervais stiffened, whirled about, peered into the whispering gloom of the park. Then he broke into a run, pounding along the pavement, back toward the path he had just quitted. The scream and the shot seemed to emanate from the place where he had left the girl.

He reached the path.

Among the dead leaves beside the bench, at the foot of the massed bushes, he saw the fawn coat, the little red hat. The girl lay motionless and silent beside the path. Gervais had almost reached the huddled form when he heard a sharp snapping of twigs and branches, the thud of footsteps and the scuffling of leaves farther ahead.

He plunged past the body by the bushes, and ran on up the path. Then, over to one side, he heard the footsteps again. He went scrambling through a thicket. Away off in the gloom beneath the trees he saw an indistinct figure, running swiftly.

Gervais whipped out his revolver.

"Stop!"

Head down, racing toward the friendly shadows, the fugitive paid no heed.

Gervais fired a shot over the man's head. The fellow did not stop. He dodged to one side, plunging into the undergrowth. Gervais lost sight of him, but stumbled across the grass in pursuit.

The fugitive had miscalculated. He was hampered by the clinging bushes. There was a tremendous commotion as he strove to free himself. Gervais came up just as the man lurched wildly out of the crackling tangle. The fellow tripped over a root and went sprawling.

Gervais pounced on him as he groaned and struggled to rise. He clapped a heavy hand on the man's shoulder and dragged him to his feet.

"All right," snarled the prisoner. "What's it all about?"

The same metallic voice. Gervais peered at him. In the dim light he distinguished the hard features of the man he had accosted on the path.

"You again, eh? Come out here!"

He hustled his captive out into the open.

"Honest to God, officer, I don't know nothin' about it," the fellow blurted. "I went right away like you told me to, and—"

"Shut up!"

Gervais ran his hands expertly over the man's pockets. He encountered a suspicious bulge, and on investigation discovered a heavy automatic.

"That," he said, with satisfaction, "fixes you."

The prisoner was silent. Gervais snapped handcuffs about his wrists. "Come along!" He gripped his captive by one arm and jostled him roughly across the grass.

"So it was a bumpin' off, was it?" Gervais said grimly.

"I never done it, I tell you."

"You're under arrest," the constable told him, in the formula. "Anything you say may be used against you."

The fellow plodded along with a docile, sullen resignation. Once in a while the steel links jangled.

Gervais hastened. He could still hear that dreadful scream, like a shaft of steel piercing the cloak of night. Dead gray grass swayed in the wind. The open sward, vivid under the ghostly moon, was bare.

They reached the path. Here the prisoner's steps became more reluctant.

The girl still lay among the leaves beside the bench.

Gervais switched on his flash light.

Dead in the center of its circular radiance she lay, head flung back, fists clenched, and the impudent little red hat awry.

Very carefully, so as not to obliterate possible footprints in the gravel, the constable crouched over her.

His prisoner stood gloomily submissive, like a statue in the moonlight, his head bowed, his shackles reflecting little glints of silver.

Gervais looked down at the dead face of the girl. Pity and wrath gripped him. He muttered something in a husky voice.

She was beautiful, and she had died in fear.

CHAPTER II
AN OPEN-AND-SHUT CASE

HE afternoon business in the Fleur de Lis Tavern did not properly begin until Mr. Michael Brent slipped into his favorite chair at his usual table and quaffed his customary mug of dark beer, medium.

The afternoon business for Mr. Michael Brent did not properly begin until the rite at the Fleur de Lis had been concluded, and inasmuch as the fame of the tavern's special brew of dark beer had spread among Mr. Brent's cronies and kindred spirits, often luring them to the place at indecently early hours to begin the day's guzzling, it was frequently well on in the afternoon before the lawyer clambered the stairs of the old stone building across the road and entered his office.

In this two-room lair, the windows of which were apparently never washed, and the desks seemingly never cleared of a wilderness of papers, lurked Minton.

A word as to Minton.

His value, the lawyer often asserted, was above rubies. He was Michael Brent's clerk, stenographer, bookkeeper, office boy, messenger, adviser and confidant.

Minton had waded through a large legal library and remembered it all. He ordered his life by an invisible time clock. He did not drink; he did not smoke; he did not swear; he was a bit apologetic concerning his one vice of chewing gum; he was an elder of the church, and father of a minor domestic congregation numbering seven.

Minton wrote excellent briefs, handled all Brent's office routine, and never asked for an increase in salary. He had innocent eyes, scanty hair, big ears, a small mouth, a meek expression and an Adam's apple that bobbled when he talked, which was seldom.

"The perfect clerk!" said Michael Brent, discussing this treasure with his crony, Dryborough, owner of the secondhand bookshop across the way. "He looks after the detail. I do the heavy thinking."

Dryborough, a fat little man who always looked sadder and wearier than any fat little man has a right to look, raised his mug of dark (large) and sniffed.

"You mean he looks after the work, and you do the heavy drinking."

" I don't drink. I like beer, but I don't drink."

Dryborough ignored this sophistry.

"Some day," he said, "that paragon of meekness and efficiency will get wise to himself and go work for somebody else. Then where will you be?"

Having delivered himself of this prophecy and propounded this inquiry, Dryborough squinted sorrowfully into his beer, sighed and took a gurgling drink.

"In the first place," answered Brent, smoothing his neat black beard, " Minton will never leave me."

"Don't be too sure."

"He is perfectly happy and contented where he is. Minton has found his predestined niche in the social structure. He is well paid, we understand each other, he enjoys his work, and I see that he gets lots of it."

"I have no doubt of that."

"In the second place, if Minton ever *should* leave me, which is absurd, I would simply get another clerk. I would not get one quite as admirable as Minton, but I would get a good one. The woods are full of earnest, industrious toilers who have an enormous capacity for detail, but who lack the broader vision."

Michael Brent thereupon took a sip of beer, with an air of great complacency. He was a picturesque, genial-looking man with twinkling blue eyes, a mop of curly black hair above a good forehead, and firm white teeth beneath his carefully trimmed mustache.

He was picturesque, first because of a beard in an age when the beard is in disfavor; secondly because of his attire, which was odd, careless, and suited him amazingly. He wore a soft black felt hat, exceedingly battered, a soft white shirt with a low collar that showed his fine neck to advantage, and a black silk necktie.

Although he was the *enfant terrible* of the Montreal bar, he did not in the least look the part of a man of law, nor would any one have guessed his age as being but thirty.

Minton and I," he was saying, "team up beautifully. He is a shark in the office, but a dub in court. The drudgery of preparing a case annoys me, but in court—aha! With Minton's spadework, with my generalship—"

"And your copious supply of hot air," suggested the crony rudely.

"With my command of language, I proceed to confound the opposition, convince the bench, move the jury to tears of sympathy or murmurs of indignation as required, and walk out with a verdict. Without Minton, I admit, I might not do so well. But then, on the other hand, where would Minton be without me? He has a head chuck full of legal facts, but who wants 'em? You can buy a library of legal facts for so much down and so much a month. I know, because the draft on mine is due to-morrow."

"Why buy a library when you have Minton?"

"I have asked myself that question over and over again. But, as I was saying, Minton's truly appalling stock of knowledge would be a drug on the market if he didn't have me to present it in its most salable form. Minton himself couldn't go into court and do anything but make a hopeless ass of himself in the simplest of cases. But toss him a dozen scrambled facts in a real estate tangle in the privacy of the office, and the man can do juggling feats that would surprise you. I could defend a confessed murderer on five minutes' notice and make a fair fist of it—"

"But ask you to draw up a bill of sale!"

"It would give me such a severe headache that I would have to hurry over here and tell Alphonse to draw me my usual mug of dark, medium. In fact, the very thought of it gives me a headache, so—"

He raised one forefinger in a gesture well known to Alphonse, who promptly drew the usual mug of dark, medium.

"Sometimes," said Dryborough, "you amuse me. At

other times you give me a pain. You call yourself a lawyer, but you act like a son of the idle rich, and you dress like the movie idea of an artist. Or is it a Bolshevik? I confess that it puzzles me. Why don't you shave?"

Pleased, the subject of these remarks glanced at his reflection in the mirror and fondled the black beard lovingly.

"Frankly, I don't like shaving. I'm too lazy. But I try to convince myself that it is because I believe the Creator meant that men should be bearded. And then, the average jury has a tremendous respect for a lawyer with a beard. It gives me added years, dignity and wisdom. When I was first called to the bar, I was very shy—"

"Impossible!" breathed Dryborough.

"It's a fact. I lacked confidence. But I found that behind the protection of a beard, my other self had a chance to assert itself. I also found that I picked up a number of clients, who mistook me for a Frenchman, who would not have intrusted their cases to an Irishman under any circumstances. That disposes of the beard and this very elegant mustache. As for my black hat, my silk tie, and my annoying habit of always finding you in the tavern when you should be in your shop—"

Michael Brent's explanation of these Bohemian details was interrupted by the appearance of Minton, who had entered the Fleur de Lis with the apprehensive timidity of a maiden setting foot in the red light district.

"What's the trouble, Minty?"

The faithful servant blinked reproachfully at his

employer through silver-rimmed spectacles. "Have you forgotten the Lewis case, Mr. Brent? You promised to see him this afternoon."

"The Lewis case? H-m! Thank you, Minty. Thank you. As a matter of fact, I *had* forgotten the Lewis case. I have a recollection of being dragged out of bed at some unholy hour last night by a telephone call from Hinky Lewis or a detective or somebody. The inconsiderate ass has killed somebody, hasn't he?"

"It's quite serious this time," said Minton. "Murder."

"Hinky is progressing. Last time it was robbery, wasn't it?"

Five years, Mr. Brent. He just got out a week ago."

"He stayed out of trouble an entire week! Well, I suppose I'd better go down and see him. He was remanded this morning, wasn't he?"

"Yes, sir."

"I was busy in another court. I didn't have time."

"He is very anxious to see you, sir."

"All right. I'll be there." Brent waved Minton away, and as the apostle of righteousness glided off to the comparative purity of the street, he murmured: "I don't know what I'd do without that man. I really don't."

"I do," said Dryborough. "You'd starve."

Unperturbed, the lawyer beckoned to Alphonse. "To-day's newspaper."

Alphonse produced the paper from behind the bar, and Brent quickly scanned the front page. "Here it is," he said at last, and read: " 'Girl brutally slain in Mount Royal Park.' "

"Your client is in deep," remarked Dryborough.

"H-m! Looks like it. Somehow, it doesn't sound like Hinky. However, we'll see."

Brent rapidly perused the newspaper account. A girl about twenty years old was shot, shortly after nine o'clock the previous night, in one of the park pathways. Her identity has not yet been established. An arrest was made: John ("Hinky") Lewis, thirty-eight, who had been released from St. Vincent de Paul Penitentiary just a week previous, a man with a lengthy criminal record.

Lewis was seen running from the scene of the crime, and was taken into custody by a constable who had heard the shot. An automatic was found in his pocket. One shell had been ejected. Footprints of Lewis were found in the path, close by the body.

Constable Gervais, who made the arrest, had noticed Lewis following the girl into the park and he had warned the man away. Less than five minutes later he heard a scream, followed by the fatal shot.

Brent read the account through to the end.

"I think you have a job on your hands," observed Dryborough.

"It looks like an open-and-shut case, I'll admit. No wonder my client wanted me down there on the run. I guess he's about ready to yelp for another lawyer by now. But I was so confoundedly busy this morning I didn't have a minute to spare—and then Hinky slipped my mind."

"Those hard-boiled detectives will probably have a complete confession out of him by now."

"Oh, no. Hinky is an old-timer. 'Beyond asserting his innocence, Lewis maintained a stubborn silence under a severe grilling by detectives at headquarters.' I'd better go down and see him. He'll want a little encouragement."

"You'll defend him?" asked Dryborough, scandalized.

"Of course," Brent answered airily. "A prisoner is assumed to be innocent until he is found guilty, you know."

"In theory. You know perfectly well that most people assume he must be guilty; otherwise he wouldn't be a prisoner. Your client may be an estimable and persecuted citizen, but if that newspaper account is correct, I think he ought to be lynched."

"How bloodthirsty we are this afternoon! The newspapers don't always get all the facts. Hinky is not a killer."

"Oh, no!"

"No! He's yellow! He might beat a woman up, but he wouldn't kill her."

" Charming fellow."

"Very interesting. I'll have you meet him after he has been acquitted."

"I'd rather have a ticket for the hanging. I've never seen a hanging, and this looks like a good opportunity."

"Long life to Hinky!" said Brent, drinking the rest, of his beer. " It's too bad he's only been out of the pen a week. My fee will be small. Still, he has friends."

Mr. Dryborough shook his head slowly and helplessly. Brent was too much for him. Then he reached for the newspaper to read the account for himself.

Brent set the black hat at a rakish angle, patted the silk necktie, gave the little black mustache a twirl and smoothed the black beard that gave him the aspect of an amiable Saracen. With a flash of white teeth the lawyer bade his crony good afternoon, flipped a coin to

Alphonse, and left the tavern.

CHAPTER III
A THOUSAND-TO-ONE SHOT

TWENTY minutes later, Mr. Brent was in conference with Hinky Lewis.

His client, shifty-eyed, and with the penitentiary pallor still upon him, tried to affect a lofty confidence, but was obviously frightened. The nervousness was in no way allayed when Brent, after hearing his story, remarked that it sounded very thin.

"Juries are saps, but it will be hard to find twelve saps who are sappy enough to swallow that one. Think again, Hinky."

"But I'm tellin' the truth, Mr. Brent," protested Hinky. "I never bumped the dame off. The flattie picked me up just because he saw me runnin' away."

"Can you blame him? Come clean with me now, Hinky. They got plenty on you. You were in the park."

Lewis nodded sullenly. "Yeah."

"And you were following this girl?"

"Well—it was this way—"

"Why?"

"Mr. Brent, I'll give you the straight dope on this. I

was just driftin' along the street when this dame ankles past, and as she goes by she kinda gives me a look, see?"

"The come-hither?"

"Well, I dunno. I couldn't figger it out. But you know how the janes fall for me—"

"Sure. You've always considered yourself quite a sheik, Hinky. If a woman even glances at you, you think you've made a hit. You got it into your head that this jane might be easy pickings, eh?"

"Well, she was alone, and down around the park you often pick up some pretty swell frails. Anyway, I figgered maybe she was givin' me the eye, so I trailed along."

"You think well of yourself, don't you, Hinky?"

"She turned up into this path, see? And just when I was catchin' up with her, along breezes this cop. Well, he looks me over kinda nasty, so I kept right on goin'. But when he got outa sight I beat it up the path after this jane. She was standin' right by one of the benches. Well, I figgered she had been givin' me the eye, after all, so I steps up and was just goin' to pass the time of day, when along comes the cop again. He'd spotted me."

"He put the bee on you, eh?"

"Well, there would have been an argument, but this jane kinda stood up for me. I figgered I was in for it, because when I got close I seen she was a lady—a flapper, you know, but a lady. But she seemed kinda nervous and queer, and when the cop was itchin' to get his hands on me, this jane said there wasn't no trouble and everythin' was all right. Well, I was mighty relieved, I can tell you. So the cop buzzes off, sore as a boil, after tellin' me to beat it."

"So I suppose you came back again?"

"Well, I figgered the dame couldn't be very sore at me, and mebbe she wanted me to come back."

"Your conceit has landed you in a fine mess."

"I was just comin' back down the path, and I could see her a little way ahead, when I saw her turn around sudden, toward the bushes. Then she lets this screech out of her. Honest to God, Mr. Brent, I never heard nothin' like it in all my life! I was so damn scared I just stood there, stiff. And then came the shot. And the jane tumbled over."

"And you beat it?"

"I wasn't goin' to stick around. First thing I figgered was that it wouldn't look so hot for me to be nabbed right there, after the bull puttin' the bee on me a little while before. I beat it, but this flattie came up so quick I didn't have no time, and he got me."

"Where did the shot come from?"

"Near as I could figger, it come from the bushes. I think she must have heard the guy in there move when he stood up, and she saw him just as he was bringin' the gun down. She hollered, and then he fired."

"How about your footprints?"

"They got there when I come up to speak to this jane the first time."

" And the gun?"

"Well, I was packin' a rod."

"One shot fired."

"That's where I get a tough break. There was a little caper over in Verdun the other night, and I had to scare a guy."

There was a long silence. Michael Brent lit a cigarette.

"You're damned if you do, and damned if you don't, Hinky."

"If I don't what?"

"Tell the truth. If you cover up, you're hooked on circumstantial evidence. If you tell the yarn you just told me, they won't believe it. You haven't an alibi. You'll have a tough time explaining why you were following that girl around. Honestly, Hinky, it doesn't look good. It makes it a lot easier for me when I can believe the yarn a client tells me, but this one gags a bit."

"It's the truth."

"Come clean, now."

"I never bumped her off!" insisted Lewis doggedly, his voice rising.

Michael Brent had been looking directly into the man's eyes when he told his story; not once had they narrowed to betray a lie; now he sat back.

"All right, Hinky. I believe you. But it's mighty few that would."

"I got a tough break. Evcrythin' worked fine for the guy that did the job. The cop was so busy chasin' me that this other bird just walked away."

"The only point in your favor is that nobody saw you do it. But if they don't find the other guy, it's curtains for you."

The prisoner moistened his lips.

"They're liable to look hard for him, too," he muttered ironically.

"That's just the trouble. They've got you, and there's a nice, open-and-shut case against you, all built up and ready-made. They're not going out looking for more work. You've only got one chance, Hinky, and that's the chance that something will break to turn up the guy who did kill her."

"A thousand-to-one shot."

"Maybe we can shorten the odds. I'm going to nose around a bit. You don't know any more about this girl than what you've told me?"

"Never saw her before, I tell you. They ain't even found out her name yet."

"Funny they can't find out who she is. I'm going to trot over to the morgue and have a look at her."

"You won't throw me down, Mr. Brent? I've come clean with you."

"Keep your mouth shut and sit tight, Hinky. I'll poke around and see what I can pick up. When they identify this girl I may be able to get a better line on things. I'll see you later."

He put on his hat.

"Don't run away, Hinky."

And, with this pleasantry, Mr. Michael Brent left his client and departed for the morgue.

CHAPTER IV
IN THE TRANSOM

UCK flipped a valuable card to Michael Brent. He reached the morgue just a few minutes after the murder victim had been identified. Even before the news could be flashed to police headquarters, he was talking with the frightened woman who had recognized the body on the slab.

This woman was housekeeper of the home in which the girl had lived. As she answered Brent's hurried questions she sobbed convulsively, dabbing at her reddened eyes with a handkerchief.

The name of the murdered girl, she said, was Margaret Hilliard. She was the only daughter of a wealthy Nova Scotia family, and she had been living in Montreal for two years, as a university student, at the home of her aunt, a widow. The aunt was away from the city at the time.

"I didn't think there was anything wrong when she didn't come back last night," sobbed the woman. " She said she might stay with a girl friend. It wasn't until noon that one of her chums called up and asked why Margaret had missed lectures this morning. Then I happened to pick up the newspaper—" She broke down and wept hysterically.

Do you know any reason why any one should seek her life?"

At first the woman could not answer. Then she stammered that the whole affair was unbelievable. Margaret, she insisted, hadn't an enemy in the world.

Overcome by shock and grief, she fell to sobbing uncontrollably. Brent knew he had little time, for detectives would reach the morgue in a few minutes. Apparently headquarters had neglected to station a man there to pick up clews, as is usually done in murder cases, which was another lucky break for the defendant. Even at that, whatever advantage Brent might gain would have to be gained quickly.

"A love affair?" he suggested.

Evidently this struck a responsive chord. The woman looked up at him, her plump, homely face stained with tears.

"She had. Oh, yes—she had. She had a love affair. They were engaged."

"His name?"

But the woman was weeping too violently to reply.

"Do you know his name?"

"Paul!" she gasped.

"His last name?"

"Gregory."

"He will have to know. Can you tell me where he lives?"

"It will—break—his heart," she said in a choking whisper. "They loved each other so much."

"His address?" insisted Brent.

"The Majestic Apartments. It's—it's on Sherbrooke East."

An attendant approached them, solicitous about the woman, who was being detained for questioning. Brent could ask her nothing more. He had learned something at any rate.

When he saw that she was being looked after, the lawyer departed quickly and unobtrusively, hailed a taxi, and within ten minutes arrived at the Majestic Apartments.

The Majestic belied its name. It was one of those shabby old stone buildings that rise in solid phalanxes on the residential thoroughfares of down town Montreal. It was the same to-day as it had been yesterday and would be tomorrow; a house that differed scarcely a particle from the houses on either side and those that ranged away to left and right the length of the block—cold, gray and inscrutable.

They all had the same flight of steps from the street, the same impersonal bay windows, the same dingy card in the door, indicating that apartments were to let, the same air of having come down in the world.

In the lobby Michael Brent studied the inevitable card rack, and found that Paul Gregory occupied No. 12, which was presumably on the top floor.

So he went up two flights of stairs through the usual strata of cabbage odors to a more rarefied atmosphere where the fragrance was compounded of illuminating gas and the weekly wash. There, in a dark and narrow hallway, he discovered the door of No. 12.

His peremptory knocks, however, brought no response. He began to reflect that he had been unduly hasty. Gregory would not be in his rooms at this hour of the day. Probably, like the girl, he was a university student.

Brent was about to turn away with the intention of seeking out the janitor for further information, when he happened to glance up at the transom.

It was slanted at a sharp angle, at such a degree that the glass had become a mirror reflecting more or less clearly the interior of the room beyond. And although Michael Brent's first glance had been casual, he stiffened abruptly, then raised himself on tiptoe and stared.

Distorted, fragmentary and inverted was the reflection, but it was clear enough to reveal the figure of a man sprawled on his back on the floor of the little living room.

As the lawyer moved forward in his astonishment, the transom glass became transparent again and the dreadful picture vanished.

He recovered the angle of vision; the room leaped into view once more; there lay the man on the floor, arms outflung, face up—a dead body.

For almost a full minute the lawyer gazed at this astounding reflection. Then he murmured "Lovely dyin' Dora!" and hastened in search of the janitor. In a short time he returned with that functionary, who received with surly indifference the news that there had been an accident in No. 12.

"What kind of an accident?" he growled, fumbling for his keys.

Brent indicated the transom. "You can see the reflection. There's a man lying on the floor."

The janitor glanced up.

"Somethin' wrong," he admitted grudgingly. "Mebbe he's only drunk."

He opened the door. They stood on the threshold of the little apartment. The transom glass had played no tricks. A young man in trousers, slippers and white shirt lay rigid in death in the middle of the room. There was a queer noise in the janitor's throat.

"He's dead!"

"Who is he?"

The janitor turned a vaguely astonished face toward Mr. Brent.

"The guy that lived here. Gregory. Don't you know him?"

"I've never seen him before. I just called on business."

They stepped into the room and the janitor circled the body warily.

"Good God! There's blood here—look at his head! Why—say—he didn't just die. He was *killed!*"

"Murdered!"

"His skull is all caved in. Look!"

The janitor was gibbering; he stared at the gruesome object at his feet, with a sort of horrified fascination.

"And that's Gregory?" asked Brent.

"Sure it's him. Say—I'd better call the police, eh? This is a dirty mess. A hell of a note. It 'll be hard to rent this apartment again."

Brent stepped gingerly across the floor and looked down at the distorted face of the dead youth.

"Looks to me as though he's been dead for some time. When did you see him last?"

"I dunno. Yesterday mornin'."

"At what time?"

"About eight o'clock. I was sweepin' the steps. Gosh—to think he'd be lyin' here like this! The police—"

"Do you know what he did for a living?"

The janitor shrugged.

"I dunno. He was in an office somewhere."

"What time did he come back yesterday?"

"I never seen him. He usually got back about six o'clock and changed his clothes and went out to eat."

"But you didn't see him come back yesterday afternoon?"

"No."

"You didn't hear him? Didn't see a light in his room?"

"No. I'm downstairs mostly."

"You don't know whether the light was on in his apartment last night?"

"No. Say, mister, what's—"

"Did any one call here for him yesterday?"

"How should I know? People are comin' and goin' all the time, around here. I never pay no attention."

"You don't know if any one called on him last night? Some one must have been with him—did you see anybody coming into the building or going out that you didn't recognize?"

The man shook his head. "I was down in the basement. That's where I live. There was different people goin' up and down the front steps, but I never looked out."

"What kind of a chap was Gregory?" asked Brent, gesturing toward the rigid form on the floor.

"I dunno. He never had much to say. He paid his

rent regular."

"Quiet?"

"Sure."

"Didn't give you any trouble?"

"No. He wasn't like some that are always throwin' wild parties and raisin' hell. He seemed a nice sort of a guy."

"Did he have many friends? People who came to see him?"

"Not that I ever saw."

"Women?"

"I never saw none. I don't nose around upstairs much. I mind my own business."

"How long has Gregory been living here?"

"About five months, I guess. What are you askin' all these questions for anyway? What were you callin' on him for? I'm gonna call the police about this, and you'd better not go away, neither."

Brent realized he could learn little more from the janitor.

"Don't worry about me," he said. "I'll stick around."

The man went over to the wall telephone and called police headquarters. While he was excitedly and almost incoherently telling of the discovery in No. 12, Brent looked about him.

The apartment consisted of three small rooms, living room, bedroom and bath. The living room had one window overlooking a dingy courtyard; it was plainly furnished, with a table, a bookshelf, a few chairs. One of these chairs, over by the window, was overturned. The lawyer eyed it reflectively.

"There must have been a bit of a fight," he said to himself.

The door of the bedroom was open, and he glanced casually into the chamber. The small bed was made, but carelessly, as though by a masculine hand.

A fragment of paper on the floor caught Brent's eye. He stepped into the bedroom and picked it up. There were a few words in a feminine handwriting. He read:

so please don't go any . . .
No. 90 for I am a . . .
dangerous pl . . .
that man . . .
love you too m . . .

Brent smoothed his beard in the characteristic gesture. He turned the paper over. The other side was blank. The note paper was of good quality, and when he sniffed at it he was aware of a faint, subtle perfume.

He heard the janitor's voice: "You'll be right up, eh? No, we won't touch nothin'." Then the telephone receiver clicked, and Brent impulsively thrust the fragment of paper into his pocket. He was well aware that he should disturb nothing, pending arrival of the police, but this fragment of paper interested him, and he wanted a chance to study it further.

The janitor appeared in the doorway, staring at him curiously.

"Police are comin' up right away."

"That's fine. By the way," said Michael Brent, "can you tell me if Mr. Gregory made up his own bed?"

"I guess so. There was a woman came in once a week to clean up, and she made the bed any time she was here."

"When was she here last?"

"Day before yesterday."

"Then Mr. Gregory made his own bed yesterday morning?"

"Wasn't nobody else to do it."

"H-m! The bed hasn't been slept in. That means he was killed last evening."

"It might 'a' been this mornin', after he got up and made his bed," suggested the janitor.

Brent shook his head.

"I think he's been dead quite a while."

He moved out of the bedroom and glanced again at the corpse on the floor. There is something infinitely terrible in the spectacle of a man overtaken by death at the very height of youth and vigor.

The strong fingers were clenched, the lithe limbs were pitiful in their impotence; he was a powerfully built young fellow, and it seemed incredible that the flame of life had gone out of him. He was a man of about twentyseven, tall and broad shouldered, with black hair that still seemed electric with vitality, strong, regular features, white teeth clenched in the death agony.

"Good-looking chap," remarked Brent.

"Too damn bad!" said the janitor, wagging his head. "I can't figger why anybody should want for to bump him off. Right in this house, too! And none of us heard a sound."

"He probably never knew what hit him. Caved in his skull."

The janitor grimaced.

"Rotten way to croak."

They stirred about the room uneasily, waiting for the police. Brent lounged over toward the wall telephone. The directory hung beneath it. Idly he glanced at the blue cover.

On it he saw a few penciled figures, dollar marks, circles and triangles—aimless scribblings that apparently were meaningless. But Brent scrutinized these casual marks closely when he saw dominating the maze, in heavy, black figures, the number 90.

Ninety!

His thoughts flew back to the fragment of paper he had picked up in the bedroom. "Number Ninety," it said. And here was the same number, scribbled on the cover of the telephone directory! It might mean anything. It might mean nothing. But he scanned the cover with a new interest.

A four-figure number, prefaced in each case by "UP," had been written several times—evidently a telephone number in the Uptown exchange. Then there were several diamonds, some large, some small, traced over and over again in pencil, as though done by some one waiting at the telephone for a connection.

Diamonds. They meant nothing. Everybody had some pet hieroglyphic; some people drew circles, some drew faces, some drew squares, while absent-mindedly scribbling.

Brent jotted down the telephone number on the back of an envelope and then gazed, with a puzzled frown, at that heavy, black figure 90.

Had it not been for the fragment of the letter he had found, he would have passed over the number without a second glance. But now it assumed a baffling importance.

Heavy footsteps in the hall heralded the police, and with their arrival the case of Paul Gregory automatically became a public matter, a sensation and a mystery.

Two calm, casual-mannered detectives took charge of Apartment 12, briefly questioned Brent and the janitor, then dismissed them. As the lawyer left, they were methodically going over the apartment in search of fingerprints.

The machinery of the detective bureau had been thrown into gear, and experts, photographers and reporters were hustling on their way up to the Majestic.

CHAPTER V
THE ACE OF DIAMONDS

ICHAEL BRENT went to his office, where he found Minton working industriously, as usual. The faithful servant looked up mildly as he entered.

"A mystery, Minty!" announced Brent, flinging his hat on the desk. "A deep, dreadful, impenetrable mystery!"

"Indeed?"

"Does the number 90 mean anything to you, Minty?"

"Not yet, sir."

Michael Brent subsided into a chair and put his feet up on the desk.

"Not yet? Then there is hope. Put on your thinking cap and we'll ponder."

He took the fragment of paper from his pocket and gazed at it moodily.

"A girl was killed last night. She was shot, Minty. Just a few minutes ago I discovered the body of her *fiancé*, when I went to break the news of the girl's death.

He had been knocked over the head. Our client, Hinky Lewis, is already in jail, being held for the girl's murder, and unless he can prove an alibi it looks very much as if he will be accused of the second killing too."

Having thus begun, Brent told Minton the entire story, interrupted by frequent ejaculations of "Dreadful!" as the clerk's pale eyes bulged perceptibly. He concluded by tossing the little fragment of letter paper across the table and telling of the coincidence of finding the number 90 scribbled among the diamonds and numbers on the cover of the directory.

"I do not aspire to show these very efficient detectives where to get off at," said Brent, after lighting a cigarette. "However, my job is to clear Hinky Lewis, and to clear Hinky Lewis I must prove that some one other than Hinky murdered the girl. The detectives, having a settled conviction that Hinky did murder her, will reason that he also murdered Gregory. My reasoning is that the same person who killed Gregory killed the girl, and that person—"

"Was not Lewis!"

"Exactly. Question—who was it?"

Minton examined the piece of note paper. "You think this should offer a clew?"

"It should help."

"H-m! Good quality paper. The lower left-hand corner of the page. Possibly, Mr. Brent, we could make a guess at some of the unfinished words."

Minton rummaged in a drawer until he found a sheet of personal stationery that he judged would be about the same size as the sheet from which the fragment had been torn. Methodically, he pasted the piece of paper over the lower left-hand corner of the complete sheet.

"Good!" approved Brent. " We should be able to tell fairly accurately, by the size of the handwriting, just how many words would be needed to fill out the lines. Ah! There's our first line already. We already have 'so please don't go any' and there is just about enough room left for one good-sized word or a couple of small ones. The next line follows up with 'Number Ninety,' which is evidently a house number, so we can guess that the missing words were 'more to.' "

Catching the spirit of the game, Minton nodded admiringly.

" 'So please don't go any more to Number Ninety.' That's it, Mr. Brent. That's it!"

He wrote in the two words and surveyed the result.

"In the last line," suggested Minton, "the last word begins with 'm.' Don't you think it should be 'much'? In view of the context I imagine—"

"Right! Put it down, Minty. 'Love you too much' is what we want. And we can take a guess at the broken word in the second line. You will notice she didn't write 'Number Ninety' in full, just the abbreviation and the figures. There is room for a few more small words in the line, but we'll get rid of one of them now. 'Afraid.' "

" 'Number Ninety for I am afraid.' " Minton wrote it down.

"You say, Mr. Brent, that you think this Number Ninety is a house number. Then wouldn't the word in the next line, the one beginning 'pl,' be 'place'?"

"Exactly. It all hangs together. We're making progress. What have we now?"

Minton completed the word and handed the paper to Brent. It now read:

so please don't go any more to . . .
No. 90 for I am afraid . . .
*dangerous pl*ace . . .
that man . . .
*love you too m*uch . . .

Brent was exultant. "It begins to make sense, eh? Now the second line, the whole phrase, is as clear as mud. Three small words to finish up the second line, Minty. Write 'em down. 'It is a.' Do you see?"

"Oh, yes. '*So please don't go any* more to *No. 90 for I am afraid* it is a *dangerous place.*' She was warning him, Mr. Brent!"

"We've got something valuable here. There's no doubt that this letter was a warning. Some woman knew Gregory was in danger. And that danger, somehow, is associated with the number ninety, presumably a house address."

"It disposes of the theory," Minton observed judicially, "that Gregory was murdered in the heat of passion. It was premeditated."

"If we could only find the woman who wrote this letter!"

"Miss Hilliard," suggested the clerk. But Brent shook his head emphatically.

"Evidently she was in danger, too. She and Gregory met the same fate. The warning might have been for her as well."

"But the last line—'love you too much.' The girl was Gregory's *fiancée*, wasn't she?"

"There may have been another woman who loved him too much. And in that case we have a possible murder motive lurking around somewhere. No, I don't think Margaret Hilliard wrote that note. But I'm going around to dig up some more information. If there was a rival in the case, we'll be getting somewhere. As I see it, I must find out who wrote that note."

"And," said Minton, indicating the fourth line of the message, "who is 'that man.' "

The two words had a sinister significance. Behind them loomed a darkly anonymous figure, a cowled shadow of menace.

" 'That man,' " muttered Brent thoughtfully, as he donned his hat. "There are thousands and thousands of men in this city, eh Minty? And one of 'em is 'that man'! We'll hunt him out. We'll find him! I'm going to talk to the housekeeper again and learn all I can."

All eagerness and excitement, he was at the door. Minton was as calm as the proverbial graven image.

"You mentioned seeing diamonds scribbled on the cover of the telephone directory," he said mildly.

Brent paused, one hand on the doorknob. "I don't think they mean anything," he said carelessly. "Just scribblings. When I'm waiting, with a pencil in my hand, I scribble circles. Everybody does something like that. Gregory scribbled diamonds. Some draw faces. The real clew on the directory cover was the number. Ninety!"

"Possibly," agreed Minton. "I was just thinking—of course it mightn't mean anything, but it's just a suggestion—"

"Out with it!"

"It just occurred to me that there is a taxicab company in the city that has a diamond trade-mark. Of course there may be no connection whatever, but it just seems that perhaps Gregory may have had that on his mind."

Michael Brent bestowed a look of approval upon his clerk.

"The Diamond Taxi, of course! Minton, you're a genius! When I find 'that man' and send him to the scaffold, I'm positively going to raise your salary."

CHAPTER VI
A LETTER FROM MARGARET

R. BRENT sometimes claimed that he had eminence in the difficult art of loafing without boredom. His crony, Dryborough, would never admit this.

"When you have no pressing business in hand," said Dryborough, "you are undoubtedly the laziest of all God's creatures, with the possible exception of the great-toed sloth. But when you tackle a bit of work that interests you, I am reminded of a terrier digging out a rat."

Brent didn't like this simile particularly, insisting that inasmuch as work never interested him under any circumstances, nothing that interested him could be termed work, but certainly there was truth in it. Now that he had his teeth in the Hilliard-Gregory case, he was as feverishly eager as any young college graduate going after his first bond sale.

From an afternoon edition he learned the address of the house where Margaret Hilliard had lived. The identification of the girl's body and the discovery of her lover's murder monopolized the front page.

On his way to the house, Brent read the newspaper account of the double tragedy, but it held nothing that he did not already know. Hinky Lewis, he found, had been subjected to another inquisition, but had stubbornly maintained total ignorance of the Gregory murder and complete innocence in the death of the girl.

The atmosphere of the house was one of grief, excitement and dread, like an overwhelming shadow. Brent learned that the name of the woman who had identified Margaret Hilliard's body that morning was Miss Mills. The change in her appearance was startling. Her face was swollen, her eyes red-rimmed from weeping, she seemed dazed. The shock of the girl's tragic death had left her in a state of numbed bewilderment.

She explained, in a voice little higher than a whisper, that detectives had questioned her, and that the ordeal, coming swiftly on the heels of the dreadful experience at the morgue, had been so trying that she was not prepared to discuss the case again. Brent, sympathetic, said he would take up little of her time.

"You know, of course, about Mr. Gregory?"

The woman nodded. " I heard. It—oh, well—it's all too terrible. Unbelievable. I can't believe I'm really awake, and that these things have happened."

"I went to his place because you told me he had been engaged to Miss Hilliard," the lawyer explained. "Now I'm conducting a little independent investigation of my own in this dreadful affair, and, if it isn't too painful for you, I'd be glad if you could tell me a little more about both these young people."

"The engagement—I shouldn't have told you. I

spoke before I thought."

"Why shouldn't you have told me?"

"The engagement hadn't been announced."

"I see."

"It wasn't a formal betrothal. Margaret's family—" She hesitated.

" Yes?"

"She was afraid they wouldn't like Paul. Her aunt wanted her to break it off."

"Had she anything against the man?"

"Nothing, except that he was poor."

"And her people are wealthy?"

Yes. Her aunt wouldn't let Paul come to the house. He was a lovely boy. Clever. He worked for a firm of architects, and of course he wasn't very well off, although he would have been some day. I'm sure of it."

"Gregory's people do not live in the city?"

"No. I think they are farmers."

"I see. Now, I don't suppose you know if any other girl was in love with Gregory?"

"Not that I ever heard of. He was crazy about Margaret."

"Any other chap in love with Miss Hilliard?"

"There was a man," she said slowly, "but she didn't care for him very much, although her aunt favored him. He took her out driving a few times, but she refused most of his invitations. He was a friend of her family."

"Do you know his name?"

"Mr. Starr. Pelham Starr, I believe."

"Living in the city?"

"Yes."

"A friend of the family, you say. Wealthy?"

"He drives a very expensive car."

"You don't know much about him?"

"No. Margaret didn't care for him. He drinks a lot."

"Did he know Gregory?"

"I couldn't say."

"There was no question of rivalry between the two men, as far as you know?"

"I don't know."

Brent switched to another angle.

"Have you any idea why she went to that place in the park last night?"

The question broke the last vestige of the woman's self-control. She sobbed outright, then pillowed her head in her arms, crying softly. After a while she looked up.

"I told the detectives," she said brokenly. "Margaret used to call Paul up often, whenever her aunt was out in the evening. Last night she telephoned some one—I think it was him—and went out immediately afterward."

"Did you overhear the conversation?"

"Some of it. Whatever he said, seemed to disturb her a great deal. She kept saying: 'But why? Don't you know why?' And then she said: 'Can't you possibly tell me?' And finally she said: 'All right. I'll go.' "

"You didn't overhear all her side of the talk?"

"Not the first part. It wasn't until she raised her voice. She seemed excited."

"And then she went out?"

"Immediately. I saw her before she left. She looked very puzzled and worried."

"She didn't offer any explanation?"

"None. When she didn't come back, I was alarmed,

but she often stayed with girl friends when she was out late at parties or dances. In any case, I didn't imagine anything had happened to her. Not until noon, when I saw the newspaper—"

She was on the point of breaking down again.

"Just two things more, Miss Mills. First of all, what is the telephone number of this house?"

She told him. It was identical with the number he had found scribbled on the cover of the directory in Gregory's apartment. That, at least, was cleared up.

"And now, could you find a specimen of Miss Hilliard's handwriting for me?"

She looked at him doubtfully for a moment, then excused herself and went upstairs. She returned shortly with a letter, which she handed to Brent.

"One of the letters Margaret wrote me during the holidays."

Brent glanced at the address on the envelope. The writing was identical with that on the fragment of note paper he had found in the dead man's bedroom.

He was not unprepared for this; nevertheless he was surprised. It at once shattered his theory that another woman had been in love with Gregory. He would have to abandon that lead, unless he found something else to support it. The endearments in that warning note had been penned by Margaret Hilliard.

Brent became aware that Miss Mills was looking at him curiously as he scrutinized the envelope.

"Thank you—thank you," he said hastily. "This is just what I wanted." He gave the envelope back to her and got up. "You've been very patient with me, and I shan't bother you any longer."

"I hope I've been able to help you. Do you know—if

the police have learned anything new?"

"I couldn't say. Speaking of the police, perhaps it will be just as well if you don't mention anything to them about this talk we've just had." Brent smiled at her disarmingly. "Of course, everything is perfectly fair and above board, but I'd like to work on this case in my own way, without interference. Do you mind?"

"I shan't say anything."

The door closed slowly. Brent strode jauntily away.

CHAPTER VII
A GIRL NAMED NORAH

INTON seldom offered suggestions, but when he did they were usually good. His remark that the scribbled diamonds on the cover of the telephone directory might have some connection with the emblem of the taxicab company bore fruit.

An obliging manager produced office records for his inspection, and Brent found that there had been three calls to the Majestic Apartments during the week.

One of the drivers was readily located and summoned to the office; Brent drew a blank here, however, for the man said his fare had been an old lady with a great deal of baggage. He had driven her to the station, and she had tipped him five cents.

Brent had better luck with the other drivers.

The first had some difficulty in remembering the call, but at last brought it to mind. Yes, he had picked up a fare at the Majestic—a young fellow. He couldn't just recall the fellow's appearance, but he was good looking and well dressed. Where had he gone? Somewhere on the Main.

"St. Lawrence Main? Just where?"

The man shrugged. He couldn't remember the exact corner. It was down around a bad neighborhood.

The records showed that this trip had been made at eight ten on the Monday evening before the murders.

The third and last record concerning the Majestic was for five thirty of the afternoon of the day Margaret Hilliard had been slain.

"The same day," murmured Brent as they awaited the arrival of this driver, the other man having been dismissed. "This may mean something."

It was half an hour before the third driver was located, but when he appeared he briskly announced that he remembered quite well his call to the Majestic Apartments the previous afternoon.

"Why do you remember it so well?" asked Brent.

The man fished a newspaper from his hip pocket.

"When I read about that murder up there I began to think back, for I knew I'd been up at the place some time this week, and then, when I saw this guy's picture, see, I knew it was the same guy."

With a stubby forefinger he pointed to a photograph of Paul Gregory on the front page.

"The same man?"

"Sure. I remember him from his picture. I was sent up to the Majestic, and this guy told me to drive him down on St. Lawrence Main."

"Where did he get out?"

"It was below St. Catherine Street, at the corner of Chat Noir. He told me not to wait."

"Chat Noir? I didn't know there was such a street?"

"It's a nickname. I forget what it's really called. Just

a short street leading off the Main, down in a pretty tough part of the town. Some of us call it Chat Noir because it's like having a black cat cross your path to go down that street after dark."

"Why?"

The man shrugged. "Ten chances to one you'd get knocked on the dome—unless they knew you."

"You didn't see him come back?"

"I didn't wait."

Brent reached for his hat. "Drive me down to Chat Noir," he said.

Down below "The Main," that noisy, gaudy, jangling, colorful thoroughfare of cheap movie houses, penny arcades, chop suey joints, waxwork shows, fortune telling parlors, taverns, souvenir shops, dance halls and dubious lodging places, where the mechanical pianos and the sidewalk barkers are never still, where the electric lights are always twinkling, where a perpetual carnival blares to the open street and artificial lights and artificial music inspire an artificial gayety, where "Krausemeyer's Alley" plays on and on before shifting audiences, and the grease paint drips from the comedian's nose, where shills and suckers, harridans and hustlers, rubes and racketeers, dicks and dubs jostle one another on the crowded pavements—down below the roaring Main, he came to the corner of Chat Noir.

Ever afterward, when Brent had learned the real name of this sinister street, and when he had learned nicknames other than the one the taxi driver had given it, he still called it Chat Noir—the Street of the Black Cat.

There was something peculiarly significant and appropriate, because the cheap, shoddy thoroughfare had a wretched look, as though it seeped with misery and poverty and vice, as though the contamination of evil and misfortune might touch whomever came near.

Gregory, the driver assured him, had got out at the corner and gone into Chat Noir.

"I'll get out here, too," said Brent. "I can drive you up Chat Noir, just as well."

"No. Wait for me here. I may not have far to go."

"Watch your step, mister," advised the man.

"This is daylight," returned the lawyer confidently. "I'll be back in a few minutes."

He left the Main, passed the inevitable corner tavern, and went on up the narrow pavement of Chat Noir. It was like stepping into another world. The roadway was cobbled, and two vehicles would have had trouble trying to pass one another without infringing on the sidewalk.

The buildings were of brick and stone, so old that they had attained a common dinginess and blackness; for the most part they were lodging houses of the most squalid type. Through open doors directly at the street level, Brent had glimpses of evil halls and rickety stairways; in some of these doorways lounged hard-visaged, unshaven men, or fat women with piggy eyes and untidy hair.

Out in the cobbled road, children with pallid faces and old eyes played with a sort of vicious earnestness, screeching like savages.

The street was so narrow that the grimy buildings seemed in imminent danger of toppling forward, and one had a sense of insecurity, a feeling that at any moment there might be a cataclysm of aged bricks from above. The old, old houses were jammed and wedged together, presenting a solid front of wretchedness; a little shop managed to squeeze forward with a proud display of unwashed plate glass, a flamboyant tin beer sign and a flyspecked assortment of groceries—one bright oasis in a desert of dirt and misery.

Brent looked for a number plate. The first three he saw were rusty and indecipherable, but over the next doorway he read the number, 74.

This was promising. He could not be far from No. 90. He was on the right side of the street, so he walked on quickly to the end of the block, where the number of the corner house was 84, crossed the road and looked eagerly for the number that had attained such significance.

He passed a brick tenement with two doors. The plate over the first was cracked and bent, red with rust; he could not distinguish the number. Over the second door was the number 88.

And beside the tenement was a vacant lot, fronted by a billboard advertising somebody's cigarettes.

Brent hesitated, stared at the huge sign, then hastened to the next house. The number was 94.

He looked across the street. A solid row of dirty brick buildings presented an inscrutable front. Their numbers were plainly visible—87, 89, 91, 93, 95.

There was no No. 90!

Brent tugged at his black beard. He had been so confident of locating the place that this unexpected development took the wind out of his sails. He saw that there was no use going farther, so he turned and retraced his steps.

He knew better than to ask questions. The people of

Chat Noir look askance at inquisitive strangers. He would learn nothing, and might cause trouble for himself. Yet he could scarcely bring himself to return to the taxicab; his clew had dissolved into thin air just when he felt that he was on the point of gaining valuable information, and he could not get rid of the conviction that this sinister street still held the secret of No. 90.

Deeply puzzled, Michael Brent went on back toward the Main, toward the corner of Chat Noir where his taxicab was waiting. There was nothing for it but to return uptown and seek more information about Paul Gregory.

He had butted full tilt into a blank wall on his confident journey up this blind alley; there had been some little slip, but if he could only put his finger on the one fact he had overlooked he felt sure that Chat Noir would yet yield a solution.

He was near the corner when he met a girl named Norah, and her strange companion.

Absorbed in thought, he had been trudging along with his gaze fixed on the pavement. The harsh voice of the man aroused him when he was only a few steps away.

"God knows I don't blame you for bein' disappointed, Norah, but I'm doin' the best I can. Where d'you want to stay? The Windsor Hotel?"

Brent looked up hastily, then stepped off the narrow pavement to let them pass. He had time only for a fleeting glance, but in that moment the image of the girl was stamped as indelibly upon his memory as though he had known her for years.

Against the sordid background of Chat Noir, in all

its squalid dirt and misery and vice, her beauty had a quality that was infinitely appealing, her evident timidity caught at the heart. Her childish face, her dark eyes, the pink and white purity of her complexion, the delicacy of her features, reminded one of mignonette and hollyhocks and the scent of clover in country fields.

She was small and slim. Two little parentheses of silky black hair peeped from beneath the brim of her tiny blue hat, caressing her cheeks. She wore a blue dress and a blue coat. Brent, who seldom noticed women's clothes, saw only that she was dressed neatly and quietly; he did not observe that the coat and dress were inexpensive and had known much wear.

Michael Brent was not a lady's man, but he had a proper appreciation of the beautiful, and this girl had all the mystery and loveliness of one's first sweetheart. He was not so rude as to stare, but he carried away with him a complete and ineradicable impression. He would remember her, he felt, forever. This, in spite of the fact that he had looked at her for little more than two seconds and heard her soft voice in only a few words:

"I never thought you lived in a place like this."

And the man said:

"I ain't done so bloomin' well in this country that I can live where I like."

Then they passed on out of earshot. Brent had no clear impression of the man save that he was a rat-eyed little scoundrel badly in need of a wash, and was carrying a battered suitcase. A queer couple.

At the corner, Brent looked back. They were going into one of the frowzy lodging houses of Chat Noir.

CHAPTER VIII
THE LILY IN THE MIRE

IDGE TAPLEY was one of those people who are born with a grudge against life. Nothing went well with him. Nothing ever had gone well with him. Nothing ever would.

As a baby, he squalled his resentment more vociferously than any of the other tiny beings who yelled their impotent rage against the destiny that had introduced them to life in a London slum like mosquitoes in a cesspool; as a boy he was sullen and envious, bitter and lazy; as a man he was confirmed in his resentment against "them," the shadowy legions of luckier men conspired to grind him under foot.

Like most men who gravitate naturally to the dregs of existence, he could explain it by blaming everything and everybody but himself. His life was one sustained, snarling excuse.

And now, as he ushered his foster daughter into a dark little room on the third floor of one of the most squalid lodging houses on Chat Noir, he whined his customary philippic against " them."

"You made a big mistake comin' out to this 'ere rotten country, Norah. I've cursed the day I ever left England. Look at the place I've got to live in. Look at it! And think of the nice little place we had back home."

Norah looked. She was dismayed.

The room was a cell. A small, grimy window presented a view of roofs and clotheslines. The ceiling was cracked, the wall paper was peeling off in strips, the floor was bare; there was a narrow bed, a washstand, a dubious chair. It was a cheap room, a common room, a dirty room.

Tapley put down her suitcase and the girl sat wearily on the bed.

"You never told us, father. In your letters you always said you were getting along well. Mother and I waited and waited. You said you would send for us."

"How could I send for you? How could I, when I was hardly earnin' enough to keep body and soul together? Thank Gawd, yer mother had the little shop to keep things goin', or we'd all have starved. I'd have sent for you if I could, but how could I? Answer me that!"

Norah Gray looked at her stepfather. She scarcely recognized in this stoop-shouldered, bleary-eyed denizen of Chat Noir the jaunty, assertive, gaudy man whom her mother had married. In those days Midge Tapley had been cheap and flashy, but she was too young to be analytical, and he had seemed rather wonderful to her then.

Even now she did not realize the full extent of his degradation, but it was quite obvious that Midge had altered for the worse. He was a man of graying hair and unshaven chin, red nose that looked as if it had been given a polish, squinty eyes and blotchy skin, a scrawny neck and a dirty shirt, dressed in coat and trousers that didn't match, shoes down at the heel. His voice alone had not changed; it was the same thin whine.

"You promised to bring us both out to Canada when you got settled," she insisted.

"Of course. And I would have, but I never got settled. Wait until you've been here a while, and see how hard it is fer an honest man to get steady work. Just wait. Don't blame me, Norah. It ain't been my fault I ain't done well. You shouldn't have come out here, anyway, and if I'd known in time I'd 'a' warned you, so I would."

"Perhaps not." She looked solemnly at the floor. Her voice trembled slightly. " But when mother died—there was nobody. After all, you're my stepfather."

"Yes, yes," he said hastily. "Don't think I'm complainin', Norah. I'm glad to see you. It's my dooty to look after you, and I'm not the man to dodge my dooty. But if you'd told me in time I would have arsked you to wait a while until things got better with me."

"Well—I'm here, now, and I suppose I'll have to make the best of it."

"That's the spirit!" exclaimed Midge, rubbing his hands together. "That's the spirit, gal! Be cheerful.. Everythin' will turn out all right somehow. I'm sorry I can't afford to put you up in better lodgin's than this, but I'm livin' here in this house myself, and I wanted you to be near me. When things are goin' better, we can move."

"I don't like it here," she said simply.

"Well—it ain't exactly a palace, Norah, but I can't do no better. Rents is high in Montreal, and I don't make much money."

"Are you working now?"

He looked injured. "Why, of course I'm workin'."

"Where?"

"It's a part-time job. I'm helpin' a man," he explained vaguely. "I'm expectin' somethin' better soon."

"Couldn't we move somewhere else? This is a horrible place. If you can't afford it, I have a little money—"

A glint came into Tapley's red-rimmed eyes. He rubbed his stubbled chin with the back of his hand.

"I wouldn't think of takin' any of your money, Norah," he said virtuously. "How much have you got?"

"About forty pounds."

"Two hundred dollars! That's a lot. Where did you get it."

"Mother's insurance."

"I never knew she had any insurance."

"She had a little. After the shop was sold and debts paid and the funeral was over, I had enough to buy my ticket out to Canada and have some left over."

"Have you got it with you?"

" Yes."

"That's a lot of money for you to be carryin' around, Norah. I won't take none of it for myself, but mebbe you'd better let me have it to take care of for you. I'll put it in the bank."

Norah Gray was not versed in the ways of the world, and her recollections of Midge Tapley had not been wholly unpleasant; she was only a child when he left home, and she still retained an odd affection for the man, simply because her mother had cared for him, in spite of his worthlessness. Nevertheless, the caution that experience teaches the poor bade her keep the money in her own hands.

"It's safe enough, I think," she said mildly. "But if you need some money to move away from here to a nicer place, or to help you get a better job, I could let you have some."

She meant it in all goodness of heart.

"You always was good-hearted, Norah. Even when you was only a nipper, I said it of you. Matter of fact, I have got somethin' in mind just now, and I ain't been able to handle it just on account of needin' a few dollars."

"How much do you need?"

"It all depends," said Midge judicially. "The more capital a man has, the better chances he's got of gettin' ahead. I'll take a look around and I'll let you know."

"And in the meantime, must we stay here?"

"There's plenty worse places, gal. Plenty worse. This ain't the Ritz-Carlton, in course, but people minds their own business—and it's cheap. Besides, it's handy to my work."

Midge did not enlarge on the nature of these mysterious labors.

Tired, disappointed, frightened, disillusioned—Norah was on the verge of tears. This dingy room in the heart of a strange city almost suffocated her with its ugliness, stifled her in an atmosphere of evil.

"It doesn't look like a very nice neighborhood," she observed faintly.

"You can't always judge by appearances," Midge said, with the air of one delivering a great moral truth. "It's pore, but the people is good-hearted."

He had left the door open, and now they heard shuffling footsteps in the hall. Norah looked up just as a man shambled into view; he peered into the room, standing in the doorway, his eyes blinking, his lips twisted in a thin smile.

He was a cripple. His right arm hung limply at his side as though it were withered. The hand was like a claw, dry and yellow. He was a homely fellow, with a sharp sallow face, and a shrewd expression. He looked narrowly at Norah as he said:

"Hello, Midge. Got company?"

Midge cast him a sullen glance.

"This is my gal," he muttered. "Just come from England."

The cripple raised astonished eyebrows. "I never knew you had a kid."

" This is her."

"Well, I hope she likes it here." His voice had a sardonic note. He darted a piercing glance at Norah, then turned away and went down the hall.

"Nosey!" snapped Midge, when the man was out of earshot.

"Who is he?"

"No friend of mine."

"He seemed to know you."

"He knows everybody. He lives here."

"What is his name?"

"Burger, he calls hisself."

"He's a cripple, isn't he?"

"One of his arms is dead."

"What does he do for a living?"

"He's a crook. Don't you go bein' nice to him and givin' him no sympathy, Norah. There's lots of people around here I don't want you to have anythin' to do with, for I don't like 'em, and he is only one of 'em. But this here Burger is a bloody noosance. He's always pokin' his nose into what don't concern him. He didn't have to call to stop here and ask questions."

"I hope we won't stay here very long. I don't like the place."

Norah opened her hand bag and produced a baggage check.

"You've got a trunk?"

"I forgot to give you the check when you met me. Could you have somebody send the trunk up here?"

Midge took the pasteboard.

"Takes money to have a trunk sent up," he suggested delicately.

In silence the girl opened her purse and produced a bill. She handed it to Midge, who glanced at it and stuffed it into his pocket.

"Thanks. I'd pay for it myself," he explained, "but I'm a bit hard up just now. It took my last penny to pay the landlord for your room, and I don't get no pay till to-morrow."

"I don't mind."

"That's the gal!" said Midge, greatly cheered. "Some 'd take it out in bein' nasty. I'll make it up to you some day, that I will." He edged toward the door. "Are you hungry?"

"No, thanks. I think I'll lie down and have a rest."

He seemed relieved. "It 'll do you good. I'll go and look after your trunk." At the door he paused. "If you go out for a walk, don't go far. This is a bad city for a gal to be out alone."

With this righteous admonition, Midge Tapley left his foster daughter and descended the rickety stairs to the street, tenderly clutching the crisp bill in his pocket.

There was a transfer company's office near by, but Midge did not go there directly. Instead, he stopped off at the corner tavern, where he made a barely perceptible sign to a waiter with yellowish face and roving eyes. The waiter brought him a glass of beer, and at the same time slipped him a little paper packet beneath the table. Midge handed over the bill and got back a dollar. He drank his beer and went into the lavatory, the paper packet in his trembling fingers.

Ten minutes later, with eyes shining and a feeling of great benevolence toward the world in general, Midge Tapley handed in the trunk check at the transfer office, paid the charges, and went out with the air of one who has done his duty.

"Funny the difference a little shot of snow can make," he mused. "I been needin' that."

He felt exhilarated.

"Wonder how much of that money I can wangle out of her. Mysto and me can make a neat bit o' coin if we only have some capital to get goin'. I wonder if she'd stand for me touchin' her for a hundred?"

He peeped through a tavern door and looked at the clock.

"About time I was goin' around to No. 90," reflected Midge. He hesitated on the pavement "There might be somethin' on."

Then he thought better of it.

"What's the use? I got a gal to look after now. Guess I can take a little holiday wunst in a while. It don't happen every day in the week."

Presumably No. 90 was deprived of Midge Tapley's company that evening, for he turned in the direction of the lodging house.

CHAPTER IX
AN ENCOUNTER WITH LABOEUF

HILE her stepfather was out attending to the matter of the trunk, and incidentally treating himself to a deck of cocaine, Norah Gray sat on her cot in the shabby cell and bit her lips to keep from crying with loneliness and disappointment.

She was pitifully young and inexperienced, a girl in years, but a child in her innocent outlook on life. Midge was all she had in the world now; she felt an instinctive affection for him because she was in a strange country, far from the scenes she had known, and because he was the only familiar figure left in her life.

That she should find him living in this wretched slum had been far from her expectations. Midge's letters had been infrequent, but they had given no indication of his descent. He was invariably on the point of leaving Montreal to take up land in the West; he was always faithfully saving his money; he was continually promising that in a few months he would send for

Norah and her mother, that they might all enter upon an unprecedented era of prosperity and pastoral peace.

Of course a freeborn Englishman had a hard time in Canada; he always stressed that. The country was backward; people didn't do things as they did them in England; the Canadians were a stubborn lot, and were strangely independent of advice, although they were only a pack of ignorant colonials. But, even here, wrote the brave and undiscouraged Midge, hard work and ambition would tell in time.

Norah's mother had privately opined that her husband was engaged in his customary occupation of "waitin' for a bit o' luck," but she had no idea that he had abandoned himself to the underworld of Montreal.

And Norah, even now when she looked around this shabby room, had no suspicion that Midge Tapley was a derelict, a dope fiend, a denizen of Chat Noir, one of those who lurked in mysterious dens by day and emerged by night into the streets of shadow.

The gloom deepened, and although she resolutely tried to put out of her mind all the warm, delicious thoughts of the life she had left behind, they thronged her memory, and she had not the heart to banish them.

She thought of the little shop in the English village, of her kindly, patient mother behind the counter, the smell of spices and buns and groceries, the bell that tinkled when customers entered, the pretty garden back of the house, her little white room upstairs, with the gable windows looking out to the green meadows and the hedgerows and the blue sea far away.

It had all been clean and fresh and friendly, and as

she looked at this dingy room with its grimy window opening on a view of roofs and chimneys and smoky sky, she suddenly yielded to homesickness, flung herself on the hard bed and sobbed wretchedly.

After a long time she sat up, wiping her eyes. The room was dark. She was lonely and frightened; she wished Midge would return.

She felt that she could not endure the narrow cell of a room a moment longer, so she got up and washed away the tear stains, powdered her nose, and then put on her hat and coat. The room was dark and close; she resolved to go outside and wait for Midge.

The lodging house seemed deserted as she went down the rickety stairs. There were rows of dismal, uncommunicative doors in the two hallways. She saw no one. She went out into the street and was surprised to find that it was not as dark as she had thought. Her room had been so gloomy that she thought night had fallen.

Two greasy-faced old harridans were jabbering fiercely at one another in French, from adjacent doorways, each with a bawling brat clinging to her skirts.

A drunken man was sitting on the pavement, his back against a telephone pole, singing a maudlin song.

A screeching child blundered against Norah and disappeared into a doorway, hotly pursued by another ragged little savage who halted on the steps and hurled a half brick into the dark hall.

In an upper window of a house across the street a gross old man leaned out like a fat gargoyle, his arms and shoulders bare, his chest covered by a dirty undershirt. An arm emerged from a window above and a jug of slops was emptied into the street; the gargoyle vanished hastily, but popped into view again when the deluge was over; curses ascended in a throaty rumble; the arm and the jug disappeared and the upper window banged.

Norah faltered. She wanted to turn back, but when she thought of the dark little room she had just left, she forced herself to go on.

The two harridans stopped their jabbering at once, stared at her frankly, and then forgot their animosity in a muttered parley as she passed. The gargoyle in the upper window leered at her.

She would just go to the end of the block and turn back. The atmosphere was oppressive; strange odors emanated from the doorways. Chat Noir is foul. Norah's room was close and stifling, but the street was little better.

The English maiden knew nothing of the nameless things masked by these drab house fronts, and, although she shrank from the grossness and poverty of Chat Noir, she viewed the pulsing life of the street with a tremulous curiosity. She was too innocent to know fear, too ignorant of the dangers lurking in the shadows, but she knew instinctively that Chat Noir was vicious and evil.

Looking back, she could see the twinkling lights of the Main just beyond the distant corner, and hear the roar of the trolleys. She wished she had gone in that direction.

The farther she went down Chat Noir, the dirtier and more sinister it became. She reached a corner where a narrow lane cut a slanting gulf among the huddled tenements, and here she was just about to turn back when a terrifying group emerged from the alley and confronted her.

Two huge mastiffs, growling and snarling, leaping ponderously and straining at the leash, appeared first. Norah did not see the heavy whipcord that restrained them, and she gave a cry of terror as the animals plunged out of the gloom of the lane.

They bared their teeth and burst into a frenzy of hoarse barking, but when they would have leaped toward her they were brought up short. Then came their master.

He was a massive, broad-shouldered man, over six feet in height, with a great shock of black hair, a rugged, swarthy face, and muscular arms, bare to the elbow. One hairy hand gripped the leash, and his feet were planted firmly on the ground, wide apart, as he braced himself to hold back the plunging dogs.

Bareheaded, barearmed, with shirt open at the throat to reveal a matted chest, he was a gigantic and terrifying figure—fit master for the ferocious brutes that were now rearing up on their haunches as he doubled the leash about his wrist and dragged them back.

He was laughing insanely, his big white teeth gleaming. It was a maniac laugh: "Yeah-ha-ha!" that seemed to rise from the depths of his great chest, and his eyes were glistening slits beneath bushy brows.

When he saw Norah his laughter trailed away into a snarl and he stood quite still, then roared a command that brought the dogs slavering and fawning to his feet, bellies to the ground, their tails lashing.

"N'avez pas peur!" bellowed the master of the dogs, baring his strong teeth again in a grin.

This was evidently addressed to Norah, but as she

did not understand French, she did not know that he was merely telling her not to be afraid, and she was more frightened than ever.

"No French?" demanded the ogre.

She shook her head, then turned swiftly away. There was a subdued growling from the dogs, a heavy footstep, her wrist was seized in a firm grasp. The big man loomed massive at her side, and he swung her

Norah faltered at sight of the sinister street

about as lightly as though she were a child; he still gripped the leash and the animals circled them, padding restlessly.

"Where do you come from?"

His fingers were like steel bands about her wrist, he had drawn her toward him and he was gazing down at her terrified face. His expression was at once imperious, ingratiating and cruel.

The girl was conscious of his great strength, his animal vitality, and of a fascination akin to that of the serpent. His eyes were almost black, with a cold, steady glitter in them, and as he looked down at her, the bold possessiveness of his gaze made her feel ashamed.

Although she was very frightened, Norah was surprised at the calmness of her own voice:

"Let me go, please!"

The ogre flung back his head and roared with laughter, a vigorous bellow that trailed off in throaty chuckles.

"Let you go, little one! Not yet. I have just found you."

"Please!"

She tried to release herself, but although his grasp on her wrist appeared to be effortless, it was like a vise. The girl felt herself drawn closer to him.

"You will go with me," he said commandingly, a curiously vibrant tone creeping into his voice. She chanced to look into his eyes, and the glittering little lights were like magnets sapping the resistance from her. She felt suddenly weak and helpless, she wanted to look away, but the eyes held her in a spell.

By a violent effort of the will she managed to turn aside and the spell snapped; anger rose like a flame. She uttered a sob of sheer wrath, flung back her free arm and then slapped him across the face with all the strength she could muster.

She was not afraid any longer; she was angrier than she had ever been in her life; she had never believed herself capable of such murderous indignation. Again and again she slapped the swarthy face and each stinging impact restored her courage, deepened the hatred for her captor. But he only opened wide his mouth and his eyes squinted as he bellowed with laughter again.

"Ho, ho!" he choked. "You have spirit, eh? You have spirit! So much the better."

He spluttered and gurgled with laughter. The huge dogs, as though sharing his merriment, tugged at the leash, barking.

"You slap! It is good! They are caresses."

He released her wrist but flung his arm around the girl's waist and almost lifted her off her feet as he pressed her close to him, his grinning face hovering above her.

"Caress me again!" he invited. "Again! You have both hands free for more of those delicious caresses."

She kicked and struggled, but the arm circled her tightly. Norah's eyes blazed and her teeth were clenched at the indignity. She dug her sharp little finger nails into the tough skin of his cheeks, and she scratched with a fierce intensity of purpose. Livid streaks appeared and slowly crimsoned; but the ogre scarcely seemed to feel the scratches, for, although he leaned back so that she could not reach his face again, he laughed more uproariously than ever.

"You are a wild cat! You claw me, eh? Ah, but I like that!" He smacked his thick lips mockingly. "It will be fun to tame you."

She beat at his heavy chest with her fists, realizing the futility of opposing his. strength. One of the dogs, snarling, lunged at her with bared teeth, but the man growled and kicked the brute so viciously that it yelped with pain and slunk back. He released his hold so that Norah was able to step back a pace, but then his fingers gripped her arm.

"Not so soon! You don't get away just yet. You will come with me, no?"

He turned back toward the alley from which he had emerged, and forced her along beside him, all the while laughing as though it were a tremendous joke. Norah was exhausted from her struggles, almost crying with terror. The mastiffs brushed against her, whining.

"I live not far!" the ogre was saying. "You shall see—"

A figure appeared at his elbow.

"M'sieu' Laboeuf," said a mild voice.

The big man swung about with a snarl. He faced a stoop-shouldered, ugly little fellow in an ill-fitting blue suit, a man with dull, tired eyes, a cynical mouth, who now stood with his hands in his pockets, an expression of weary disinterest on his homely face. Norah did not recognize him at first, and then she saw that he was none other than Burger, the cripple whom she had met in the lodging house.

"Well?" demanded the ogre.

"Excuse me for butting in," said Burger, in the same mild and placating voice, "but I thought I'd tip you off about the dame."

Laboeuf stared at him truculently.

"What about her?"

"That's Midge's gal."

Laboeuf laughed shortly, and tightened his grasp on Norah's arm.

"Listen," he rasped, and waved his free hand toward the street. "Do you see any one else buttin' in?"

They both looked back. Here and there were little groups of people gazing toward them, but although, the people of Chat Noir had been watching Norah's encounter with Laboeuf, and had been taking a lively interest in the little drama, not one had moved to interfere. When they saw Laboeuf look back they turned away as if they had seen nothing.

"Do you see any one else buttin' in?" repeated Laboeuf. "You don't. They know better. In Chat Noir they know that Laboeuf is boss. *Boss*—d'you hear?" His massive fist clenched. "Burger, for that I teach you a lesson." The fist drew back. "If this is Midge's woman, she ain't his woman no more."

The fist smashed into Burger's face

He swung viciously. The fist smashed into Burger's face; he staggered back, his hat flew off his head, he sprawled on the pavement. Laboeuf glared down at him, his nostrils dilating.

"Maybe now you will mind your own business."

Mechanically Burger rubbed the back of his hand over his face. Blood was beginning to show. Laboeuf laughed.

"I did not say she was Midge's woman," persisted Burger in the same mild voice as he got to his feet. "She is his daughter. She is one of us."

Laboeuf's laughter stopped.

Blood was streaming down Burger's face now, and one of his eyes was closing. He took a dirty handkerchief from his pocket and dabbled at his nose. He seemed to take the blow as a matter of course.

"How do you know this?" demanded Laboeuf.

Burger shrugged. "Ask her?"

There was no need. Some one came running down the street; it was Midge Tapley. He hurried up, panting, mopping his brow with his sleeve.

"What's the matter?" he asked anxiously. He looked inquiringly at Norah, then cast an obsequious glance at Laboeuf. The dogs snarled and Midge stepped back smartly. "Has there been some trouble?"

Laboeuf released Norah's wrist. She was so numb with fright by this time that she scarcely had strength to step back. Midge put an arm around her shoulders.

"Was it the dogs, Mr. Laboeuf?" asked Midge. "Was she scared of the dogs?"

Laboeuf looked at him sullenly. "Is that your daughter?"

There was cold ferocity in his voice.

Midge nodded. "Yes. Yes. My daughter. My step-daughter, Mr. Laboeuf. Just came over from England this day."

Laboeuf grunted. Then, without a word, he gave such a vicious yank at the leash that the dogs went blundering against each other, gave the nearest mastiff such a kick that he yelped with agony, then wheeled about and strode down the street. The huge dogs plunged on ahead of him, tugging at the whipcord.

Thus, with bare arm thrust forward, feet wide apart so that he would not be thrown off balance by any sudden lunge of the monstrous dogs, Laboeuf resumed his evening walk. Directly down the middle of the road he went, looking neither to left nor right, head high, gazing imperiously ahead, and the people of Chat Noir bowed and nodded and muttered "*B'soir,* M'sieu' Laboeuf," fawning like serfs.

"My Gawd!" exclaimed Midge. "What's been goin' on here?"

Norah huddled close to him. She wanted to fling her arms around him then, to cling to him, to press her face to his shoulder.

"That man—" She could say no more, but wept silently.

Burger, still wiping the blood from his face, with one eye now almost closed, said: "Laboeuf scared her."

Midge looked frightened. Mechanically he patted Norah's arm.

"Nothin' to be frightened of, gal," he muttered.

She looked up, tight-lipped, and brushed the tears from her eyes with an angry gesture.

"I'm not frightened. I'm mad."

"He was only foolin'."

"He's a beast."

Norah's gaze rested on Burger's battered and bleeding face. Her expression softened. "Oh, you're hurt!"

"It's all right," mumbled Burger. "My nose is bleedin' a little, but it ain't broken."

She was touched by his humility and her compassion was aroused by the sight of his blood-streaked countenance.

"But you can't leave it like that. It must pain terribly. Come with us and let me wash the blood off."

Burger shuffled his feet and would have turned away. Midge looked dubious, but Norah was insistent. She grasped Burger's sleeve and urged him to come with them. She was all concern now.

They went back down Chat Noir in silence and entered the lodging house. The landlady was prevailed upon to provide hot water, and they went to Norah's room, where she bathed Burger's face.

He submitted to her ministrations uncomfortably, protesting that he was all right, and that his injury needed no attention, but when he finally rose to go, the bloodstains had vanished and there remained only the purplish bruise about his eye.

"Thanks, miss," he muttered gratefully, nodded to Midge, and walked out of the room without a backward glance.

Midge scratched his head.

"You didn't need to go to no fuss about him."

"If it hadn't been for Mr. Burger, that brute would have taken me away with him," Norah explained.

Midge looked uneasy.

"He wouldn't have done that. He was only foolin'. Laboeuf ain't a bad sort."

"What do you know about him?"

"Well—I've known him, on and off—he's a great hand for a joke, is Laboeuf. I guess he got sore because Burger butted in."

"He struck him in the face and knocked him down.

The least I could do was offer to wash off the blood for him."

"It's all right. It's all right," Midge said hastily. "I ain't kickin'. But you didn't have to do it. Burger didn't expect it."

Burger, in fact, had not expected it. Out in the hallway he was reflectively touching his face, his rough fingers bringing back more vividly than ever the memory of the smooth, gentle hands of the girl. She was so deft, so quick, so young and pretty. It had been years since any woman had been kind to Burger.

There was a softer light in his eyes as he went slowly down the stairs and emerged again into the shadows of Chat Noir.

CHAPTER X
A TIP PROM PELHAM STARR

NORAH would have been vastly amazed could she have known of the emotions she had inspired in the legal breast of Michael Brent. Had any one asked her if she remembered encountering an odd-looking man with a black beard and a floppy hat, on the afternoon of her arrival in Chat Noir, she would have been hard put to recollect the gentleman at all, in spite of the picturesque nature of his appearance. Chat Noir itself had occupied most of her attention at the time.

However, had any one inquired of Michael Brent if he remembered seeing a bewildered girl of sweet and childish beauty, a girl of shy and delicate loveliness, in the heart of one of Montreal's most evil slums, he would have called the incident to mind with suspicious readiness.

Moreover, he would have agreed to the description with enthusiasm and supplied any number of tender adjectives by way of elaboration, to boot.

It was not only her cameo prettiness, the charm of

her unsophisticated manner, the appeal of her evident misgivings that intrigued him and kept her image like a warm little flame in his heart. She had caught his interest largely because she was so obviously out of her accustomed world and so obviously aware of it; against that sinister background she was out of place.

Thence the puzzle. Why was she there? Who was her companion, that skulking little rat with the shifty eyes?

And although Brent told himself, with a sigh, that he was too old to permit himself surprise at any strange thing he saw in the streets of shadow, although he tried to dismiss the whole matter with the reflection that he would never, in all probability, see the girl again, the incident stuck to his mind like a burr.

He found himself improvising a dozen theories as to the girl's presence in Chat Noir, and each time he impatiently asked himself what possible concern it was of his, anyway.

But somehow, for no apparent logical reason, it seemed a concern of the greatest importance.

He was thinking more of the girl than of the immediate business in hand as he ascended the steps of a formidable residence in an exclusive district of Montreal next morning. It irritated him, for Michael Brent, although only thirty years old, had prided himself on being a dyed-in-the-wool degree bachelor, wholly immune to the lure of a pretty face.

"The big secret, my boy," he often told Dryborough, when that benedict confided his woes as a member of the great majority, "is not to remember 'em. When they're out of sight, keep 'em out of mind. But once you start thinking about the little blonde you met at the party last night, or when you start remembering what kind of a dress your stenographer had on to-day —that's the time to go and get drunk, or drown yourself, or something. For the skids are greased and you're beginning to slip, and you'll have to move fast or you're done for."

This had all sounded very well at the time, and with a few notable exceptions in his eighteenth year—before the virtues of the scheme had occurred to him—it had always been gratifyingly effective.

No wonder, then, that Michael Brent was irritated when he found he couldn't forget the girl of Chat Noir; it was disturbing to realize that he didn't want to forget her. His only comfort was in the reflection that he would never see her again, but somehow that thought was not quite as consoling as it should have been.

"What's wrong with me?" he inquired testily of his inner self as he rang the bell. "I'm acting like a young calf in high school."

So, while he waited, he valiantly thrust the persistent vision into the remote recesses of his mind and sternly dwelt on the immediate problem of extracting information from Mr. Pelham Starr, whose name had been given to him by the housekeeper of a certain girl who was murdered in Mount Royal Park.

He had with difficulty contrived an appointment with Mr. Starr for that morning, but it had been managed finally through the good offices of a client whom Brent had once successfully defended in a ticklish case, and who was, incidentally, a close friend of Starr.

Only by representing Michael Brent as an implacable foe of the police, for whom Starr had no love, following several scrapes in which he had figured during the sowing of a luxuriant wild oats crop, had this friend obtained consent to the interview.

Brent was evidently expected, for a maid took his hat and coat and ushered him into the library, informing him that Mr. Starr would be down directly. He sank into the depths of a commodious leather chair and accepted a cigarette from a mahogany box that the maid left at his elbow.

Soon, with smoke drifting lazily about his head, the attorney was idly mapping a campaign to clear his client, Hinky Lewis, who was languishing in jail within the shadow of the scaffold.

As an admirer of the late Margaret Hilliard, the wealthy Mr. Starr might have information of consequence, but whether he had or hadn't, it was a foregone conclusion that he would keep a tight rein on his tongue. The Hilliard-Gregory case was monopolizing the headlines, and it was only reasonable to assume that Starr would shy at becoming involved; he would not welcome publicity of that sort.

Not that Pelham Starr was unused to objectionable publicity. He was thirty years of age, and he had gone through two years, three months and four days of university, five automobile smash-ups, one divorce, and two very exclusive scandals; he had been kicked out of two clubs, and had maintained a consistent record of at least one good jag a week since his twenty-fourth birthday, not counting a month at a sanatorium.

Publicity of such nature, however, is far removed from the publicity of front page participation in a murder mystery.

A silken swishing heralded the arrival of Pelham

Starr, who came in just then, clad in pyjamas and dressing gown, growled a curt greeting and subsided into a deep armchair. He had a heavy, pulpy face with sallow skin of coarse texture, brown hair that was already thinning on top, and the eyes of a sleepy cat. His expression was habitually weary and sullen, for nothing interested him any more.

"Well?" he asked, ungraciously.

"I've been doing a little investigation work in the Hilliard case, and I thought that as you had been a friend of Miss Hilliard, you might be able to help me out," Brent said directly.

"Why come to me? I don't know anything."

"You knew Miss Hilliard."

"What's that got to do with it? I'm not the only person who knew her."

"I believe you went out with her a few times."

The maid entered the room just then with a bottle of Scotch, a siphon of soda, and glasses on a tray.

"Want a drink?" inquired Starr.

"No, thank you. It's a bit early for me."

"Then you'll excuse me."

Starr dismissed the maid and mixed himself a generous drink.

"I have to have an eye-opener," he explained. "Rotten headache." He drank, and sat back with a sigh of satisfaction.

"Did you know Gregory?"

"I met him."

"You didn't know him intimately?"

" I didn't care to. He wasn't my sort."

"Were you, in any sense of the word, rivals?"

The heavy-lidded eyes closed. "Margaret's people

are good friends of ours. That was all."

"You weren't sentimentally interested?"

"Not at all."

"Did you ever discuss Gregory with her?"

Starr glanced at his interrogator over the rim of the glass. "I told her I didn't think he was in her class."

"What did she say to that?"

"None of your business," Starr retorted, and drank again.

"She told you it was none of your business?" said Brent amiably.

"No. I'm telling you it's none of your business."

"Pardon me if I seem inquisitive, Mr. Starr, but I'm just trying to clear up a few points that have puzzled me. Outside the matter of social position, you had nothing against Gregory?"

"He wasn't any lily."

"What do you mean by that?"

"I mean, she thought he was one of these holy-holy chaps, but I found out a few things about Gregory."

"For instance?"

"Margaret had a few things to say because I like a little drink now and then. Well, her precious Paul was no saint."

"No?"

Presumably the headache was yielding to the beneficent effect of the eye-opener. Starr's voice had lost some of its surliness. He leaned forward.

"He certainly wasn't. He had some queer friends."

"Oh, I can hardly credit that, Mr. Starr," said Brent, shrewdly. "From what I have learned, he was an exemplary young man."

Starr rose to the bait. "That shows all you know

about him. I've *seen* him."

"With whom?"

"Women."

"Other women? Oh, well—any young man may have friends, other than his *fiancée.*"

"I mean," blurted Starr, "that I've seen him with streetwalkers."

"Really?"

"Yes, I've seen him with 'em. And pimps. Talking to 'em. I saw him down at the Acadia one night with three women at his table."

"You're sure of this, Mr. Starr?"

" Would I lie about it?"

"I'm not insinuating that."

"I know what I'm talking about, I tell you. He used to hang around some mighty tough parts of the city."

"Where?"

"Sanguinet and De Bullion Streets, for instance, and those back streets off St. Catherine near St. Lawrence Main."

"Not so good."

"It made me sore. Here was this willy-boy putting it across on Margaret that he was a white-haired saint, and then sneaking off by himself on jaunts into the cheap night clubs and down into the worst streets in town. I got more dope on that boy than he imagined."

"You were interested?"

"Well—I made inquiries. Frankly, it galled me when Margaret kept throwing him up to me all the time. I found out plenty. Why, do you know that fellow was having an affair with some woman in that street they call Chat Noir, for two weeks before he was killed?"

"Well, well!" exclaimed Brent, greatly astonished

and inwardly excited. "You're quite sure of that, Mr. Starr?"

"Absolutely. I'm just telling you that to show that he wasn't the innocent he made out to be."

"Miss Hilliard evidently believed in him."

"He had her fooled. But it wasn't as if she hadn't been warned against him."

"She knew?"

"I told her."

"You warned her against Gregory?"

"I told her what I had learned."

"What did she say?"

Pelham Starr shrugged. "You know how women are. She wouldn't believe me, of course."

"And it ended at that?"

"The detectives were here last night," said Starr, with seeming irrelevance. "They asked me a lot of questions, too, and they went away with damn little information. I've already told you a lot more than I told them, Mr. Brent, and if you'll promise to keep me out of this mess and not go spilling this dope to the newspapers, I'll tell you some more."

"Don't worry about the newspapers," laughed the lawyer. "This is my own little private investigation, and anything you tell me will go no further."

"Tommy Macallister told me about the jam you pulled him out of, and he said you were a decent chap, so I'll play with you as long as you don't drag me into the affair. So far as the police are concerned, they can go to the devil. They've never done me any favors, and if you're out to crimp their game, I'm with you."

"I'm trying to clear the man they've arrested for the girl's murder."

"Well—where was I? When I told Margaret what I knew about Gregory, she challenged me to tell it to his face. Frankly, I liked the girl, and when she told me I had no chance because she cared for Gregory, it made me sore. I saw him in the Acadia with these tough babies one night, so that gave me a line on him, and I had him looked up. That's how I got my information. She thought I was lying. So, to prove that I wasn't, I did tell it to Gregory's face, and Margaret was there."

"Did he deny it?"

"That's just it," declared Pelham Starr, triumphantly. "He did not. He admitted he had been down around Sanguinet and De Bullion, and that he had been seen talking to loose women, but he had the nerve to bluff it out. Said he had a good reason."

"What was his reason?"

"He wouldn't say. He was as white as a sheet, and nervous, and I guess he couldn't think up a good lie quick enough. He just said she would have to believe in him."

"But he didn't explain?"

"How could he? I had him cold. I have a few friends in the right places and when I want to get the goods on a man I can do it without much trouble. I had the goods on him and he knew it."

"Didn't Margaret question him?"

"Perhaps she did when I was not around. But Gregory got away with his bluff at the time. He got nasty and we had a few words."

"Oh, you quarreled?"

Starr looked up, a gleam in his eyes. He was instantly on the defensive.

"Don't get me mixed up in this," he said, distinctly.

"I warn you, it won't do you any good. If you're hinting that I might have had anything to do with the murders—"

Brent laughed disarmingly.

"It never entered my head. You've taken me wrong, Mr. Starr."

Mollified, the man sank back in his chair.

"I didn't have anything to do with the murders. I want to make that clear," he muttered.

"Your little difference with Gregory was simply because he resented your interest in his affairs."

"You can put it that way. I didn't like the beggar—I don't deny it. He was as poor as a church mouse, yet he had the presumption to hang around a girl of Margaret's position. A fortune hunter, in my opinion. Nothing more nor less. A damned fortune hunter."

"Miss Hilliard's family didn't approve of him, eh?"

"They didn't know. If they had, there would have been trouble. Mrs. Hilliard had better plans for Margaret. But I wasn't interested in Gregory's affairs. He

"It was very unpleasant all around," said Starr

could go to the devil his own way, as far as I cared, and I told him so. It was entirely on Margaret's account that I butted in. I hated to see her made a fool of."

"Naturally."

"It was very unpleasant all around," said Starr, with an aggrieved air. "I did my best to save Margaret from the fellow—and now we know what happened."

"Tragedy. Have you any theory?"

"Gregory's woman, of course."

"You're sure there was another woman?"

"Haven't I told you? Didn't I tell Margaret? Didn't Gregory himself admit visiting a woman in Chat Noir?"

"He admitted it?"

"Quite. He couldn't deny it. But he was stubborn. He said he would talk it over with Margaret when I wasn't around, but he refused to tell me anything. I could easily see what was behind that. The fellow thought he could tell her lies she might swallow but that a man would see through."

"You given me a valuable clew, Mr. Starr. Did you learn anything more about this woman?"

"No."

"Her address?"

"Nothing. He made several trips to Chat Noir, and he was seen there once with a woman, so I assume that's why he went there."

"Your warning seems to have been justified."

"If Margaret had listened to me she would probably be alive to-day. My own theory, as I said, is that Gregory's woman finished them both. Gregory wouldn't break with Margaret—not while there was a chance of marrying her for her money or being bought off by her parents. It meant money to him, either way. But he tried to keep this other woman in tow at the same time. Probably she called for a showdown, got jealous, and when he kept up his double game she ran amuck."

"It's a much more reasonable theory than any one has advanced yet. But, of course, you have had information denied to the police."

"Are you going to tell 'em?" growled Starr.

"Not me."

"If you can use this dope without dragging me into the mess, all right. But if you double cross me and get me on the witness stand, by the Lord Harry, I'll close up like a clam, and you'll get nowhere."

Pelham Starr got up, indicating that the interview was closed. Brent did not question him further. At the door he expressed his thanks.

"You've given me a new lead, Mr. Starr."

I hope it gets you somewhere."

Brent thought he detected a sardonic note in the man's voice.

"If only Gregory had been killed, I wouldn't have told you a thing," continued Starr, holding the door open. "Good riddance to bad rubbish, and more power to the killer's elbow, *I'd* say. I would not raise my little finger," he declared venomously. "But *I do* feel badly about Margaret. She was a damn fine girl.. I hope you find out who did *that* job."

The emphasis, Brent reflected, as he went down the steps, had been unmistakable!

CHAPTER XI
"CHERCHEZ LA FEMME"

ICHAEL BRENT did not stop in at the Fleur de Li Tavern for his customary mug of dark beer—medium—that afternoon, and his crony, Mr. Dryborough, drank in solitary state, with a newspaper propped up before him.

It goes without saying that he was reading the latest news of the Hilliard-regory affair; it monopolized most of the front page and overflowed to the second, dribbling away on the third to a thin stream of conjectures and repetition.

The tragedy that had overtaken the wealthy girl and the struggling young architect gripped the public imagination, and the headlines flared. Detectives had grilled Hinky Lewis unmercifully, convinced that he had slain the girl, and that he was involved in the obscure human relationships behind the double crime, but the newspapers and the public sought a gaudier solution. This, they argued, was not the work of a skulking gunman seeking a purse. It went deeper than that.

Mr. Dryborough, like every one else who read the papers that morning, was passionately interested because he was deeply puzzled. Almost every paragraph raised a problem.

Why had the love of this young couple brought them separately to death? Was there one murderer or were there two? Was Hinky Lewis a killer or merely a sacrificial goat? What had happened in that dingy apartment before Paul Gregory went reeling to the floor with a broken skull? Who had lured Margaret Hilliard to the sinister rendezvous in the park?

It was one of those fascinating riddles that life periodically presents to the mob, a riddle compounded of love and death, a riddle to which the answer might never be known.

Mr. Dryborough read everything the newspaper had to offer, and at the simultaneous conclusion of the final paragraph and the second mug of dark he was more bewildered than when he began. He waited in vain for Michael Brent, in the hope of gaining further information, and finally stalked off to his bookshop, muttering.

The lawyer, in fact, had completely forgotten the existence of Dryborough, the Fleur de Lis Tavern and dark beer, in his absorption after leaving Pelham Starr. He had learned much in the interview, and he was consumed by a rising excitement as he strode back toward the office. He had been right, after all. Chat Noir had not been a blind trail.

Somehow, he could not escape the impression that Pelham Starr knew more than he had cared to tell. Suspicions began to rise in his mind. Why had Starr talked so readily to him, when he had refused to talk

to the police? It was quite possible, of course, that the man's explanation had been true—that his animosity toward the police was at the bottom of his discrimination in Brent's favor, but it was also possible that there were other and more obscure motives.

Brent found that a situation often became clarified through discussion, and to this end he frequently talked over details of his cases with his assistant, the indispensable Minton. That gentleman, besides being a superb listener, had an uncanny gift for pouncing on the one pearl of truth in a sea of legal verbiage, and a positive talent for discerning absurdities and contradictions. So when Michael Brent went into the office that morning he bade the faithful servant drop the labors in hand and listen.

Minton heard the tale of Brent's interview with Pelham Starr, judicially attentive.

She was a slatternly creature with suspicious eyes

"What do you think, Minty? Was Pelham Starr trying to draw a red herring across the trail?"

Minton polished his spectacles and permitted himself a stick of gum as an aid to thought.

"From what you have told me, Mr. Brent, I imagine the man has been quite honest with you," he said finally.

"I thought so, too. But when I began to think things over, I wondered. It seems strange that he is apparently the only person who has ever heard of Gregory's association with streetwalkers, and of his prowlings in the underworld, and particularly of his friendship with this mysterious woman in Chat Noir."

"On the surface, it might seem strange," Minton agreed, "but you must remember that he was the only person sufficiently interested in Gregory's private life to seek out these things. Gregory's closest friends would never know about them unless he betrayed himself in some way. It's very easy for a young man to lead that sort of a double life, as you might call it, in a big city."

Minton wagged his head portentously, as though his own prosaic and righteous existence might mask lurid depths for all Brent could tell.

"I suppose I shouldn't be so confoundedly suspicious, but the information Starr gave me seems too good to be true. That is, from the standpoint of clearing up these murders. I've been wondering if it wasn't all a gorgeous lie."

"It's a fact that there is no one to contradict it."

"That's what makes me suspicious. It's so airtight. Where did he get his information about Gregory? He didn't say. He builds up an excellent case against some unknown woman, although diligent police investigation has revealed no hint of this woman, no hint of any such affair in Gregory's life. I have no proof beyond his word, that any such woman ever existed."

Minton reached for a sheaf of papers on the desk.

"I took the liberty of clipping the latest newspaper stories about the affair," he said. "I pasted them up so you could look them over quickly. When you speak of this mysterious woman it reminds me that the police seem to be working along that angle now."

He handed Brent a sheet on which had been pasted a photograph clipped from a newspaper.

It was a picture of a girl. She was plump, of a full-blown prettiness, with dark eyes and a heavy mass of dark hair piled high on her head. It was a full face portrait, rather dark and smudgy in reproduction, and beneath it was an explanatory paragraph:

WHO IS THIS GIRL?

Police are seeking the original of this photograph, which was found in the apartment where the murdered body of Paul Gregory, young architect, was discovered yesterday morning. The photograph, lacking all identification marks, was in a bureau drawer and police attention has been concentrated on it in view of the fact that it was the only picture of a woman, among the dead man's effects, other than a large cabinet portrait of his murdered *fiancée*, Margaret Hilliard.

Michael Brent sniffed.

"Probably an old flame. Maybe a relative."

"Perhaps," agreed Minton. "But, being the *only* picture of another woman, it is interesting."

Brent paced restlessly about the office.

"We'll sum it up. Here we have a young man, in love with a girl above his social station in life. He is known to have been seen with suspicious characters. He telephones the girl and presumably asks her to meet him. She is murdered by some one who is aware of the meeting place. It would seem that the young man murdered her himself. Possible motive she had discovered his philanderings, accused him, and he killed her in anger. But we already know that she was aware of his visits to No. 90, wherever that may be. And we find that the young man was himself murdered at about the same time the girl met her death."

Minton looked helpless.

"I am utterly and completely at sea," said Brent, sitting down again. "Oh, Starr was right. He was right.

Gregory was up to his neck in some affair—that seems certain. But why it should lead to two murders, I can't fathom. When that poor girl left the house to meet her lover, she was as good as dead."

"They say there's a woman back of almost every crime."

"Cherchez la femme! That's axiomatic. My own theory is that each murder was committed by a different person. Gregory was clubbed to death. The girl was shot. But there's a connection somewhere, and there's a woman somewhere. If we find her we can solve the whole business."

He picked up the sheet again and studied the photograph of the girl. "Pretty enough," he muttered, "but she's no raving beauty. Still, a photograph tells nothing. And if the police can't trace it, what chance have we? It's exasperating. There she is! Who is she? Above all, where is she?"

Brent was greatly agitated. Minton, accustomed to these outbursts when his employer was worried and bewildered, looked at him mildly.

"I think that is an old photograph."

"What makes you think that?"

"Most girls nowadays have their hair bobbed."

Brent gazed at the picture again.

"I must be slipping. How did I ever miss that? Sure, she has her hair dressed in the fashion of five years back." He flung the sheet back on the desk. "We can discount the picture. It's just one of Gregory's relatives or else an old sweetheart. If it were his lady friend of Chat Noir she would have bobbed hair, that's certain, for that kind can't afford to stay five years behind the times."

"Speaking of Chat Noir—you said you were down there yesterday looking for No. 90."

"Yes, and there is no No. 90."

"But Mr. Starr claims Gregory called on a woman in that street, and it appears to check with what the taxi drivers told you."

"Yes. That was one circumstance that led me to believe Starr was telling the truth. He had no idea that I knew of Gregory's visits to Chat Noir." Brent was full of enthusiasm again. "It all comes back to that confounded street! The whole solution is down there, somewhere, and I'm going to find it, No. 90 or not!"

"Of course there was nothing to indicate that No. 90 was on Chat Noir at all," Minton reminded him. "It was only a guess on your part, and it appears to have been wrong. It has confused the issue a bit, in my opinion. Perhaps if you forget about that number for the time being and concentrate on the street as a whole, you might be further ahead."

"Oh, I'm going back there. Somewhere on that street there is a woman who knows the inside story of those murders, and I'll find her if I have to question every trollop on Chat Noir."

"Perhaps the police—"

Minton wilted under Brent's glare.

"The police! Bah! I've tackled this thing alone, and I'll stay with it. I'm not going to hand over my information to the police and say, 'Please, kind sirs, this is too deep for me. I've bitten off more than I can chew. Won't you help me?' And if they fell down on the job, what would they do? They'd keep their mouths shut, and settle down to making the most of their case against Hinky Lewis, my client. If they clear up the mystery before I do, the more power to them, but I'll play my lone hand to the finish."

Minton coughed apologetically.

"I hadn't thought of it in that light."

"I'm going to find that woman, and I'm going to learn something more about Pelham Starr. I'm not altogether satisfied yet about that young man. I think he told me some facts and some lies. That remark he made about hoping I cleared up the Hilliard murder and not the other, sticks in my mind."

"It may have been just his ill temper. He made it clear that he had no love for Gregory. And, after all, he didn't say he hoped you wouldn't clear up the Gregory end of the case. He just meant that he was indifferent."

"Still, he quarreled with Gregory. There's just a chance that Mr. Pelham Starr may have been drawing a red herring across a trail that could lead unpleasantly close to himself."

"There's a possible motive, no doubt."

"It's the only definite motive, slim as it is, that I've run across so far, and I can't afford to overlook it. I'm going back to Chat Noir."

He was eager to get back to the unsavory street. His eagerness was not wholly based on a desire to learn more about Paul Gregory's mysterious visits to the neighborhood. Although he would not admit it to himself, there was a persistent hope that he might again see the girl he had encountered on Chat Noir the previous day.

CHAPTER XII
A SURE THING

MIDGE borrowed some money from Norah and treated her to breakfast at a little restaurant on the Main.

"My boss won't be payin' me until to-night," he explained. "I'm a bit short of cash, but I'll pay it back to you, Norah."

"I wish you would take it all, and let us move away from here."

"We'll see about that. I'll look around. Of course, it don't do for a man to throw up his job when he ain't got nothin' else in sight. Montreal is a hard city, Norah. It ain't always easy to get work. But, as I was tellin' you yesterday, I've got somethin' in mind if I can get a bit of capital to swing it, and I'll see the man this very day. Seein' it's your money, I want to be careful."

"I suppose I could go to work. I don't like to be idle."

"That's the spirit," he said approvingly. "We'll look over the advertisements in the papers some of these days. Just for now, I think you'd best take a good rest for a week or so."

"There's so little for me to do. I hate staying around the lodging house all day."

"Just be patient. Be patient, gal. We'll get settled down a little better after a while. If this deal I'm thinkin' of works out all right, we'll be able to do more for ourselves."

"What kind of a deal is it?"

"An investment. I don't rightly know what kind of a business it is, for the man didn't say. I was talkin' to this chap a few days ago, and he said if I had any money to spare he could put me in the way of doublin' it overnight."

"The stock market?" she said, dubiously. "I don't think it's safe—"

"Oh, no," said Midge, shocked. "Not the stock market. I ain't such a fool as to go in for that game. Unless you're on the inside, they just robs you. No, this is a sure thing. I'll find out about it to-day."

So far as it went, Midge was telling the truth. He failed to mention that the philanthropic gentleman who was to double his money overnight was a chance acquaintance he had met in the corner tavern, a derby-hatted, red-faced person with a startling taste in neckties and waistcoats, a fascinating individual who could perform dexterous feats with coins and cards.

Over a friendly quart of beer this gifted artist had confided that he had entertained vaudeville audiences from coast to coast for several years, under the billing of "Mr. Mysto, the Man Who Puzzles You." Unfortunately, Mr. Mysto had toppled from grace between the supper show and the evening performance of his first day in Montreal, and had been permitted to puzzle local audiences no longer, inasmuch as he had not sobered up for two days.

Short-sighted and narrow-minded moguls of the profession had canceled the remainder of his time, and Mr. Mysto had decided to repay this injustice by depriving vaudeville of his presence for a while.

There were, he confided, ways and means whereby his gifts could be utilized in private life to pecuniary advantage. Thereupon, Mr. Mysto winked shrewdly, produced a pack of cards from his pocket, shuffled them and nonchalantly extracted four aces.

Midge gaped. He saw the possibilities of Mr. Mysto's talent at once. His newfound friend then confided his intentions of invading a few of the gambling houses on the Main and generously offered to steer Midge in the way of a good thing should he care to put up an investment of a hundred dollars or more.

As Midge had something less than a hundred cents to his name at the time, he had been obliged to decline, but Mr. Mysto, under the influence of his third quart within the hour, professed warm affection and eternal friendship, promising that the offer would hold good for the duration of his stay in the neighborhood.

Accordingly, Midge left Norah to return to the lodging house alone and hastened back to the tavern where he had met the gentleman of talent. As luck would have it, Mr. Mysto, looking somewhat the worse for wear, was sitting by himself at a corner table. The derby hat was tilted at a less jaunty angle, and he was wearing the same gay waistcoat and the same remarkable necktie, regrettably stained with beer. He nodded gloomily to Midge.

"And how," inquired Midge, "have things been going?"

"So-so," returned the artist, tilting his glass. "Are you going to buy a drink?"

"Certainly," said Midge, like a gentleman, and held up two fingers. Mr. Mysto brightened up perceptibly.

"I don't suppose you heard about the rotten break I got last night."

"What was that?"

Mr. Mysto leaned confidentially forward. "I got in a game up at a dive a few blocks away and cleaned up. I guess I must 'a' been more'n a grand ahead, and what do you think hadda happen?"

"The cops come in."

"No. The cops don't come into this place. A couple of guns stuck me up on my way back to my room. Can you beat it? Took all the jack I had won. They even got my watch."

"Ain't that tough!" sympathized Midge.

"I would 'a' been sittin' on top of the world right now if them two lads had laid off. Ain't that a hell of a note? And here I am back where I started, without even a sawbuck to edge into the crap game in the back room."

The waiter served their beer. Midge paid. Mr. Mysto gulped long and loudly, wiped his mouth with the back of his hand, then continued querulously:

"Damn if I can see why I deserve a piece of rotten luck like that. It took me two days to crash that joint, and just when I was sittin' pretty, this had to happen. Not even masked. They stood me up against a wall, and one of 'em held a rod on me while the other guy took the collection. I must have a jinx."

Midge listened sympathetically to the tale of woe, and after Mr. Mysto's spirits began to revive under the influence of the beer, he broached the subject in hand.

"I think," he said, cautiously, "I can put up a bit of money, like you was askin' me the other day."

"How much?" asked Mysto with interest.

"It all depends. I'd have to know more about how you plan to use it. Maybe I could raise as much as fifty dollars."

"Fifty! Don't be a piker. You double your money on a sure thing."

" Well, then, a hundred."

"That's better. And for my end, all I want is ten bucks to buy my first stack. Your hundred will help me make plenty, but I give you it back and an extra hundred besides."

Midge licked his lips. "Fair enough," he said. "But what if you lose?"

"I don't lose. That's the beauty of it."

"If it's in a card game you might lose. If you couldn't lose, you'd be a millionaire," insisted Midge, reasonably enough.

"I tell you, friend, this is a sure thing. A sure thing. And the reason I ain't a millionaire is because you can only work this sure thing once in a game, and only once in the same company. Look! I'll show you."

Out came the pack of cards again. Mr. Mysto lowered his voice.

"You're the only man around here that knows I'm handy with the pasteboards, see. If it ever got around, why I wouldn't get into no more games. But I'll show you, because I know you're a man that can keep his mouth shut. Now watch!"

He shuffled the cards, then flicked them out on the table in four separate five-card hands.

"Suppose I'm sittin' in a poker game, and it's my deal, and there's four other guys at the table. Well, there's the way I'd deal 'em. You didn't see anything phony, did you?"

"No!"

"Well, then, look." Mr. Mysto turned up the cards. His own hand consisted of the ten, jack, queen, king, and ace of hearts. There was no need to look at the other hands. Mysto's was unbeatable.

"Cripes!"

"Ain't that a sure thing?" asked Mysto softly.

Midge rubbed his chin with his knuckles. "There couldn't be anything surer than that," he admitted. "How do you do it? Are the cards stacked? Could you do it with another deck?"

"I can do it with any deck. It's all a matter of trainin'. Shuffle 'em yourself!"

Midge shuffled the cards and handed them back. Mr. Mysto then shuffled them once more, explaining that the trick could be accomplished only on his own deal. Out flicked the cards. He dealt himself another royal flush.

Midge was convinced.

"Can you get into a game tonight?"

"Yes. I met a guy who says he'll bring me up to another joint. Lapierre's."

"I know the place. But where does my hundred come in?"

"Listen," said Mr. Mysto expansively. "I'll tell you what I'll do. Give me a ten spot to start me in this game to-night, and when I'm ready to deal myself the unbeatable hand I'll give you the high sign. You can give me the hundred before the game if you like, or you can slip it to me then, just to show everythin's fair and above-board. You can stand behind my chair and see the hand for yourself, and then slip me the jack. I'll bet it for you. That's all I do. I bet it for you. The hand can't be beat. I win the pot and you double your money. Unless, of course, everybody else checks out and nobody calls me or raises me, but that ain't likely. Could anything be fairer than that?"

"No," said Midge. "Nothin' could be fairer than that. I'll get the money right away."

"If you can get more than a hundred, bring it along. I'll bet it for you just the same, and you'll double it. You can see yourself that you haven't a chance in the world of losing. It's a sure thing if ever there was one."

"I don't have to give you the money until I see the cards in your hand?"

"No. You can't lose."

"And all you want is ten dollars?" Midge could not rid himself of the impression that there was a catch in this munificent offer somewhere.

"Ten bucks to get into the game. By the time I'm ready to deal myself the royal flush I should have that ten spot built up so high that I'll make a killing on the big hand. I'm not worrying about *my* end of it. I'll let you share in it just for get-away money."

Midge finished his beer.

"Do you want the ten right away?"

"Right away."

"Sure you won't spend it?" Midge asked cautiously.

"Say, listen!" demanded Mr. Mysto with an injured air. "What do you think I am anyway? A crook? Here I just go and let you in on a sure thing, just because you're a friend of mine, and you're afraid to trust me with a ten."

"I didn't mean that," said Midge hastily. "I'll go and get it right now."

"I'll wait here," Mr. Mysto growled.

Midge left the tavern and returned to the lodging house. He found Norah sitting on the front steps, playing with two of the children of the neighborhood, ragged, dirty-faced youngsters who were as shy as savages, but she had contrived to win their confidence and was laughing with them as though she had known them for years. She was a friendly little thing, and although her pleasant "good morning" to the landlady had been rewarded with a glare of surprised suspicion, the youngsters had proved more amenable to her good nature.

Swiftly, then, Midge explained that he had seen the man of whom he had spoken, that by great good luck the offer was still open, and that he needed ten dollars at once to bind the bargain.

"It's a business deal," he lied glibly. "He's buyin' a bit of property that he can sell to-night and double his money, and he says I can come in on it, seein' he's a friend of mine."

"How much more will it take?"

"As much as you can spare, Norah. I had to promise him I'd put in a hundred dollars anyway, but if you've got more than that I'd put it all in. We can't lose. It's a sure thing. You'll have the money back tomorrow morning—doubled."

"Are you quite sure it's safe?"

"Would I advise you to put up your money if I thought there was any chance of losin' it?" asked Midge. "It's a sure thing, I tell you. There ain't no chance of losin'. I know about these things, Norah, and I never heard of anythin' surer than this. It would be a crime to let it go by."

She yielded at last to his persuasions, went up to her room and returned with her purse. She kept only a few dollars for herself and gave Midge the rest.

"A hundred and sixty," said Midge, counting the money. "That means we can put in a hundred and fifty, not countin' the ten he wants now. This time tomorrow mornin' we'll have three hundred dollars. It's a pity we ain't got more."

He scuttled off, thrusting the money into his pocket.

Norah sat on the steps, the purse in her lap. The children, who were afraid of Midge, had withdrawn. Norah fingered the few remaining bills. One hundred and sixty dollars was a lot of money, but the sum had not seemed so great when she knew it was all she had in the world. However, possession of the plump little roll of bills had given her a feeling of security; now she was suddenly afraid.

After all, money was important. What if Midge were wrong? What if he lost her little fortune? They would have to stay on in this poor lodging house, in this dreadful street, and poverty would stalk at their heels. This thought frightened her.

A footstep on the stairs aroused her. She moved aside to let a lodger go by, and then looked up when a throaty voice said: "Mornin', miss."

It was Burger. He was the same homely figure of the previous afternoon, his appearance in nowise beautified by the puffy and swollen black eye. The helpless arm hung limply by his side. He was an ugly and repellent figure, but there was something respectful in his manner and something kindly in his voice. Then she remembered the man as he had been the previous night, his humble gratitude as she bathed his bruised face, and she smiled at him.

"How's the eye?"

He stepped down onto the pavement.

"It's all right. It don't hurt—since you fixed it up."

"I'm awfully grateful to you for saving me from that brute."

Burger looked uncomfortable, and shuffled uneasily.

"He didn't know who you were, or I guess he wouldn't have bothered you. But he's a bad actor. I'm glad I came along."

"I was frightened to death," she told him earnestly, her delicate chin uptilted and her eyes wide.

"He's kinda used to havin' his own way around here. Everybody is scared of him. I think he's cuckoo."

"Cuckoo?"

"Crazy," explained Burger. "We can't say much, for Laboeuf runs things in this street, and he's a bad guy to cross, but I think he's nuts. Them dogs of his scare the livin' tripe out of everybody, and he thinks it's a great joke. There's plenty would shoot the brutes if they dared. But Laboeuf is boss, see? I suppose you know he's Midge's boss?"

Norah was startled.

"My stepfather works for that man?"

"Didn't he tell you? I guess he was scared to, after last night. Yeah, he works for Laboeuf. That was why he didn't dare put up no argument when he took you away from Laboeuf. He's afraid of him."

"But what kind of work does he do?"

Burger rubbed his stubbly chin. "I guess Midge 'll have to tell you that. But if you don't mind me tellin' you somethin', miss, I wouldn't stay around here any longer'n you can help."

"I don't like living here. But I suppose it's all my stepfather can afford."

Burger looked at her strangely. "It's been a long time since you seen him last, huh?"

"More than five years."

"Well—you know him better'n I do, and it's none of my business, but if you can get him to move away you'll be better off. This ain't a good neighborhood for a nice girl like you."

"I've asked him to move somewhere else."

"And what did he say?"

"He said we couldn't go just now, but when things got better—"

"Keep harpin' on it, miss. Midge 'll stay here till the crack of doom if you let things ride. Get me? Make him move. He'll stick unless you pry him loose. If he won't go, why you pack up and go anyway, and maybe that 'll waken him up. Don't think I'm buttin' in, kid, but it's for your own good."

"You see," she faltered, "I don't know any one else in Canada. I have no friends and no relatives but him. I have to stay with him. There's no place for me to go."

"You can always get a job, and there's worse things than bein' alone. Of course, maybe Midge'll brace up now that he's gotta look after you, but don't let him put anythin' over on you." Burger looked down at the toes of his shabby boots. "Not that I'm runnin' him down, or anythin', but the less you stick around this part of town, the better, see?"

He looked around, nervously, as though fearing he may have been overheard.

"I gotta be goin' now. Listen, you won't spill any of this to Midge, will you?"

"You mean, I'm not to tell him?"

"Don't say nothin'. If he thought I was talkin' to you he might be sore." Burger began to edge away. "I'm just tippin' you off because I hate to see—well—I don't like to see you livin' around here, for you're too good—I mean, it ain't your class at all—"

He shuffled off down the street. Norah watched him go; she had an impulse to run after him, to question him, to ask him to explain more about her stepfather, about Laboeuf, about the dangers at which he had hinted. But he went away, and she sat there on the steps, fumbling at the worn purse in her lap, the purse that was now so thin and empty. Chat Noir, even in the clear morning sunlight, seemed more sinister than ever.

CHAPTER XIII
THE DEAD HAND

APIERRE'S place was a dingy apartment over a dry-goods store on the Main. It was only a small gambling joint ignored by the bigger fry among the gambling fraternity because it was reputedly in constant danger of being "knocked over" by the police and its clientele was largely of the tourist variety, steered there by taxicab drivers and hackmen.

However, one could usually find a moderate game in progress, and chips could be purchased reasonably. Mr. Mysto, accompanied by a friend whom he introduced as Levy, met Midge in the corner tavern shortly after nine o'clock that night and the three set out.

Levy was a short, fat little Jew with greasy hair. Midge took an instant dislike to him, and Levy, on his part, paid Midge scant attention.

"C'mon," the Jew said. "It ain't everybody can get into this place, y' understand, unless they got somebody wit' 'em, but any frien' of mine is welcome."

Mr. Mysto bestowed a surreptitious wink upon

Midge, for whom a great light promptly dawned. He astutely divined that Levy was a touter for Lapierre's place, and Mysto was playing the role of the lamb, innocently eager for the slaughter. Midge shook with inward laughter. If Levy only knew!

There was a poker game in progress at Lapierre's place when they arrived, obtaining admittance after an impressive series of signals in the way of knocks and double knocks at the outer door, and Mysto played the part of sucker to perfection. Levy clapped him on the back, introduced him to Lapierre, and extolled his merits as a good fellow, while Mysto chafed with evident impatience to get into the game. Midge, when he said he had come only to look on, was ignored.

"If they only knew he ain't got no more than ten dollars in his pockets they'd sing a different tune," opined Midge.

Before he sat in, Mysto sidled over to his financial backer. "Do you want to slip me the dough now or when I get the big mitt?" he whispered.

"D'you think you'd better have it now?"

"They might see you slippin' me the jack and raise a row. If you give it to me now I'll put it in this pocket, see," and he slapped the left hand pocket of his trousers, "and play it when the time comes."

Midge gave him the money and Mysto counted it.

"A hundred and fifty. Good! That means three hundred for you when I win with the big hand."

Mr. Mysto pocketed the bills and plunged into the game.

Any wavering doubts Midge might have had as to Mysto's ability to invade a game on limited capital swiftly vanished when his friend won the first hand with three queens and raked in a pot that must have amounted to thirty dollars. The game was draw, and there were four others at the table, but shortly after Mysto's entry one of the players dropped out, penniless. Levy slipped into the vacant chair.

Midge almost hugged himself with elation. The touter, in all probability a card sharp, planned to participate in the spoils. He thought Mysto would be easy pickings, eh! He would get his fingers burned. The po-

His skull seemed to crack into fragments

etic justice of the situation delighted Midge beyond measure. He looked forward with keen anticipation to Levy's downfall at the hands of the man he had sought to entrap.

The room was heavy with smoke. The players were in their shirt sleeves, but they kept their hats on, and each puffed at a cigar or cigarette. Their faces were gray and expressionless; they glanced at one another occasionally, confining their brief words solely to the game.

One was a thin, misanthropic individual with high cheek bones and a prominent Adam's apple above his rumpled collar. Another was young and pimply-faced, with stubby fingers. The man beside him was a ponderous, slow-moving fellow with pallid countenance and a heavy black mustache.

The misanthropic man had been winning until Levy entered the game, and then his luck turned. However, he was cautious, and tossed in his cards frequently after the deal, refusing to stay on anything but a strong opening hand.

Levy, apparently, had stolen his luck. He won three big pots in succession, then lost heavily when he put too much faith in the strength of a small straight as opposed to Mr. Mysto's two-card draw. When Levy finally called he found that Mysto's confidence had been well founded, and a full house won the substantial pot. Midge slapped his knee appreciatively. Levy glowered at him.

More men entered the place; some sat in at another game in the next room; others looked on; a few idled about the little bar in the kitchen.

Midge placed himself directly behind Mr. Mysto's chair and watched the rise and fall of his companion's fortunes. The gentleman of talent was not attempting any sleight of hand as yet, so far as Midge could see, but his luck was consistently good, and he played his cards well.

Half an hour passed. The place was dim with smoke. Voices droned. Cards flickered under the green-shaded light. Midge was tired, but he was afraid of losing his position behind Mysto's chair, for there were more onlookers now.

Levy and Mr. Mysto were the heavy winners. The sad-faced man was almost broke, despite his caution. Time and again he was nosed out of the pot by a narrow margin. The pallid fellow caressed his mustache and seemed to be holding his own. The pimply-faced youth skirted insolvency several times, but had an uncanny faculty for holding a winning hand just when it appeared that he was about to succumb.

At last Mr. Mysto casually scratched his left ear, the signal that he was about to exercise his peculiar talent. It was his deal. Midge tried to appear bored. The cards flicked about the table, so swiftly that one could scarcely follow the rapid motions of the white fingers.

Mysto laid aside the deck and picked up his hand, cupping the cards. There was a jack on top. One by one the others edged into view as Mysto separated them. The ace was next. Then the ten. Then the king, and finally the queen.

Midge gulped.

The fellow was right. He had dealt himself the unbeatable hand.

Ten, jack, queen, king and ace. All diamonds. A royal flush—pat!

It was miraculous. If only the others stayed in to fight it out. What a profitable slaughter this would be! They stayed. Mysto raised the initial bet and still they stayed.

"Cards?"

Levy drew three, and sat back, his face expressionless. The sad man asked for one; the fellow with the mustache drew two and the pimply-faced youth took three.

"I'll play these," said Mysto.

The sad man raised his eyebrows and looked reflectively at the dealer. Mustache bet a dollar and Levy promptly raised. The sad man put down his cards with a sigh, but the pimply young man was a glutton for punishment and stuck with the ship. Mysto raised again. Mustache peered down into his hand and met the raise, but Levy boosted it once more. The pimply youth decided that he had enough, and when Mysto again raised he looked vastly relieved that he had dropped out when he did.

"I guess you have 'em," Mustache muttered and dropped out.

"Gotta show me," said Levy, and came back with another raise.

Mysto hesitated. "See you and bump you again."

Levy nodded. "How much?"

Mysto thrust his hand into his pocket and drew out the roll of bills. "A hundred and fifty bucks to say I beat you."

Levy counted the money, peeled an equal sum from a fat wad of bills, met the raise and called.

"It's a shame to take you like this," said Mysto.

"Show 'em."

The gentleman of talent flung down his hand.

"Nobody can beat 'em," he said quietly, and reached for his winnings.

"Hey—hold on!" Levy rose halfway out of his chair. "You can't take anything with that hand."

"Why not? It's a royal flush, ain't it?"

"The hell it is! You dealt yourself an extra card."

Levy thrust aside Mysto's hand. There lay the royal

flush, but there also lay a seven of clubs, peeping out from beneath the ten.

Mysto's mouth opened. The other players leaned forward. The sad-faced man shook his head.

"One too many, brother."

"But I had 'em, I tell you!" protested Mysto. " I never saw that seven. It musta been lyin' on the table."

"Nope!" grumbled Mustache. "It wasn't lyin' on the table. It's all in your hand."

The pimply youth clucked sympathetically.

"'Too bad," he said. "A royal flush ruined. On your own deal. You give yourself one too many."

"Well, it was the last card!" declared Mysto. "It don't count. I had the flush before I got the seven. The cards must 'a' been stuck together. It was on the bottom. My flush still holds good."

"It does like hell!" snapped Levy. " ou can't pull anythin' like that around here. It's a dead hand. I win the pot."

"How do you get that way? You couldn't beat my royal flush."

"I can't beat a royal flush, but I can beat a dead hand, no matter what cards I got."

"We all oughta get our money back," ventured the pimply-faced young man.

"Bull!" said Levy, emphatically. "It's a dead hand, and he and I was the only ones in. I get the pot. That's the rules."

The sad-faced man nodded.

"It's the rules, all right."

"I don't believe it," declared Mysto.

Levy called Lapierre. The gambling house proprietor heard the case and scratched his head dubiously.

"I never heard of anyt'ing like dat before. But I t'ink M'sieu' Levy is right. Wait. I got a book."

He went out into the kitchen and the argument was resumed. Two or three of the onlookers joined in. Some supported Levy, but one thought everybody should get their money back. Midge squeaked a mild word in favor of Mysto, but no one heard him. Lapierre returned with his book—a paper bound edition of Hoyle.

The authority covered the situation. Levy, it appeared, was right. The extra card rendered Mysto's hand dead and Levy was entitled to the pot.

"I told you so," he grunted, and raked in his winnings, which included the side bet. "After this, count your cards, friend."

Midge was utterly dazed. He turned away as the game was resumed. Mysto, after a great deal of grumbling, had decided to continue. Midge stumbled toward the door, left the flat, and went down the stairs into the street.

He shivered, but not because the night was cool.

Three hundred dollars! It had lain right there before him, to all intents and purposes his, and his alone. Now the fat, velvety wad of bills reposed in Levy's pocket.

"It's mine, by rights," mumbled Midge.

Mysto, the infallible, had blundered. One little slip, and the unbeatable hand had been beaten.

"How in hell did he ever come to do a thing like that? Pick up an extry card! Gawd! And the money as good as in my purse."

People jostled him as he shuffled down the Main, and some cursed when he blundered against them, scarcely seeing where he was going. He paid no attention, muttering to himself:

"It's always the way. I've never been lucky. Somethin' always happens. There couldn't have been nothin' surer than that. Nothin'. And somethin' had to happen."

He entered Chat Noir. Head down, hands thrust deep in his pockets, he went down the dark street until he was a few doors away from the lodging house, and then he turned abruptly and vanished into the depths of a black little alley.

So far it had not occurred to him that the real loser was Norah. In a vague way he knew he would have to make some explanation to cover the disappearance of her money, but this did not greatly bother him. The gall and wormwood was in the blow to his own pride; he had thought himself sufficiently shrewd to "put one over" on Lapierre's poker game, and something had gone wrong.

CHAPTER XIV
THE BOSS OF CHAT NOIR

IDGE TAPLEY ascended a rickety flight of wooden steps leading to the rear veranda of a house at the rear end of the alley. There were no lights in evidence when he shuffled up to the door and rapped three times sharply.

A woman's voice said: "Who's there?"

"It's me. Midge."

The door opened. The woman, sullen and slovenly, stood there. She had once been beautiful, and although she was not yet old, the flame and the spirit of youth had left her. She had dark, tragic eyes, a discouraged mouth. Her thick black hair was untidy.

"Where's Laboeuf?"

She gestured toward the next room. Midge went in.

He found Laboeuf, boss of Chat Noir, just finishing a late supper. He glanced up indifferently and growled a surly greeting.

"Got anything for me?" asked Midge.

Laboeuf looked surprised.

"What? You look for work?"

"I need some money, right away." Laboeuf grunted.

"So? Maybe I find somet'ing for you."

He picked up a match from the table, thrust it between his big, strong teeth and stared at Midge reflectively.

"That girl," he said. "Is she really your daughter, eh?"

A crafty expression crept into Midge's eyes. So Laboeuf was interested!

"She's my gal," he answered. "I married her old woman."

Laboeuf grunted.

"What are you going to do with her?"

Midge shrugged. "Dunno. Get her a job somewheres, I guess."

"If she wants work," suggested Laboeuf, "send her to me."

Nervously, Midge groped for a cigarette.

"Not that kind of work," he said.

Laboeuf spat the match viciously from his mouth. "Are you sure she's your girl?" he grinned.

The cigarette drooped sullenly. "Yes. She's all right. You ain't got no chance there, Mr. Laboeuf."

The big man swung his feet from the table, stood up and stretched his arms as he yawned. On the wall his shadow was like an enormous cross.

"I guess maybe she'll do what she likes," he growled. Then he stared at Midge again until the little man became uncomfortable and chewed the cigarette to a pulp. Little flecks of tobacco dribbled over his lower lip.

Then Laboeuf said: "I see you hangin' around today wit' that fellow who says his name is Mysto. What game are you up to wit' him?"

"We had a little deal on."

"How comes he let you work in wit' him?"

"He's a friend of mine."

Laboeuf flung back his head and laughed uproariously, his eyes squinted, his mouth wide open. "So!" he said. "A friend? Did he show you card tricks?"

Midge knew better than to lie to Laboeuf. The boss of Chat Noir had an uncanny way of knowing nearly everything that went on in his bailiwick.

"Yes." Then Midge's grievance surged up. "We would 'a' made some money, too, if things had only gone right."

"You?" sneered Laboeuf.

"Yes, me! Mysto and me was workin' together on somethin' that would 'a' made me a nice piece of change. It was a sure thing, so it was. I tell you, Mr. Laboeuf, that fellow is smart. He can make the cards eat outa his hand, so he can. We had it all doped out together and he was to make a hundred and fifty bucks for me tonight over at Lapierre's."

"How?"

"He can do tricks, this Mysto. When it's his own deal there ain't nothin' he can't do, and he does it smart. He used to be on the stage. When he wants to, he can deal himself a royal flush, and to-night I raised me some money, and Mysto, bein' as he's a friend of mine, bet it for me when he dealt himself a royal flush, see? It was a sure thing, but I don't know what went wrong—he slipped up somehow and give himself a card too many. And I lost. Every cent I had in the world."

Laboeuf slapped his thigh, delightedly.

"And you lost?" he roared. "And you lost your money, perhaps, to a Jew named Levy, eh?"

Midge nodded. "All I had. A hundred and fifty."

Laboeuf chuckled.

"And yet you do not know how it was done?"

"It was an accident. Mysto give himself an extra card by mistake. He lost a lot of money, too."

Laboeuf clucked his tongue sympathetically.

"Triste!" he muttered. "It breaks my heart." And then, as Midge detected a mocking note, Laboeuf roared savagely: "You fool! You live here in Chat Noir for one, two, how many years? And you learn nothing. You are a worse sucker than any the taxi drivers bring down from the big hotels."

"How?" Midge was gaping pathetically.

"I am ashame that I have anybody work for me who is so damn stupid. Look! I know this Mysto. He is a crook. He come into a card game that I run, last night. He does his stuff, and he is smart, but he does not fool me. When he go, I tell Emil, and Emil goes out by the back way and meets this Mysto and takes away from him all the money he won. There were a lot of suckers in the place that night, so I get it all, and Mysto is another sucker, because all the time I just let things ride, so he is working for me and does not know it, and because he thinks he is cheating me, I take his money and pay him nothing."

Midge wagged his head admiringly. "He was tellin' me about that. He thinks it was an ordinary stick-up."

Laboeuf snorted. "I know a few tricks he does not know yet. And as for him and Levy, they are working together, but some of these nights something is going to happen."

"How do you mean, workin' together?"

"Bah! Why should I tell you? Mysto finds a sucker like you and shows him how he can deal himself a hand nobody can beat, and he says he will bet your money for you. A sure thing! Don't you know yet that nothing is sure, where somebody is going to make money for you, except that he is going to make some for himself. You went into that game, Mysto and Levy are working with Lapierre, and they win easy, and then Mysto deals himself the big hand. But he hides the other card from you, or else he picks it up when everybody else is busy watching the bets. And what happens? He loses. Levy wins, and to-night they split your hundred and fifty and Levy curses Mysto for getting drunk and picking a cheap sucker like you instead of a big one."

The scathing contempt in Laboeuf's voice made Midge's ears burn. He realized now how completely he had been duped by the plausible Mysto.

"I'll get that dirty blighter!" he gritted. "I'll get him—"

"Shut up! You get nobody. You have lost. It is a lesson. Now I have work for you, and after this do not believe people when they say they will make money for you. If you do your work well for me you will not have to worry about money."

Midge brightened up at this.

"What's on?"

Laboeuf leaned across the table, his heavy knuckles pressed against the wood, his bold eyes gleaming. "There is a man," he said, "who wants to know things. A dick, I think, but I am not sure. He is a strange man who wears a beard and a black hat, and he came to Chat Noir yesterday looking for numbers. And when he saw there was not any No. 90 on Chat Noir he went away."

"A dick, huh?"

"Perhaps. Perhaps not. I want to know."

"Seems to me I saw that guy," said Midge reflectively. "I'm try-in' to remember. Seems to me he was on the street when I was comin' home with Norah yesterday. Black whiskers and a big hat. That was him."

"You would know him if you saw him again?"

"Sure."

"I want you to keep your eyes open for this man. If you see him around here again, tail him."

"All right."

"If he's askin' questions, I want something to happen to this fellow."

"You want him beat up? You know I don't go in for that kind of work, Mr. Laboeuf," whined Midge. "I ain't got the size, nor the strength."

"You are yellow, you mean," Laboeuf said contemptuously.

"I'm not yeller," Midge retorted, showing his teeth. "But if there's beatin' up to be done, you've got guys what can do it lots better than me."

"Bah! Some of my best men are only boys. They will help you, if you need help."

Laboeuf looked up sharply. They were aware of a distant knocking. It was at the front door. His woman appeared in the room and looked at him questioningly. He spoke rapidly in French, and she went out into the hall, closing the door behind her. Midge and Laboeuf listened. They heard the front door open, heard a muffled interchange of voices, and then the door closed again. The woman returned.

She said something to Laboeuf, and the big man's face underwent a startling transformation. He wheeled about, grasped Midge by the shoulder, almost lifting him out of his chair.

"It is the man!" he exclaimed. "The man we talk about. In the big hat. He was at the door."

"Yeah?"

"You want money, eh? You do this job right and I get your money back for you."

Swiftly he gave Midge his instructions. At first the little man demurred, but Laboeuf raged at him, cursed him, shoved him to the door and thrust him out into the street.

Midge, frightened but obedient, hastened in pursuit of Michael Brent.

CHAPTER XV
NUMBER NINETY!

ONTREAL, being very old, is a gray city seamed with the story of its years. Its streets have the fantastic irregularity of the wrinkles in an old man's face. They seem to follow no set plan, they twist and curve and merge with one another and divide into smaller wrinkles, which are a network of lanes and alleys, to the confusion of the stranger and often to the bewilderment of the native. And the old streets, the narrow streets, the tortuous streets, are streets of shadow.

Michael Brent had resolved to follow Minton's suggestion and concentrate on Chat Noir as a whole. It was quite possible that a few judicious inquiries might put him on the right trail immediately, whereas if he simply settled down to a house-to-house canvass in the hope of locating No. 90, he might only be wasting time.

He reached the shabby neighborhood before darkness had fallen and strolled down Chat Noir. It occurred to him that there were dark and devious thor-

A final push and the body vanished

oughfares branching off the street that might be investigated with profit while the light was good.

Most of these, he found, were nothing more than lanes, dirty, garbage-strewn alleys, and although broken-down houses had managed to squeeze themselves in here and there he found neither street signs nor numbers.

One such evil lane caught his eye when he had been prowling about the neighborhood for more than half an hour. Mr. Brent had reached the vicinity of the signboard on the vacant lot where he had expected to find No. 90 the previous day, and a few paces farther on he came to a dirty, rutted road.

It was flanked on either side by a hideous brick house, and at first he took it to be merely an alley leading to the back yards. Then, at one side, the attorney caught sight of a plank walk. It consisted of but two boards, side by side, almost obscured by mud, and it led down the side of the brick house, continued at an angle along the base of a wooden fence and was then hidden from view by the other building.

From the angle, Brent judged there was a street or alley of some kind beyond, which merely crooked sharply from this outlet to Chat Noir. It was almost dusk now, but he decided to investigate this one remaining thoroughfare, if such it were.

Mud squelched under the planks as he walked down into the shadow of the brick house, and when he came to the fence he found that his surmise had been correct. Before him lay a short, narrow street, in length about half an ordinary block, opening at the far end on a more or less regular thoroughfare where lights were twinkling.

This passage was as sinister as it was dirty. The narrow, plank walk continued down one side past half a dozen grimy old dwellings. On the other side of the street were a ditch, a fence, and a jungle of rubbish heaps.

The first house was deserted. Its windows were shattered and the front door sagged drunkenly open. The number plate by the open door had been torn loose and hung down backward by a single nail. It was a forlorn, dismal house, haunted by evil ghosts.

The next building apparently was occupied, for the front door was closed and Brent caught a glimmer of yellow light beneath a drawn shade. There was a number plate, cracked and blistered, but the figures were almost illegible, and the gloom had deepened so that

Brent was obliged to draw close to the steps before he could decipher it.

Faintly he discerned the number.

Ninety-four.

"Getting warmer," the lawyer said to himself. He felt a glow of excitement as he hastened on to the next house.

It was a squat little frame shack, old and weather-beaten. A lamp shone through the front window, and he could hear a baby squalling. The number plate beside the door was rusted, but he thought he could distinguish the figure two.

The next was a brick house, a little better than the others in the row, with a flight of wooden steps leading to a door above the street level. There were two upper windows; in one a pane of glass was broken and the aperture was stuffed up with rags.

There was no sign of light or life. The house had an aloof and secretive air, as though its dingy brick walls guarded mysteries.

He could barely see the number plate, defaced by the sun, the wind and the rain, warped, cracked and rusted, but by venturing close he was able to discern the number he sought. There it was, faintly visible—No. 90!

Brent paused only long enough to make sure he had read the number aright. Then, trying to assume a casual air, he slowly moved on down the board walk.

He felt, intuitively, that this was the house with which the destiny of Paul Gregory had been so strangely concerned. This dark, silent dwelling on a squalid side street knew something of the hidden events that had culminated in the young architect's murder. Some one in this abode had known Gregory, had talked to him, doubtless knew the motives behind his death!

And there the building stood, aloof, reticent, inscrutable, guarding its secrets.

Brent had an impulse to turn, to retrace his steps, to walk up to the door, to knock, to demand the names of those who lived within, to ask what they knew of Paul Gregory and of his visits to Chat Noir.

This impulse was, of course, insane. He would learn nothing; at the best, he would meet suave denials: at the worst, he would be knocked on the head as a meddlesome spy.

He went on to the end of the sinister little street and came out upon a more respectable thoroughfare. He was puzzled as to his next course of action. He had found No. 90—he was sure of that—but what now?

Brent went into a tiny drug store, made a purchase, and engaged the clerk in conversation. What was the name of the little street to the left? The clerk did not know. Who lived there? The clerk shrugged and looked suspicious. Was it a tough street?

The clerk had heard that crooks lived there, mostly, and he wouldn't go up that street alone after dark for several million dollars. What kind of crooks? Just crooks, and what did Brent want to know for anyway?

"I was looking for a friend's house. He lives down this way, and I forgot the name of the street."

"If he lives up that street, brother, you've got some funny friends, *I'd* say."

"Oh, he's quite respectable—"

"Then he don't live up there. And lissen, if I was you I just wouldn't go around asking questions. People might think you're a dick or something, and you might get into trouble."

Brent affected virtuous surprise.

"A dick? You mean a detective?"

"I'm just tipping you off, although it's none of my business. As long as you don't ask questions down around here nobody will bother you, but when you get curious—watch your step."

"Dear me! I didn't know. I hadn't the slightest idea—I *thought* I was in a rather queer part of town, but if you hadn't told me, I might have blundered into all sorts of trouble. Henry doesn't live in this sort of a neighborhood, at any rate, so I must be away off the track. I *do* wish I could remember the name of that street. Well, thank you very much, young man, for your warning. Goodness knows what might have happened me if I'd gone nosing around these streets—and it's getting dark now."

Michael Brent mopped his brow nervously, and backed out of the shop with all the agitation of a peaceful citizen who meant to lose no time in taking himself off from this criminal neighborhood into which he had unwittingly wandered.

As he went away, he knew he had effectually disarmed any suspicions the clerk may have entertained, but he saw that he would have to be careful. He had been given some excellent advice. It would not do to ask questions in the neighborhood of Chat Noir.

And yet, if he did not ask questions, how could he learn anything about No. 90?

Then he recalled an individual by the name of Kremberg, a close personal friend of Hinky Lewis, to whom he might talk with safety. On a number of past occasions, Kremberg had gone bail for Hinky, and there was undoubtedly some sort of alliance between the pair.

Michael Brent searched in his address book and discovered that the man was at the present time engaged in the night club racket, holding forth at the Pleasure Garden on Sanguinet Street.

This was not far away, so Brent got his bearings and returned to the Main, thence up to St. Catherine. He continued on to the black little gulf on either side of the great traffic artery and turned to his left into Sanguinet, one of the most forbidding of all the vicious thoroughfares in down town Montreal.

It was a very quiet street, with red brick houses jammed close together facing one another darkly. There were few street lights; no windows glowed; here and there a taxi waited at a doorway; occasionally a car bumped its way down the street, drew up at the curb, two or three men got out and went up the steps of one of the houses, a door opened discreetly and they disappeared.

But in spite of the quietness and darkness in such contrast to the booming glare of St. Catherine Street, just a few steps away, there was a brooding sense of hidden life.

CHAPTER XVI
THE WOMAN AT NUMBER NINETY

HE Pleasure Garden had no outward evidences to distinguish it from any of the other buildings in this grim and gloomy row save a crimson lantern that hung above the door.

Brent, however, had been there previously on the occasion of one of Hinky's major peccadillos, so he strode up the steps jauntily and pressed the bell. The door was glass fronted, but no light shone from beyond. He was aware a few seconds later that he was being subjected to scrutiny from within, as he stood in the ruby radiance of the lantern. Then the door opened silently.

He entered a dark hall, the front door closed, another opened, and a man in shabby evening dress escorted him into a small lobby.

"Kremberg around?"

The doorman scrutinized Brent carefully.

"I remember your face, sir," he said in a respectful voice, "but I can't place you."

"Brent."

"Oh, yes. I remember now. Mr. Kremberg may be upstairs. I just came on duty myself."

"It's a bit early, I know."

"Just go in and sit down, Mr. Brent. I'll see if I can find him for you."

To the right was a flight of stairs; to the left a door led into the Pleasure Garden itself. At the end of the hall the hat check girl presided, but the rows of empty hooks indicated that Brent was the first guest that evening.

Brent retained his hat and went into a long, low-ceilinged room, extending the entire length of the house and widening out at the rear to cover most of the ground floor space with the exception of the entrance hall.

It was festooned with colored paper and there was a cheap attempt at a gaudy decorative scheme. Tables were ranged along the sides, about the shimmering dance floor, and at the back was a kitchen, divided from the main room by a counter door. On a low platform three young fellows were tootling and twanging and tinkling on saxophone, banjo, and piano.

Two waiters were lounging about the kitchen entrance. One hastened over and Brent ordered an illicit highball that he didn't want, paid seventy-five cents for it, and tipped the waiter a quarter. Then he sipped his drink and pondered on the vast hocus-pocus of the whole business.

In a few hours, toward midnight and after, the Pleasure Garden would be going full blast for the benefit of a flock of misguided citizens and tourists—thrill-seekers who were willing to pay dearly for the privilege of drinking illegally, preyed upon by all the dubious men and women who consorted in this place.

"Kremberg must be cleaning up," reflected Brent. "It's an easy graft."

The doorman appeared.

"Do you mind waiting, Mr. Brent? He is out just now, but we expect him any minute."

"I'll stick around. I want to talk to him about Hinky."

The doorman's plump face was impassive, but his eyelids flickered, ever so slightly.

"As soon as Mr. Kremberg comes in, I'll have him told that you're here. It isn't very gay just now. We don't usually liven up until after the shows."

"That's all right. I didn't come in to be entertained."

"I hope you didn't pay for that high ball, Mr. Brent," said the man reprovingly.

"Why not?"

"I can't let you do that, Mr. Brent," the doorman explained. "Mr. Kremberg wouldn't like it. You must let me give you a better one." He snapped his fingers. The waiter came over. "Take this away and bring Mr. Brent a good high ball. When this gentleman comes here, he is to have the best," he added significantly.

And, as the waiter slithered off with the condemned drink on a tray, the doorman put three twenty-five-cent pieces on the table. "You must consider yourself Mr. Kremberg's guest," he went on in his soft voice. "The waiter made a mistake. Your high ball was—uh—a bit weak."

Brent grinned and pocketed the money.

"I feel flattered. When a night club takes back cut booze and gives me the real McCoy instead, I may consider that I've graduated from the sucker class."

As one initiate to another, the doorman smirked.

"We all have our tricks of the trade, Mr. Brent."

A telephone bell trilled just then, and he went out into the lobby. Brent sipped the new high ball and found it an immense improvement over the other one.

Minutes passed. The doorman did not return. The musicians idly rehearsed a number. The waiters were out in the kitchen, exchanging stories with the chef, otherwise known as the barkeep.

Brent whiled away the time by trying to compose an epigram stating his conclusion that the only place more depressing than a cheap night club before any one has arrived, is a cheap night club after every one has gone home; but he found this great thought difficult of concentration.

Then he pondered for a while on the relative points of similarity between a telegram and an epigram, but decided they had nothing in common beyond brevity. This led to a consideration of epigrams in general, and he wondered why people who achieved epigrams are considered exceedingly clever, when the feat is simply a matter of making a statement in one of half a dozen hackneyed formulas.

Thus musing, he finished the high ball. The doorman had not returned and Kremberg had not appeared, so he ordered another, and was charmed to find that the waiter apparently expected neither tip nor payment.

This high ball was quite as potent as its predecessor and induced a number of moral reflections on the high cost of inebriety in night clubs. Was it not dishonest to charge seventy-five cents for a drink of weak liquor; on the other hand, did it not promote temperance by rendering the sucker penniless before he got drunk? And, after all—oh, well, who cared?

Abandoning this train of thought, Michael Brent reverted to a consideration of the mystery of No. 90. He now saw clearly that boldness was the proper course; he should have gone right up to the door.

Under the stimulating influence of the excellent high balls, and far removed from the sinister shadows of the street, his heart was brave within him. He had erred on the side of caution. There was little to fear. Every one knew that criminals were invariably cowards.

Quite reckless and valiant, Mr. Brent got up and wandered out into the lobby, firmly clutching his hat.

The doorman heard him and hastened downstairs.

"How about Kremberg?" Brent asked impatiently.

"He will be late this evening, Mr. Brent. I am sorry. But if you care to wait half an hour longer—he telephoned to me just a few minutes ago."

"I won't wait. I may be back later on."

"Very well."

Urbane as ever, the doorman let him out into the street, and the lawyer swaggered along Sanguinet, up St. Catherine and down the Main with a purposeful stride. He was not at all drunk; he was simply at that stage where one's powers are magnificent and obstacles are but pebbles to be kicked aside.

His confidence diminished in some slight degree when he plunged into the darkness of Chat Noir, and by the time he had returned to the entrance of the lane he was beginning to wonder if, after all, it might not have been better to have waited for Kremberg. It was certainly a very black little alley in a very disreputable neighborhood.

Then the two high balls asserted themselves again and Michael Brent observed audibly that he would be damned if any street in Montreal could scare *him.*

So he stumbled along the precarious board walk, stepping off into the mud more than once, until he came to the end of the fence and saw the little street before him, with the twinkling lights of the cross thoroughfare in the distance. The lights reassured him. He had no distinct plan of campaign, but he meant to at least catch a glimpse of the occupants of No. 90, and, with any luck, perhaps learn something about them.

When Brent reached the house he saw a thin sliver of gold at the bottom of one of the window blinds, indicating there was a light within. He hesitated a moment, then went up the steps to knock.

Scarcely had he left the board walk than there was a deep-throated bellow from the back of the house. Then another, and another. Three dogs set up a hideous clamor. Their hoarse barking was coldly ferocious.

The sound was so utterly unexpected that the visitor stepped back, uncertain whether to proceed. Then he heard a man's voice, and the clamor subsided as suddenly as it began. Chains clanked, he heard the man's voice again; then a door slammed; there was silence.

Brent shrugged. No. 90 was evidently well guarded against intrusion.

He went boldly up on to the veranda and knocked at the door. There was no response. After a while he knocked again.

Footsteps beyond the door. A light shone dimly

through the little glass. The dirty curtain was drawn back and he faintly saw a human face. The door opened slightly.

"Oui?" A woman's voice, tremulous.

"Does Mr. Robinson live here?" asked Brent.

"Non!"

"Isn't this No. 90?"

He was trying to discern the face of the woman. She stood back in the shadows, however, and he could see her but vaguely.

"Who are you looking for?" she asked in a sullen voice.

"Mr. Robinson."

"Do you know which house he lives in?"

"He doesn't live here."

The door opened a trifle wider. In the light of the hall he could see the woman more clearly now. She was a slatternly creature with wild dark hair and suspicious eyes. Her lips drooped.

"He doesn't live here."

"You don't know where he lives?" persisted Brent.

"Not here."

The door closed. He heard the click of a lock. There was silence beyond. He sensed that the woman was eying him through the curtain.

Brent turned away. He walked down the steps to the board walk.

He had at least seen the woman's face, and he had an odd impression that he had seen the slattern before.

This, on the face of it, was absurd. He had never been in this part of the city until the previous day. But the face was familiar.

He probed in the recesses of his memory. Clients, women of the street, prisoners and witnesses—none of them. But he had seen that sullen, tragic face recently, somewhere.

The connection eluded him. He walked on slowly, head down, puzzled. The woman was in No. 90. He must, therefore, have seen her in connection with his investigations since Gregory's death. But what women had he seen? The Hilliard girl, her chum, the beautiful girl of Chat Noir—none of them.

Abruptly the solution clicked into his mind.

The photograph Minton had clipped from the newspaper! *The picture found in Gregory's room!*

It was the same woman. There was no mistaking the features. She had aged by several years, but the eyes were the same, there were still traces of the plump, girlish beauty. There was no doubt of it. This was the woman mentioned by Pelham Starr, this was the woman Gregory had visited in Chat Noir, this was the woman of No. 90!

CHAPTER XVII
THE MANHOLE

HERCHEZ LA FEMME! And he had found her. As Michael Brent went on toward the corner he experienced a great exultation. He had stumbled on a rich vein of ore in his discovery of No. 90.

The woman was good-looking—beautiful, in fact—yet he could not help but wonder how Paul Gregory had become involved with her. After all, she could be nothing more than a drab.

Brent, however, had seen enough of the world to be aware of the perverse inclinations of the human heart. He believed that deep down in every man was the impulse toward the sty; in most of us it is buried, suppressed—an abomination—and in some it manifests itself only to be scotched by forces of self-respect; in a few, it rises to be obeyed. He had known of rich and influential men who had become entangled with the lowest of water front women.

His next move? He did not know. Clearly he must see this person again, question her. But would he learn anything? He had no authority, and he knew that the denizens of the streets of shadow resent prying—viciously and forcibly.

Should he go to the police with what he knew? Undoubtedly, he considered, this would be the wise course. They were seeking this woman. He had found her. Under expert questioning she would undoubtedly explain her relationship with Gregory.

It would be sheer vanity to continue alone, and vanity might earn him a broken head. He concluded that he had gone as far as he could, singlehanded. It was now time to turn his information over to the police.

Thus deliberating, Michael Brent reached the corner and looked to left and to right, trying to define his position. There was a trolley line somewhere off to his right; he could hear the roar of the cars, so he struck off in that direction.

The lawyer did not know this quarter at all, and he was somewhat confused. He looked in vain for a taxi, but at that hour on the quiet street there was no traffic of any kind.

There were few lights, and although the street was wider than the alley he had just quitted, it was every bit as villainous and sinister in appearance. The houses all had that dark, tight-lipped aspect common to buildings in these neighborhoods—catacombs of secrets.

He passed a lane that led up behind the houses on the street of No. 90. It was blackly mysterious and forbidding.

The next corner was not far away. He had almost reached it when he heard footsteps pattering along the street behind him. He did not look back, but when a man fell into step with him he looked and saw a shabby little fellow who seemed somehow familiar to him.

"Mister," said a soft voice.

Brent did not answer. One is accosted at all hours of the day and night on Montreal streets by persons temporarily down on their luck and plaintively anxious for the "loan" of a dime wherewith to buy a "cupacaw fee." Brent had found that deafness was the best defense against these pests.

"Mister," came the soft voice again.

Michael Brent walked on, looking straight ahead.

"I'm not makin' a touch, mister," persisted the shabby man. "If it's information you're after, you'll find it worth while to talk to me."

Brent looked down at his companion. The fellow was certainly not prepossessing. He was a slinky little rat, his lips were drawn down at the corners as though they had never been permitted to curve in a smile—and then, as the corner light fell on the sharp face, came recognition.

This was the little man he had met with the girl of Chat Noir!

For a moment, Brent could scarcely credit the circumstance. He stopped short and peered at the fellow. There was no mistake. The same pinched, peaked face, the same ruddy nose, the same weak chin. The coincidence surprised him, but the fact that the little man had sought him out, promising information, thoroughly astonished the attorney.

"Information about what?" he asked.

"No. 90."

It was like a blow in the face. How did this stranger

know of his concern with No. 90? *This* man, above all! Even without mention of No. 90, Brent would have been interested in this bum by the very circumstance that he had first seen the fellow with the beautiful girl who had so intrigued him the previous day. But here he was, obsequiously hinting at revelations in the mystery of No. 90!

Brent had sufficient presence of mind to conceal his surprise.

"What," he asked, "is No. 90?"

"Mister," said the little man, "you don't need to sidestep with me, see? We can understand each other if you'll let me. Of course, I know I'm not in your class, mister, and don't think I got too much nerve talkin' to you like this, but if you want to know somethin', mebbe I can help you. I know my place, mister. I know my place, but I like to help a gentleman when I can."

Cautiously, Brent said: " It's very good of you. What makes you think I want to know anything about No. 90?"

"I *know*, mister, I *know!* You can't do much down in these parts without it gettin' known around. You're a stranger, see, and you ask questions. Mebbe I can answer some of them for you."

"Why would you?"

"I got my own reasons, mister. You're a dick, I figure. Am I right or wrong?"

Brent made no reply. The little man went on.

"I got my own reasons, and if there was certain people in No. 90 got what was comin' to 'em, I wouldn't do no cryin'. None at all."

"I see. And what could you tell me?"

"I could tell you plenty, mister. It all depends what

you want to know. And would it do me any good to spill it?"

"You mean you want money?"

The little man put out his right hand, palm downward, in a curt gesture.

"Not a penny, mister. Not a penny. It ain't money I'm after. I wouldn't take a penny for what I can tell you. But I gotta be sure you'll use it."

He halted on the street corner. Brent halted, too. He studied the thin, oldish face, the shifty eyes. The down-and-outer was typical of the quarter, perhaps a cheap crook with a grudge against some one in No. 90. He had evidently mistaken the lawyer for a detective and considered it an opportunity for a fine bit of revenge.

"What could you tell me?"

"Will you use it?"

"In what way?"

"Mister, there ain't no sense in sidesteppin' like that. Do you want to know anythin' about No. 90?"

"Yes."

The little man cocked his head on one side and peered up, wisely.

"Good!" he said, with an unmistakable air of satisfaction. "Mister, that's *all* I have to know. Absolutely *all!* I don't want to know nothin' about why you're askin' questions about No. 90, or what you're workin' on. All I want to know is that you'll use the dope."

"What makes you think I'm interested?"

"I told you before, mister, I *know.*"

Brent hesitated.

"Who is the woman living there?" he asked.

The little man looked around. Across the street,

some one was trudging along the pavement, coming in their direction.

"Mister," said the shabby man, placing a thin hand on Brent's sleeve, "would you mind steppin' off this street while we talk. I'm known around here, see, and if the blow-off came and somebody remembered I was talkin' to you, where would I be?"

He leaned closer.

"Where would I be, eh, mister? I'd be floatin' down the little old St. Lawrence with a slug in me, wouldn't I? That's the way they do things down here, see? If you don't mind walkin' up this here side street instead of stickin' to the main drag, I could talk better."

The side street was dark and narrow, but it was not very long, presumably ending in Chat Noir. There was a red lantern glimmering in the middle of the road, and Brent could see the dim outline of a wooden inclosure fencing off the scene of some repair work.

The little man was already edging off into the gloom.

"This bird comin' down the other side," he whispered, "he knows me, see. I can't take no chances, mister. Let's beat it."

Brent followed, slowly. He was cautious, but there was an earnestness about the shabby little man that convinced him the fellow really had something to tell. And it was quite reasonable that he would not care to be seen in conversation with one whom the people of the quarter had already marked as a detective.

"You wanted to know—" inquired the little man, slackening his pace.

"About the woman."

"In No. 90?"

"Yes."

They were drawing near the red lantern in the middle of the road. Somehow its crimson glow gave Brent an odd sense of discomfort. Red meant danger.

"Mister," said the little man, pressing closely against him, "just why do you want to know about her?"

His face was just a pallid blur in the gloom. Brent suddenly sensed a sharp menace.

"Why all this shilly-shallying?" he snapped impatiently. "I didn't ask you to tell me anything."

"Mister, don't get sore. Don't get sore. I gotta be careful, see. I can give you plenty of dope on that place, but I gotta watch my step, mister."

Brent frowned. Abruptly he wheeled about.

"Look here," he said. "I don't like your manner. You offered to tell me something and now you're stalling. What's the big idea? I'm not going to waste any more time on you."

"Mister—" pleaded the little man, and grasped at Brent's arm. But the lawyer wrenched his arm free and strode back toward the entrance of the dark street.

He had gone but two paces when he heard a scuffling footstep, a sharp intake of breath. He swung around. The little man was right behind him, arm upraised.

Brent lunged to one side as the arm descended. Something struck him heavily on the shoulder.

He grappled, punching at the other's body. They strained to and fro, bodies close together.

Brent tried to seize the little man's right arm, but the fellow was too quick for him. He knew the blow was coming, but he couldn't dodge.

His skull seemed to crack into fragments, with an explosion of white light, oblivion swooped over him.

Brent slumped on the roadway. He sprawled there, one arm bent under him, and he did not move at all.

Midge, breathing heavily, looked down at the inert figure. He put the short length of lead pipe back into his pocket and wiped his hands reflectively on the front of his coat.

"That 'll teach him a lesson," he muttered.

It occurred to the assailant that his proximity to this unconscious figure in the middle of the road was dangerous, so he scuttled off into the shadows at the side of the street; he disappeared down a narrow passage between two houses.

Brent lay where he had fallen.

The street was deserted.

The red lantern glowed beyond the wooden fence. Far away a bell was tolling; the notes sounded clearly and distinctly above the confused hum of the city. A taxi sped past the street entrance, with a harsh screech.

Brent had not moved. The tolling of the bell died away. The city hummed on.

After a while some one emerged from the passage that had swallowed up Midge. He was a huge man, but he moved as silently as a cat. He stood over the prostrate form.

He hesitated, looked over at the red lantern, then bent down and seized Brent's shoulders. He dragged the lawyer toward the wooden fence.

Inside the flimsy guard rail there was a round black hole in the surface of the road. The big man let Brent slump to the pavement, and quietly let down one end of the rail.

Then, with a quick movement, he grasped the body again, and thrust it to the edge of the manhole. It slipped forward, the head and shoulders disappeared. A final push and the body vanished. There was a distant, significant splash.

The big man stood beside the black hole, looking down. He turned aside, methodically replaced the guard rail, and walked away. He went into the dark passage.

The street was deserted again.

The ruby light glowed over the hole.

CHAPTER XVIII
EVIDENCE OF FOUL PLAY

INTON usually reached the office at nine o'clock in the morning. He was occasionally five or ten minutes ahead of time; he was never by any chance five or ten minutes late. A less conscientious man might have taken advantage of his employer's notorious tardiness, but Minton, as has been said, ordered his life by an invisible time clock.

He let himself into the office on the morning after Michael Brent's visit to No. 90, precisely as a distant clock boomed the hour, took off his hat and coat, hung them up, donned his worn jacket and sat down at his desk. He gave no thought, of course, to Brent's absence. Never, since he came to work for Brent, had the lawyer reached the office first.

Noon came. No Brent.

Not until the afternoon did a few vague misgivings disturb him. He reached for the telephone and called Brent's apartment. There was no answer.

Minton got up and went out, carefully locking the

door. He went across the street to the Fleur de Lis and asked Alphonse if Brent had been in that day.

The waiter shook his head. "Not dis afternoon, not dis morning. First time he miss coming in here, so far back I can remember."

Michael Brent's afternoon visit to the tavern was almost in the nature of a religious rite. Minton coughed doubtfully and went on to the bookshop.

He had to do considerable exploring before he finally discovered Mr. Dryborough sitting on the floor at the back of the shop, behind a rampart of books, immersed in a dusty volume.

"Has Mr. Brent been in to-day?" asked the faithful servant.

Dryborough looked up, blinked, and put the book aside.

"I haven't seen him for two days," he announced, looking at Minton severely.

"He hasn't been at the office today."

"Is he sick?"

"He's not at his apartment."

"In court?"

"He would have called at the office first."

"Out of town?"

"He would have let me know."

"Got run over and sent to the hospital?"

"I'd have been notified."

This appeared to exhaust Mr. Dryborough's stock of possible explanations, but he thought deeply for a few moments and ventured:

"On a drunk?"

"Mr. Brent never goes on drunks," Minton responded stiffly.

"That's true, too," Dryborough said. "Still, you never can tell."

Minton refused to consider this explanation and departed. He made his way up to Dorchester Street on a visit to the little apartment house where Brent stayed. He went up a heavily carpeted flight of stairs and tapped at the door of Brent's apartment, but there was no answer, so he went down into the lobby.

The *concierge*, a grandmotherly old lady in a little white cap, emerged from some mysterious region, and after Minton had stated his business she went over to a marble-topped table and shuffled a few letters lying there.

"See? This mail came for him this morning."

"He may have gone out before the mail arrived."

The old lady pressed a bell. In a little while a maid appeared on the landing. They exchanged a few rapid words in French. The old lady turned to Minton again.

"M'sieu' Brent he did not come in at all last night."

"Oh!"

"The maid she says his bed was not slept in."

Minton thanked her and went away. He had an uneasy feeling that something had gone wrong. However, he had a whole-hearted fear of making a fool of himself, so he did not pursue his inquiries further, although he scanned the afternoon paper with particular attention to the accident list.

He finished the afternoon in a state of anxiety, and went home to exchange theories with the family at the supper table. By a majority vote it was decided that he should not worry.

Next day Minton waited nervously until almost noon, but Brent did not appear. Then he went over to the Fleur de Lis and found Dryborough disconsolately drinking a mug of beer. He confided his perturbation to the old bookseller, but that skeptical man affirmed that Brent must certainly be on a drunk, a very big drunk, because even the best of 'em went on a toot once in a while.

But Minton knew better. He made inquiries at the apartment house, the hospitals, the courthouse, and even the morgue, but there was no trace of Michael Brent, so he went reluctantly to police headquarters.

"Missing, eh?" said the official to whom he told his story. "Perhaps he went out of town."

Minton shook his head.

"I happen to know he was making some investigations that might have taken him into a bad neighborhood. It's just possible that some harm may have come to him."

"H-m! That's different. What neighborhood?"

"He mentioned a street called Chat Noir," Minton said cautiously.

"Chat Noir! And you haven't seen him since? I'd say it was high time you came around to tell us about it."

"Say!" spoke up a plain-clothes man lounging near by. "How about that hat I found? It was in an alley near Chat Noir."

The sergeant nodded. "Bring it up." He turned to Minton. "One of the boys found a hat down around that neighborhood. There was blood on it. We'll let you have a look at it."

Minton turned perceptibly paler. "What kind of hat?"

"I dunno. I didn't see it. The hat was brought in, just in case it might be useful. There's a lot of funny things happen around there."

Minton waited, trembling. After a while the plain-clothes man returned and tossed a black hat carelessly on the desk.

"It's his," Minton said dully.

"Huh?" The plain-clothes man lost his casual air at once.

"It's Mr. Brent's hat. I'd know it anywhere."

The floppy black hat that was Michael Brent's most

"It's Mr Brent's hat," said Minton

picturesque affectation looked battered and forlorn. Minton recognized it immediately. He had seen that hat too often to be mistaken. He picked it up.

"Yes, it's his hat. I'd know it by the dents in it, if nothing else. Same size, same material, same shape."

He glanced inside, and gulped.

Sticking to the sweatband were several black hairs, in a russet stain.

"Something terrible has happened to Mr. Brent!"

"Black haired, was he?"

"Yes."

The plain-clothes man examined the hat, inside and out, with professional interest.

"I'd say that whoever was wearin' this hat got a nasty knock on the dome. I guess we'll have to get busy on this."

"Where was it found?"

"I was on a case down around Chat Noir yesterday and the cop on the beat told me about findin' this hat. It was lyin' beside the curb, he said, and when he saw the blood on it he picked it up and turned it over to me. But we didn't have no report of any trouble around there, so I never thought any more about it."

"I've wasted so much valuable time," Minton said plaintively. "I should have known there was something wrong."

"It would 'a' been better if you'd come in right away, but I guess you thought he'd turn up, huh? Well, you come with me and we'll get the particulars and mebbe we'll find out what happened him."

Then ensued various formalities, after which Minton left headquarters. He was frightened and rather dazed. Every time he thought of that dreadful blood stain on the sweatband he shuddered.

He had given the police a complete description of Brent as he had last seen him, but he had omitted mentioning the reason for the lawyer's descent into Chat Noir. In that respect he remained cautious. More than once he was tempted to make some mention of No. 90, but he suppressed the impulse. Brent might still be alive. Only as a last resort would Minton divulge the clews on which his employer had been working.

He went back to the office, but he couldn't work. He was no stranger to crime and violence, in the academic sense; such things had been part of his daily routine for years, but this was the first time anything of the sort had obtruded on his personal life. He was profoundly shaken.

Just as he was about to leave the office, the telephone rang.

Tremulously he answered. A gruff voice bade him come down to police headquarters immediately.

"Is—is there any trace of him?"

"We got something. It may be a clew. You come on down and take a look at what we've found."

Click!

Minton was sweating as he struggled into his coat and seized his hat. There was something grimly indefinite about that "take a look at what we've found." What had they found? A body? In a state of shivering suspense he hastened to headquarters.

Their discovery was not what he feared. It was only a coat—a soggy, bedraggled garment that lay limply across a table, with a paper tag attached to one of the buttons. A bored officer gestured toward it.

"This was brought in a little while ago. It was found in an ash can a couple of blocks from where Mr. Brent's hat was picked up. See if you can identify it, will you?"

Minton picked up the coat gingerly. It was damp to the touch. It had evidently been very wet, and it had lost its shape, but he saw that it was Brent's coat, without a doubt. He looked for the tailor's tag on the inner pocket. That settled it.

"Mr. Brent was wearing that coat when I last saw him," Minton told the officer.

The man took the garment from him indifferently.

"It's his, eh? You're sure?"

"Quite sure."

The officer examined the collar.

"Did you see them?" He indicated a few rusty stains.

"I—I didn't notice. Is it—"

"Blood. That's what made us think mebbe it was his coat. He got knocked on the head, sure enough, and the blood stained his hat and went over the back of his coat collar, see?"

Minton was almost speechless with dread.

"Do you think he's been murdered?"

The officer shrugged and tossed the coat back on the table.

"Where was it found?"

"In an ash can."

"Near where they found the hat?"

"No. That's what makes it kinda hard to figger out. One of our men fished the coat out of an ash can in an alley about five or six blocks away."

"Wasn't there anything in the pockets? No papers?"

"Not a thing."

"The coat," said Minton, vacantly, "seems damp."

"It rained like hell the night he disappeared."

"Yes, that's right. It did rain."

"Well, you identify the coat, huh?"

"Yes, there's no doubt of it. He was wearing that very coat the last time I saw him. The very coat."

Minton looked sadly at the limp garment on the table. The rusty stains on the collar seemed to grow larger and redder as he gazed at them in fascination.

"And that's that. I guess your boss was bumped off, all right. Don't worry. We'll find his body somewhere. It 'll turn up."

With this consolation, Minton had to be content. He was subjected to further questioning before he left headquarters, but stubbornly resisted the temptation to tell the detectives why Brent had invaded Chat Noir. There was still a chance, he told himself, still a chance that his employer was alive.

But on his way home that evening he bought a newspaper and read a bristling headline that seemed to confirm all his apprehensions

LAWYER MISSING; FOUL PLAY FEARED!

There was something grim and authoritative about the heavy black type. It summed up everything, coldly, tersely, and left scant room for hope. Minton was surprised to find, on reading the news story beneath the headline, that the paper had already learned of his identification of the coat; it did not occur to him that the police had merely awaited this identification before releasing the story.

The bald facts related in the account almost frightened him. Until this time he had been blindly confident, refusing to admit to himself that Brent might be dead; it seemed that the newspaper refused to consider any other theory.

Michael Brent, a well-known criminal lawyer, had ventured into an unsavory quarter of the city at night on business. He had not returned. His hat, battered and bloodstained, had been found in an alley. His coat, also bloodstained, had been found in an ash can five blocks away. Police investigation had unearthed no further trace of him. What else could one make of that but murder?

Minton crumpled the newspaper in his thin hands and stared morosely at the vest buttons of a strap hanger standing before him in the crowded trolley. He might have been carried past his stop had not the habit of years brought him mechanically to his feet exactly when the car slowed down at his street corner.

At the supper table he found himself, for the first time in years, the center of importance, but he was too depressed to enjoy the novelty of the experience. The family actually listened to him with respect. When he told of identifying the coat, and of seeing the ominous stains of blood, two of the younger Mintons began to howl with fear, and were packed off to bed, weeping.

Next morning, before he set out for the office, he telephoned to police headquarters and asked if there had been any further trace of Michael Brent.

"Nothing yet," he was told.

Minton was not stampeded out of his daily routine. He went to the office as usual, arriving a few minutes before nine o'clock. He hung up his hat and coat, donned his jacket, sat down at his desk. In a few minutes the door opened and Dryborough came in. The old bookseller looked questioningly at him and Minton shook his head.

"No news at all?"

"None."

"I read about it in the paper last night," said Dryborough. "It's the damnedest thing, isn't it?"

"It is very serious," agreed Minton.

"Blood stains," muttered Dryborough, sitting down. "Blood stains! You're sure it was his hat and coat?"

"Positive."

"With blood stains on 'em?"

"I saw them myself."

Dryborough shook his head sadly, mumbling to himself. Then he stared at Minton in a challenging manner.

"Do you really think he's dead?"

"I hope not. But if he's alive he would have got in touch with somebody by now, don't you think? Then, there are the blood stains."

"That's true."

"Perhaps," suggested Minton hopefully, "he's being held prisoner somewhere."

Dryborough sniffed.

"That happens in books. Who would hold him prisoner? What for?" Minton had no reply.

"Poor Brent!" sighed Dryborough. "I always liked him, you know. I'll miss my afternoon glass of beer with him."

Already, reflected Minton, the man was referring to Brent in the past tense.

"It's very mysterious, to say the least."

"He should have known better," Dryborough commented testily. "He should have known better than to go wandering around those back streets at night. Just like some silly tourist. He was inviting a knock on the head."

"It was on business."

"Funny kind of business! It 'll be too bad if they don't find his body."

"Don't talk like that," protested Minton.

Dryborough glared at him. "They don't always find 'em."

"I can't believe Mr. Brent is dead," insisted Minton.

"Well, it doesn't do any harm to hope. But—blood stains!"

"He may have met with an accident and lost his memory."

Dryborough nodded. "Almost anybody is liable to meet with an accident if they go prowling around those streets after dark."

The telephone jangled. Minton picked up the receiver. "Yes? Yes. What is it? I'll be right down."

He thrust aside the instrument and began to struggle out of his jacket.

"Anything new?" Dryborough asked sharply.

"They've found a watch. They think it might be his."

"A watch, eh? Where?"

"In a pawnshop."

"I knew it!" declared Mr. Dryborough triumphantly. "Murdered for his money! Knocked on the head, just like a silly tourist! What an idiotic and disgraceful way to die!"

Minton shook his head sadly, but in his heart he refused to admit that his master, strong, clever and resourceful, had died at the age of thirty with a double murder mystery still unsolved.

CHAPTER XIX
THE RED LIGHT

ICHAEL BRENT was unconscious when he was thrust into the manhole, but the tingling shock of his immersion in cold water brought him back to his senses.

At first he had no recollection of the battle in the street. He had not the slightest idea of what had happened to him, and he was only aware of a stabbing pain in his head, of utter darkness all about, of a great, hollow roaring, of surging waters, and of some tremendous force that was sweeping him irresistibly forward.

He was whirled about like a cork; water splashed over him; the icy cold penetrated his body. He made a few instinctive struggles and his hands slipped against a wet, slimy wall. Then he was flung out into the middle of the roaring stream again.

His brain cleared. He knew now what had happened.

The blackness was profound. The roar of the sewer was like thunder, echoing and reëchoing from the in-

visible walls. He struggled in the violent onrush of water, but his efforts were futile; the current was terrific, and in any case he was plunging down a subterranean prison.

Again he brushed against the side of the sewer, grasping vainly at smooth, wet stone, and then he went whirling out into the depths again.

Above him flashed a yellow glare; it seemed compounded of great stars set in a circle, and it vanished in an instant. He had passed beneath another manhole. But he was swept on. Blackness engulfed him utterly.

Brent was in a dazed state, and his battle for life was instinctive. His struggle in the great sewer was a nightmare. For the first time in his life he knew terror.

He had no hope of ever seeing the outer world again.

The attorney felt that this dreadful journey could have but one end. He was tossed about like a chip, submerged, flung against the slippery walls, dragged back into the current. Through his mind, like a steel thread, ran the thought, "I am dying!"

Frisco Fat stared doubtfully at Brent, who was sitting on the cot

He felt a surge of panic at the prospect of gradually losing consciousness, of perishing miserably down in the filthy darkness beneath the city streets, of becoming a limp, drenched, anonymous form washed out into the sullen river.

The drowning man caught sight of a peculiar pillar of light in the void ahead; then he was battered against the wall, his scrabbling fingers slipping vainly on the surface of the masonry, and the illumination was temporarily blotted out.

The very sight of light gave him hope, but as he was swept closer he saw that while the pillar of light was pouring through an opening in the roof of the sewer, the masonry was several feet above, and beyond his reach.

He could not hold out much longer. If he were swept past this shaft he would never live to reach another.

All his thoughts were in confusion; the crimson gleam was the one reality in a roaring insanity. It seemed to draw away from him, rising higher above, a circle of red light beyond his outflung arm, a good two feet from his finger tips.

The current swept him beneath the shaft, and then he saw something against the gleaming wall, something barely discernible in the light from above—two slim black bars of steel, with rungs between—a little ladder dangling against the side of the tunnel.

He saw it in time, just as he was plunging past, and reached for it frantically.

Desperate fingers closed about a cold, wet rung. The current wrenched at his body. He clung there by one hand.

His fingers began to slip. He tried to seize the rung with his other hand, but missed the ladder altogether.

Water was breaking over him, he could not shake the inexorable grip of the current, he was suffocating.

And then, with a last despairing gesture, his free hand found the rung and he clutched the little bar of steel. He clung there, gasping, swaying from side to side with the wash of the foul waters.

After a while Brent managed to drag himself up so that his feet were on a rung beneath the surface, and he emerged, dripping, from the water, and struggled up into the shaft beneath the open manhole.

Despite the hollow roar of the sewer he could hear the clank of machinery on the street above.

Painfully, rung by rung, he ascended toward the street. He was in that condition commonly known as being more dead than alive. He was wretchedly cold, his body ached with pain, his head throbbed. Every movement was agonizing.

It seemed an interminable length of time before his head and shoulders emerged from the manhole and he sprawled halfway over the side, exhausted, filling his lungs with the pure night air.

A few yards away a massive steel monster clanked and pounded in the gloom; he could see a cloud of rolling smoke and little jets of flame, glowing red coals, and dark figures moving about like gnomes. Immediately above him, on a tripod, was suspended a scarlet lantern; this had cast the pillar of ruddy illumination into the blackness of the sewer. The red light had saved his life!

He crawled out, thanking his stars and the city government for the circumstance that had sent a repair gang to this street on this particular night.

Brent scrambled wearily to his feet. Had any of the workmen seen that drenched, fearful apparition rising from the manhole they would have been thrown into an uproar, but it so happened that they were all engaged some distance away at the time, and his emergence was unnoticed.

His first instinctive movement was toward the ruddy fires of the great machine. Then he paused, and in obedience to a resolution not yet fully formed, he turned aside and stumbled off into the shadows.

No one had seen Michael Brent, and if any one chanced to look up a moment later in time to see the vague form beyond the circle of light, he paid no attention, for in the city streets dark wraiths come and go mysteriously on their obscure errands and no one pays them even the tribute of curiosity. The workmen were busy. Their iron monster clanked and pounded, breathing smoke and flame in the night.

Brent avoided the men and crept into the darkness. A plan was forming in his throbbing head, its basis being a determination that no one should be aware of his escape from the sewer. His enemies believed him dead; then, dead he would remain.

Wet, cold and exhausted, he lurched down a narrow street that he saw near by. He wanted to find a place where he could warm himself and dry his clothes, but he knew that he would attract attention wherever he went, because of the shocking state of his garments.

The pain at the back of his head was severe. He felt, tentatively, and when he withdrew his fingers he found that they were sticky with blood. He had lost his hat. Water was dripping from his drenched clothes.

He came to the end of the little street and found himself near a park. He had no idea of his whereabouts, and he was unable to identify the place, but he crossed the road and sat down on a bench beneath a clump of trees.

A light mist was drifting down; he had scarcely noticed it when he emerged from the sewer, but in the park it was more evident. The scattered lights were dim, their radiance diffused in the gentle haze of gray. The bulk of some great building beyond the distant street loomed fantastically through the gathering fog. The naked trees drooped limply, and the footpath was strewn with soggy leaves. The road gleamed like black ice.

Brent shivered. His immediate needs were warmth, shelter, dry clothing.

The reasonable course was obvious. He could go to his apartment, stopping at the nearest police station to report the affair. But the plan that was in his mind when he crawled out of the manhole and avoided the workmen near by predicated a course neither reasonable nor obvious.

He was, to the satisfaction of his enemies, a dead man. But who were these enemies, and why had they desired his death? He was convinced that the little man who had attacked him was something more than a common footpad. He was not playing a lone hand. There were others involved.

It all led back, of course, to No. 90. His interest in that sinister dwelling had brought swift and definite consequences. Within five minutes of his rash visit to the place, an attempt had been made upon his life.

Well, it was evidence enough that No. 90 held dark secrets that unscrupulous people meant to guard at any cost. He had learned that it did not pay to attack them in the open, and now he was resolved to fight them at their own game. Here, by a neat turn of fate, they had unwittingly given him the best possible weapon—the assumption of his own death.

But this weapon, to be effective, must be retained intact. He held the upper hand so long as they considered him out of the way forever, and to confirm this belief, to convince them that he was no longer to be feared, he must abandon his identity and resume the campaign in new guise. Michael Brent was dead, a lifeless hulk in the oblivion of the sewer. He must proceed on that premise.

It was raining now, a wretched, clammy drizzle that seemed to materialize out of the fog rather than fall from the sky, but he was already so completely drenched that it didn't bother him.

With the rain, the mist became heavier, and the great building beyond the park was obliterated, the lights became hazier, and only the trees near by could be distinguished in the enveloping grayness.

Bareheaded, drenched to the skin, utterly exhausted, Brent sat on the park bench, hunched forward dejectedly, fondling the little black beard in the gesture that was habitual with him when engrossed in thought.

A gust of cold wind shook the branches above him, and there was a heavy shower of raindrops from the wet twigs, spattering out of the drizzle.

He couldn't stay here all night. He must find shelter—but finding shelter meant coming in contact with people, and he wanted to avoid that.

No one must see Michael Brent in the flesh. It was necessary for the success of his scheme that there be hue and cry over his disappearance, and he could not risk having some casual passer-by recollect having seen him several hours after he was presumably dead.

The beard, of course, must go. This was regrettable; Brent cherished that beard. Still, he reflected, it was fortunate that he had a beard to discard. Without it his appearance would be so greatly altered that he could assume his new identity with little risk of discovery.

The characteristic black hat was gone. He would wear a cap.

His meditations were interrupted by a crunching step on the gravel. The attorney looked up.

CHAPTER XX
COMPANIONS IN MISERY

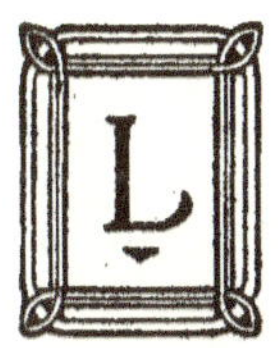OOMING out of the mist advanced a bulky figure, just an obscure shadow in the gloom. At first Brent thought the newcomer was a policeman, but the fellow shuffled down the path instead of pacing with deliberate stride, and when he was abreast of the bench he was revealed as a stout, thickset man with a jovial, unshaved face beneath an exceedingly battered hat. Brent could see him quite clearly in the radiance of the near-by light.

The stranger had stiffened, like an animal, when he caught sight of Brent. Now he halted. They peered at one another in the fog.

"*B'soir,*" growled the newcomer.

"Good night!" Brent lowered his head. He had no desire for company just then. But the stout stranger said cheerfully: "Oh, so you're not a Frenchie, huh?" and sat down beside him.

Brent did not move.

"Seems like everybody I've spoke to since I landed in this burg to-night couldn't talk English. Wet night, brother!"

"Very."

"Not so good for floppin' in the park, is it?" The man had a hearty, throaty voice that somehow imbued confidence; he was friendly without arousing that instinctive mistrust the city bred man has for strangers.

Brent studied the gravel at his feet, and one hand was cupped about his chin, hiding the beard.

"Not very good," he agreed.

A silence. Then: "Up against it, brother?"

"Some."

"Broke?"

Brent nodded, silently.

"So'm I. What of it?"

"Companions in misery."

The stranger shifted about to get a better look at Brent, and the bench creaked under his weight.

"Kind of an educated egg, huh? But I get you. Companions in misery is good. Been like this before?"

"This is the first time."

"I thought so. It gets you the first time. When you've been havin' your ups and downs as long as me you don't take it so bad. Just the same, it's too bad if you gotta sleep in the park just for the need of a dime."

Brent looked up at his companion. In the dim light he could discern the man's broad, coarse, good-natured face, with its shrewd eyes, bulbous nose and wide mouth; he was in bad need of a shave, for there was a bristly black smudge above his upper lip and on his fat jowls and chin. He wore no collar, his coat was turned up about his neck, his clothes were unbelievably tattered.

"Can you get a bed for a dime?"

"Where you been, brother? Sure you can get a flop for a dime."

"Near here?"

"There's a flop-house down the street. You'll see a sign over the door: 'Good Beds—Ten Cents.' The last part is honest."

"The beds can't be very good."

"Whaddaya expect for a dime? Feathers?"

"Are you going to sleep in the park?"

The stranger shrugged. "Oh, I'll mebbe prowl around some more and see if I can rap for a touch. It ain't so late, and people are soft when it's rainin'."

Brent fumbled in his pockets. He felt two or three drenched and soggy bills, a few coins. He found a quarter and handed it to the man by his side. "I guess I can stake you."

With no apparent surprise the man took the money. "Thanks, brother. How about yourself? Gonna sit here all night?"

"I don't know."

The derelict edged closer on the bench. He was peering at Brent's clothes.

"Say," he demanded, "where the hell have you been? Swimmin'?"

"Not exactly."

"You're soaked. I'm wet myself, but I'm not *that* wet, for it ain't been rainin' long enough." He looked closer. " And if you don't mind me noticin' it," he went on, in a quieter voice, "you've had a pretty bad crack on the dome."

"An accident."

"Listen, brother. I mind my own business, see. I'm what you folks would call a tramp, and they call me

Frisco Fat. That's all you need to know about me, and I don't want to know nothin' about you. But if you got anythin' on your mind you can spill it, and mebbe I can help. You look to me like somebody had beat hell outa you and dumped you in the river, and you ain't got over it yet."

"I'm all right. I'm just trying to figure something out."

"Gonna sit here in the rain all night to do your figurin'?"

The drizzle had become a shower. Brent came to a sudden resolution.

"Perhaps you can help me," he said. "The fact is, I want to get rid of this beard, and I don't want to have people see me until I do."

Frisco Fat sat back and raised his eyebrows significantly.

"On the lam, eh? Well, I been there myself. Looks like you had to do a little bit of battlin' and swimmin' on the get-away, too. Don't be scared of me spillin' anythin'. If you've bust outa stir, I don't blame yuh for not wantin' to go back."

From this Brent gathered that his companion assumed he had just escaped from prison, and, as Frisco Fat appeared to view this with sympathy, he did not go out of his way to correct the impression.

"I don't dare go much farther," he said, "until I get rid of this beard, you see."

"Right! And lemme tell you, brother, you're lucky you've got that trellis work to start with. Mow 'em off, and you're a new man. How come they let you keep 'em if you were in stir?"

Brent hesitated. " I—well—I wasn't really in

prison—"

"Made your get-away when they was takin' you there, huh? It's all Annie Oakley with me, brother. I don't know what it was all about, and I ain't carin' any. But gettin' down to cases, this is no place to hide. There's a flattie likely to be along any minute. What you'd best do is come along with me to this here flop-house. There ain't no danger of bein' spotted there. Keep your head down and let me do the talkin' and the guy at the door won't be able to say whether you're bearded or bald-headed."

"Then what?"

"In the mornin' you can clean up the shrubbery." Frisco Fat patted a side pocket of his coat. "I always carry my own razor, even if I don't look it just now." He rubbed his bristly chin. "The brothers and sisters are pretty strong on my own chip and chase, ain't they? I need a misbehave myself. Anyway, in the mornin' you can step outa that flop-house and your own mother won't know you."

"I suppose I can count on you to keep quiet."

"Listen!" A firm hand was on Brent's arm. "You've staked me to two bits for a flop on a rainy night, ain't you? All right. Think I'm gonna go lookin' for folks that wanta know about you? It ain't none of my biz, see! None at all. Forget it." He heaved his bulk off the bench. "Come on, brother. Let's get in outa the rain."

Brent got up and followed his new friend out of the park. Although Frisco Fat was nothing more than a hobo, he inspired confidence, and his offer of assistance was clearly genuine. It appeared to present an excellent opportunity of furthering the lawyer's plan.

They crossed the glistening road, gained the pavement on the opposite side, and advanced into the thickening fog. Brent could scarcely see the end of the block. The street lights were meager blobs of yellow in the wreathing veil that overhung the city. A taxi zoomed out of the mist and was swallowed up with incredible swiftness.

A man trudged toward them with umbrella raised against the rain—a fantastic shape that seemed to come from nowhere—and when he passed by he went on into nothingness like a figure walking in a dream.

Everything was shadowy, unreal and grotesque, and when Michael Brent looked down at his own drenched clothes and reflected on the oddity of his appearance as he walked hatless in the rain with a fat and ragged vagabond by his side, he wondered if he had not perished in the sewer after all, and if he were not now wandering in some weird hell of the imagination.

Under the stingy radiance of the corner light, Frisco Fat halted and regarded Michael Brent thoughtfully.

"You'll need a new make-up," he said.

"Make-up?"

"Duds. Clothes. I don't know where you been swimmin', but that outfit won't do no more."

"I have a little money—"

"New duds for you in the mornin'. I'll get 'em secondhand. It won't cost you much. Come on."

They went down the cross street, dark and narrow. In the fog it was a sinister defile, its gloom broken by but one light, a smudgy ruby radiance far ahead. They trudged on. Rain spattered on the pavement, drummed on the roofs, gushed from waterspouts.

They arrived at the ruby light, and Brent saw that it

was a square glass sign, on which had been painted in white letters, now almost defaced, the word “Beds.” Beneath the sign was an open doorway, and a faded placard on which some one had scrawled: “Good Beds—Ten Cents.”

Frisco Fat stepped inside. “Here we are.”

He went clumping up the stairs that ascended steeply to a landing where a lonely gas jet flared. Brent followed, his dripping clothes creating an uneven trail of moisture on the steps.

CHAPTER XXI
ALIAS SAM STEUBEN

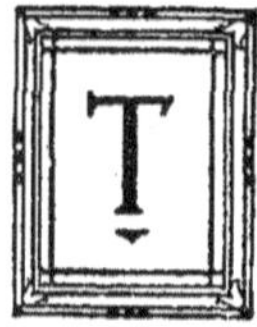

HE street had been cheerless enough, in fog and gloom and rain, but this anonymous hostelry was not much better. It was damp and clammy, the stairs were precarious, and the wavering gas flame revealed plaster walls of an astonishing griminess.

There was an open door leading into a shadowy little room, where Brent could distinguish a counter, but the room was apparently deserted.

An old, musty smell pervaded the entire place, an atmosphere of decay, of rotting wood, of dirty clothing, of human bodies, heavy and foul. Dirt and darkness, stench and shadow.

That this should be a place where men would sleep seemed almost incredible to Brent, but he followed Frisco Fat into the little room, and the vagabond went to the counter as though he knew his way about. On the counter was a cheap bell, which Frisco Fat pounded with a pudgy fist. It tinkled feebly.

"Some dump, huh?" said the fat man, leaning

against the counter. "Don't even keep a light burnin' in the office. They keep the gas on in the hall so nobody will break his neck gettin' up the stairs, and then make the light do for in here."

He banged on the bell again.

"Come on! Come on, you creepin' old buzzard!" he grumbled. "Snap out of it!" He hammered the bell violently.

They heard a stir, a wheezy gasp, a door opened at the back of the room, beyond the counter, and a voice croaked dismally. A dim light shone through the doorway and a yellowish, bald-headed old man in trousers and undershirt emerged, padding silently over toward them; he was an evil, ratlike old man with a crafty, chinless face and two prominent front teeth, filmy, dead eyes and hands like claws.

"Beds?" he croaked.

"Two," growled Frisco Fat. He put down his quarter.

A bony claw darted across the counter, seized the money and produced a nickel in change. The vulture then thrust forward a worn black book, open at a list of scribbled names, and gestured toward a bottle of ink and a pen lying near the bell.

"Gotta register?" Frisco Fat inquired. "What's the big idea"

"The law," croaked the vulture.

"You do the writin', brother. It's all I can do to make my mark." Frisco Fat stood aside and Brent took up the pen. He hesitated. "Go on. Go on. You know my name. Bill Johnson."

Dutifully, Brent wrote down "Bill Johnson" on behalf of his companion. Then he paused. The vulture tossed two metal disks on the counter. What should he write? It would not do to hesitate over his own name, but he found it difficult to think of an alias offhand. The vulture was watching.

Mechanically, he wrote, “Sam.” Sam who? Sam Smith? Too obvious. Sam Jones. Sam Brown—why couldn’t he think of something else? The name of Hartley Steuben, one of his wealthiest clients, popped into his head, and with a sort of impish delight he scribbled it in the book. Sam Steuben.

The vulture shuffled off into the gloom, there was a metallic click and a door opened in the wall at the end of the counter.

Frisco Fat picked up the disks and gave one to Brent. “That’s your flop number,” he said. They passed through and the door clicked shut behind them.

They were in a long, stuffy room, dimly lighted by a gas jet at the far end. There were windows down one side, the panes as black as ebony and streaked with rain. In the sickly radiance, Brent saw two rows of wretched wooden cots. Some of these pallets were already occupied. On the grimy walls were crudely painted numbers.

Frisco Fat looked at his disk.

“Eleven,” he said. “What’s yours?”

Brent could scarcely distinguish the figures in the dim light.

“Thirteen.”

Frisco Fat peered at the disk. “So it is! Make him take it back. He unloaded it on you.”

“Take it back?”

“The old geezer slipped one over on you. It’s unlucky, ain’t it?”

“It doesn’t make any difference to me. I’m not superstitious."

Frisco Fat looked doubtful. "It's up to you, brother," he said at last. "Mostly, he can't get rid of thirteen."

That any one driven to seeking shelter in this miserable den should fear bad luck struck Brent as the height of irony. As he made his way between the two rows of cots, breathing the foul air of the place, he caught glimpses of faces that in sleep were like masks of poverty and disease, sin and despair, and all the miseries of men.

Brent was obsessed once more by the unreality that had clung to everything since his escape from the sewer and by that queer, ridiculous idea that he had indeed perished and gone to hell.

Their shadows were enormous and grotesque on the grimy walls. Frisco Fat found his cot and sat down with a grunt of relief. As Number 12 was in the opposite row, Brent's cot was adjacent. It was hard and uncomfortable, only a few inches from the floor.

"First time you ever been in a joint like this?" asked the fat vagabond, noticing Brent's curious glances.

"It's all new to me."

They spoke in whispers. From out of the shadows came snores, gasps, an occasional muttered word.

"They ain't bad when you get used to 'em. Mighty handy when you ain't got much jack."

Frisco Fat was taking off his ragged clothes. Brent removed his soggy shoes, his drenched and filthy garments. Everything was soaked, of course. He made shift to dry his body with the blanket on his bed, but the blanket was damp and musty, so he abandoned the effort and lay on the sparse mattress, the covering wrapped about him, and shivered.

"Good night, brother," said Frisco Fat.

"Good night."

Brent did not go to sleep immediately. He lay in the darkness, listening to the snores and gasps of the slumbering men in this wretched room. It was odd that such places existed. He had known of them, in a vague way, but the reality was disturbing.

The lawyer reflected that in all the hundreds of nights he had been sleeping in a comfortable bed in a warm room, unfortunate men had been seeking sleep in just such miserable shelters as this, in the dark alleys and streets of shadow. There were hidden depths in the city, and the inscrutable buildings masked strange things.

Although he was cold, Brent fell asleep and, upon awakening, was surprised to find that it was after nine o'clock. The rain had passed; sunshine was filtering through the dust and grime on the windows.

Most of the lodgers had already departed. An old man was sitting on a cot in the opposite row; he was in his underwear and was pulling on a disreputable pair of socks. Some anonymous derelict was still sleeping on a pallet by the end wall. Frisco Fat was getting dressed. He looked over as Brent stirred.

"Mornin', brother. Sleep well?"

"Fine."

"Better get up. They don't like it if you stay too late. Some guys come in here to sleep in the daytime."

Brent remembered the program he had mapped out.

"How about that shave? And the new clothes?"

"You gimme some dough and I'll go out and pick up duds for you. I can get you a coat and a pair of pants pretty cheap. You can shave while I'm gone."

Brent reached for his sodden, useless trousers and rummaged in the pockets. To his surprise, he found that he had not very much money. There were three wet and crumpled bills, a few coppers, and about sixty cents in silver.

But Frisco Fat said: "Oh, you're well heeled. We can eat, too. We gotta eat."

Brent thrust the money into his hand. "It doesn't matter how the clothes fit."

"You can't worry about fit when you get that kind of a suit," grinned Frisco Fat. "I'll get you a cap and a shirt too. *And* a pair of socks, if you like."

"On that much money?"

"Sure. Some of these Yids could sell their whole stock for about five bucks and still make money."

Frisco Fat dressed himself and then gave Brent a package containing a razor and a cake of soap.

"It won't be so easy givin' yourself a misbehave with this," he said, "but take it easy. Too bad we can't find a pair of scissors. If it wasn't for bein' under cover, you could go down to the barber college and get the job done for nothin'."

"I'll do it myself."

Frisco Fat departed, and Brent made his way to the appalling washroom, where he achieved a lather from the cake of soap and then attacked the beard.

He suffered tortures before he had achieved an even passable shave, and he gashed himself liberally, but when it was over he was elated by the change effected in his appearance. The cracked mirror told him that there would be little danger of recognition by either friend or enemy.

Frisco Fat, returning ten minutes later with a big bundle in his arms, stared doubtfully at Brent, sitting on the cot with the blanket about him.

"Is it you?"

"It is."

"Eggs in the coffee!" declared Frisco Fat, approvingly.

"Think I'll get by?"

"Anywhere. Here's the duds."

He unwrapped the bundle and produced a shoddy coat of a sickly greenish tinge, a pair of gray trousers, a cotton shirt and a cap. They were cheap, but serviceable enough for Brent's purpose. Frisco Fat had bargained shrewdly and had persuaded the tearful merchant to throw in a pair of cotton socks free. Brent donned the new clothes.

"Don't get caught in the rain with that outfit on," Frisco Fat advised. "It'd shrink up around your neck, and you'd get yourself pinched."

He stood back and surveyed Brent critically.

"Annie Oakley!"

"All right, eh?"

"Not a dick in town would know you now. Pull that cap down over your eye a little more. There! Let's eat."

"I guess I'll leave my old clothes here. They're no use to me any more."

"Leave the pants. Bring the coat and lose it somewhere. They might trace you if you left 'em together."

Brent followed his advice and they left the flophouse together, turning in their metal disks at the counter. Two weary derelicts were just being assigned to cots as they left. At the next street corner they found a garbage can, where Brent disposed of his coat.

He did not notice the bloodstains on the back of the collar.

Frisco Fat gave Brent ninety cents in small change.

"That's what's left after gettin' the outfit. We can eat, anyway."

"It won't be much of a breakfast."

"On ninety cents? Sure. And enough left over for a smoke."

Frisco Fat knew his way about, even in a city that was strange to him. He discovered a cheap café where, for twenty cents, one could have breakfast consisting of a dubious egg, a fragile strip of bacon, a soggy potato, two slices of burned toast and a mug of coppery liquid that was at least hot. Fifteen cents bought a small packet of cigarettes. Michael Brent felt better as they sat back and puffed peacefully.

"I'm lucky to have met you," he told Frisco Fat.

The plump vagabond waved his gratitude aside.

"Fifty-fifty," he said. "You staked me to bed and breakfast. Where do you go from here?"

"I'll get a room somewhere, I guess."

"Stayin' in town?"

"Yes."

"Gonna work?"

"Perhaps."

"You won't be able to get much of a room for two bits."

This had not occurred to Brent. Hitherto he had always had enough money for his immediate needs.

"Kinda forgot that, huh?" grinned Frisco Fat. "Guess you'll have to get a job. Unless you got somethin' to hock."

Brent then remembered his watch. He had transferred it from his abandoned garments to the new clothes and found that its immersion of the previous night had done it little harm.

It was a good watch, an excellent watch. It had cost him almost two hundred dollars and he had bought it by way of celebrating the winning of his first big case. He disliked the idea of parting with it, but he saw that he must have money and already he was beginning to doubt the advisability of getting in touch with Minton. But, as Frisco Fat suggested, he could pawn the watch and redeem it later.

He showed the timepiece to his companion.

"Swell turnip! You oughta get about fifteen bucks on that."

"Fifteen? It's worth two hundred!"

"Sure. Try and get it."

They set out in search of a pawn shop. Brent found, to his surprise, that they were not far from the Main; close to the corner of Chat Noir they came upon an evil little den advertised as the resort of Square-Deal Sol.

The window was heaped with an amazing collection of guns, cameras, watches, knives and jewelry. The shop was tiny and dark. They could hear Square-Deal Sol shuffling toward them from a back room before they could see him, and he materialized from the gloom behind the counter as a dwarfish old Jew with spectacles on his nose and a bald head that seemed set awry on his hunched shoulders. He examined the watch contemptuously, sniffed at it and delivered the verdict that he couldn't give more than ten dollars if he should drop dead where he stood.

Brent was indignant at this insult to a two-hundred-dollar watch and he told the pawnbroker what it had cost.

The Jew, peering at his disreputable clothes, asked him his name.

"Er—" and then a warning kick from Frisco Fat reminded Brent of the alias. "Steuben," he corrected, hastily. "Sam Steuben."

So then the Jew thrust the watch before him, pointing a pudgy forefinger at the initials "MB" on the back of the case, and said that while he wouldn't call no man a liar and everybody said Square-Deal Sol minded his own business like no other pawnbroker in Montreal, just as a friend, y'understand, he didn't mind telling Mr. Steuben that if he went to any other pawnshop where maybe they wouldn't trust a poor man who had maybe bought the watch from a friend in the first place, he might find himself in jail for trying to pawn a watch with somebody else's initials on it, y'understand.

And then he smiled a very greasy smile and thrust his head forward and squinted over his spectacles and tapped his dirty fingers on the top of the counter until Frisco Fat muttered: "You're licked, brother. Take it."

So Brent took it, but not before Square-Deal Sol had tried to prevail on him to accept a rifle, a revolver, a suit of clothes or a diamond ring in lieu of cash. At last the money was counted out in worn, greasy bills, a dollar at a time, he took his ticket and went away.

Out on the sidewalk, Frisco Fat chuckled.

"He had yuh! He had yuh cold! Why didn't you think about them initials?"

"I almost gave him my right name."

"That wouldn't 'a' been so good. He's supposed to keep a record, see? Watch your step when you call to get that turnip back again. If he stalls you and tells you to come back—lam! Because that 'll mean the dicks are wise."

They were at the corner of Chat Noir. It seemed to Brent as though his destiny had guided him unerringly to that evil thoroughfare again. He halted.

"I think I'll get a room in one of the houses along here."

Frisco Fat nodded.

"We'll go our own ways, brother. Me, I'm goin' down to the harbor. I've had an idea about takin' a trip in a boat, just to find what it's like."

They stood on the corner. Frisco Fat extended his plump hand. "So long," he said.

"Perhaps we'll run across each other again."

"Quien sabe? Not likely, brother. The world's a big place."

"You helped me out, a lot—"

"Forget it."

Brent took some money from his pocket. "Let's split this," he suggested. "Take a dollar anyway."

"Thanks, brother. I'm goin' down to the harbor."

A wave of his hand, and Frisco Fat crossed the road. On the other side, he looked back, grinning. Then he disappeared in the crowd.

Thus Frisco Fat went out of Brent's life as casually as he had come into it.

People jostled against the attorney. He turned into Chat Noir, feeling lonelier than he had ever been since his first lonely days in Montreal. He was no longer Michael Brent, lawyer, but Sam Steuben, drifter and casual laborer, who had just parted from his only pal.

CHAPTER XXII
THE TRAIL OF THE WATCH

HEN Cadieux Street—Cadieux the notorious, Cadieux the unspeakable—was obliterated even unto its name, and when its environs were purified by due process of law, the apostles of virtue congratulated themselves that they had stamped out the underworld of Montreal.

But the underworld is not a locality; it is a social condition. The denizens of crime were scattered to the four corners of the city, and then they gravitated together again in little groups and colonies, congregating by some strange magnetism of evil.

The underworld, instead of being a little kingdom of sin in the heart of the city, a roaring republic of vice with definite boundaries, became a term applicable to a hundred scattered colonies. The black weed took root in many shadowy streets, gradually squeezed out respectability, and made these thoroughfares its own.

These streets of shadow have not the bland indifference to the stranger that characterizes virtuous neighborhoods. This, of course, is not hospitality—it is caution. The stranger is suspect.

Just as Michael Brent's first visit to Chat Noir in search of No. 90 had been duly remarked and noted, so did the arrival of Sam Steuben provoke a livelier interest than he imagined. He would have been vastly surprised had he known that any one but the landlady from whom he had rented a frowzy hall bedroom was aware of his presence in Chat Noir. That he was an object of comment and discreet inquiry was certainly farthest from his thought.

However, in the ordinary course of events, he was appraised and discussed by certain lords of the neighborhood who were interested in knowing if he were "regular," if he had connections with the detective bureau, or if he were simply a greenhorn who had wandered here all unwittingly.

Thus it came about that the matter of the pawned watch, which would ordinarily have been of profound lack of consequence to Chat Noir—inasmuch as dealings with the pawnshop are as much part of the day's routine as visits to the tavern—became extremely important as indicating the degree of the newcomer's regularity.

"His name is Steuben, and he hocked a swell turnip at Sol's place for a ten spot, and it didn't have his initials on it," was the official report made to Laboeuf by the satellite assigned to this investigation. It was one of life's little ironies that this satellite was none other than Midge.

Laboeuf's verdict, thereupon, was that Steuben must be regular—probably a gun, or a prowler on the lam. He was left alone. Had the official report indicated suspicion that the stranger might be a stoolie or a fuzz, there would have been action toward expelling the stranger from Chat Noir.

All unaware of this dispensation in his favor, Brent was settling down to life in the quarter, and incidentally finding the underworld very dull.

However, he realized the danger of forcing the issue, of making a false move, and he knew that if he were once accepted by Chat Noir he might reasonably expect to learn more about No. 90. He had decided against getting in touch with Minton. He was, in the vernacular, "waiting for a break."

On the second day, as he was on his way to the news-stand near the Main, he caught sight of a familiar figure sitting in a doorway. Even before she turned her head, he knew her for the girl who had so intrigued him.

His heart gave a little jump. The pavement became billowy and unsubstantial. She was sitting at the top of the steps of one of the brick lodging houses, her skirts drawn primly down, and she looked lonely and a bit frightened.

So little did she seem a stranger to him that it was

with difficulty he suppressed the impulse to speak to her. He wanted to stop, to go up the steps, to say: "I have thought of you often since I first saw you. Won't you tell me about yourself? Can't we be friends?"

Brent's heart gave a little jump

But the conventions must be observed, even in Chat Noir. He passed by. She was more beautiful than he had remembered her.

Norah scarcely noticed him. He was just a shabby young man, cleaner and less worldly-wise than the run of youths in Chat Noir, going about his own business.

Brent bought a newspaper and found that the press had broken out into a rash of headlines over his disappearance. On the front page he was confronted by his picture, and in the text he learned that the hat and coat had been found, that foul play was feared.

He was pleased to note that the newspaper photograph had not the slightest resemblance to the clean-shaved Sam Steuben, and, although he suffered a twinge of conscience when he reflected on the rumpus being made on his account, he persuaded himself that the end justified the means.

He returned to his room. The girl was no longer on the doorstep. Brent regretted his choice of lodging house.

For a few days, at least, he would be able to make little progress. Chat Noir had a hard, thick shell of reserve. Seemingly, no one paid him the slightest attention. No one sought his acquaintance, no one bothered him, he was quite thoroughly ignored.

This, of course, he expected. But it was difficult to make friends. The casual word, the incidental pleasantry—these were received with suspicious stares.

He was wise enough to ask questions of no one. He dared not go near No. 90. It was necessary to bide his time—to wait for the break.

It came, next day, through the watch.

The spotlight of neighborhood interest had been momentarily turned on the matter of the pawned timepiece as indicating that the mild-mannered Steuben was either a pickpocket or a burglar in hiding. It happened that a stool pigeon came across this bit of information, which would never have been otherwise resurrected from the dusty anonymity of Sol's pledges. He passed it on to the detective bureau and escaped an impending reprimand for laziness. Two detectives dropped in on Square-Deal Sol.

There was no record of a missing watch answering the description of that particular timepiece, but when one of the officers saw the initials "MB" he reached for the telephone and called up his chief.

"Sounds like Brent's," said the voice on the wire. "I'll get hold of this guy Minton, his clerk, and send him down right away."

Consequently the faithful Minton was thrown into a fever of excitement by the news that a watch apparently answering to the description of Michael Brent's had been located.

Arriving at Square-Deal Sol's place, Minton entered timidly, looking anxiously about as though expecting to see Michael Brent arising from behind the counter.

"Let him see it, Sol," growled one of the detectives.

The Jew put the watch on the counter. Although Minton recognized it at once, he picked it up carefully, turned it over in his hands, held it up to the light, scrutinized the initials, and finally said in a solemn voice:

"It is Mr. Brent's watch."

"Sure?" demanded the detective, and looked severely at the clerk, as though there was every possibility in the world that Minton was lying.

"Positive."

"You've seen it before, eh?"

"Dozens of times."

"Well, you ought to know. Did he have it on him when you last saw him? He mightn't 'a' pawned it himself, huh?"

"He wore it the day he disappeared. Mr. Brent would have no need of pawning his watch," Minton answered stiffly.

"Well, Sol," said the detective. "Loosen up. Where did this turnip come from?"

Square-Deal Sol, with great volubility, explained that he didn't know there was anything wrong with the watch, God forbid. Nobody knew better than the police that he had been in business right in this shop for fifteen years and nobody had anything on him, and everybody called him Square-Deal Sol because he was careful to keep out of trouble even if it cost him money—

"Shut up! Who brought in that turnip?"

Sol shrugged and explained that the watch had been left with him by a young man he had never seen in his life before, although he would know him if he saw him again, damn his hide! He had loaned ten dollars on the watch, although business was rotten, and he had so many watches it was a shame to take any more—

"The name! The name!"

"Steuben, he called himself, and he come in here with a fat man—"

"And the initials ain't his own. How did yah figger that?"

Sol explained this by saying Steuben claimed the watch belonged to his brother-in-law. He had seen the initials and questioned Steuben about it, for he wasn't one to let anybody put over no stolen goods on him if he knew it, but what was a man to do—call everybody a liar?—and it was hard enough trying to run an honest pawnshop when, if he wanted to turn "fence," he could make of himself a millionaire—

"G'wan, you damn old thief, you're one of the biggest fences in town, and don't think we ain't wise to you. If it wasn't for Ikey takin' the fall for you two months ago you'd be in stir right now," said the detective, without sympathy.

Square-Deal Sol was moved to lamentations and explanations concerning the regrettable business of Ikey, but the detectives did not wait.

"Do you know where this guy hangs out? Have you seen him since? How was he dressed?"

Sol calmed sufficiently to describe Steuben's attire, but declared he had not seen him since, and if the rat ever came into the shop again he'd hold him up with a shotgun and call the police.

"All right. Hang onto that turnip. If he comes in to pick it up, stall him and give us a call. If he gets away, you'll get yours, remember."

The detectives left the shop. Minton followed, meekly.

"We don't need you any more."

"I'm really not very busy," pleaded the clerk. "If I'm not in the way, I'd rather come with you."

The detectives glanced at one another. They had no love for volunteer assistants. Still, the chap might be useful in getting a line on Steuben. They permitted Minton to accompany them into the corner tavern, where they conversed for a few minutes with the proprietor, a fat, black-mustached Frenchman.

Minton looked about him curiously. There were only a few people in the tavern. Two young chaps at a corner table were sharing a quart of beer. Their heads were close together, and once in awhile Minton saw their eyes flash as they glanced over at the detectives.

Minton could not understand French, but he caught the name "Steuben," so he knew the officers were making inquiries about the mysterious man who had pawned Brent's watch. Minton was tremendously excited. The very sight of the familiar watch had been disturbing.

The proprietor disappeared. The detectives waited, silently, and appeared bored. After awhile, the proprietor came back, whispered something, and returned to his customers.

"We'll go and pick him up."

The detectives left the tavern. Minton, his heart

thumping wildly, brought up the rear.

They went down Chat Noir. Minton had not realized that such streets existed. Alone, he would have been terrified and would have lost no time in getting back to the Main. He was conscious of the sullen curiosity manifested by the blowzy women who peeped out of upper windows and the surly men who lounged in doorways. The two detectives stalked on in magnificent unconcern.

At last they halted before a drab, three-storied brick building with the inevitable placard "*Salles a Louer*—Rooms to Let" by the door.

"Here we are."

The detectives seemed to have forgotten Minton. They went up the steps and pounded at the door. In a few minutes the landlady appeared, wiping her hands on her apron. She looked defiant.

"Guy by the name of Steuben live here?"

The woman nodded. Silently, she held the door open. They went inside.

"Is he in now? Good. Where's his room?"

The landlady waddled up the stairs. On the second flight, she was puffing. On the third, she was panting. In the dark hallway she pointed to a door.

One of the men knocked sharply. There was no answer. He thrust open the door.

There was no one in the little room. The detective swung about.

"I thought you said he just come in?"

The woman burst into a torrent of French, the substance of which appeared to be a vehement protestation that she had seen the lodger going up to his room and that he had not gone out again.

One of the detectives tilted his hat and scratched his head.

"Damn funny!" he grunted.

Then he spied the window at the end of the hall. It was open. He reached it in three quick strides and looked out.

"There he goes, Emil!" he shouted to his companion. Then he hollered to some one below: "Stop, you!"

The fugitive did not stop, so the detective wrenched something from his pocket. The hollow crash of his revolver sounded twice and then he cursed and flung a leg over the window sill.

Minton gulped with horror, before he realized that the man was not jumping out of the window in his excitement, but was simply scrambling down the fire escape. The other detective followed. The landlady was screeching.

Minton ran down the hall and looked out the window. The frail steel ladder was rattling and swaying as the detectives scrambled down. The excitement of pursuit was contagious.

Carefully, he got out on the window sill, tested the first rung, then started down the ladder. Had Mrs. Minton seen her orthodox husband just then, descending a fire escape into the back yard of a dingy underworld lodging house, she would have fainted from sheer astonishment.

He did not dare look down, he gripped every rung so tightly that the rust came off on his hands, and his heart was pounding at his own temerity, but at last he reached the bottom, jumped the few remaining feet into a heap of tin cans, caught sight of one of the detectives disappearing over a board fence, and hastened across the yard in pursuit.

He scrambled over the fence, tearing his trousers, and saw the detective running down a narrow passage between two houses. Minton wondered what explanation he would give his wife to account for the torn garment. He tripped over an iron hoop and sprawled on the ground, scraping skin off his wrists, but he picked himself up and hastened down the passage.

Out on the street he saw the detectives pounding along the sidewalk. Thc foremost man turned sharply and ran into a little store. The other officer was at his heels.

By the time Minton arrived he found an excited colloquy proceeding in French, the shopkeeper stammering in a high-pitched voice and pointing to a door at the rear.

"He bust in here and out the back door!" the first detective shouted to his companion. They hurried back of the counter and through the doorway into an alley. A small boy was burning rubbish. The detective barked a question at him. The boy, wide-eyed, pointed down the alley. It was a crooked lane that wound about back of a row of tenements.

Panting, Minton followed the officers. They rounded a corner just in time to see a figure dash into a back doorway.

"We got him!" growled the foremost detective. "He's in Lepine's tavern."

They crowded through the doorway, through a little hall that was banked high with empty beer cases, into a little room behind the bar. A youth in a dirty apron was washing glasses.

"Which way did he go?"

The youth looked blankly at them.

"Which way did he go?" roared the detective.

"Nobody come here."

The detective grabbed the youth by the shoulder.

"Don't lie to me! Hurry up!"

But the youth obstinately shook his head.

"I see nobody!"

"Where's Lepine?"

"He's out front."

The detectives crowded out into the front of the tavern. One of them caught sign of Minton.

"How did you get here?" he demanded roughly. "Beat it out back and stay there. He might be hidden around here."

Meekly, Minton did as he was told.

CHAPTER XXIII
A FRIEND IN NEED

ICHAEL BRENT, alias Steuben, had been in his room when the detectives invaded the lodging house, and, although some impulse of curiosity had moved him to peep down the stair well into the hall below, he would never have suspected that the detectives were in search of him had he not caught sight of Minton.

He recognized the faithful servant instantly, and within the next second was in flight.

There was but one way of escape—the hall window. He went down the ladder in reckless haste, and he had reached the ground before the detective spied him. He heard the shots as he raced for the fence, but did not look back until he scaled the barrier. Then he saw the first officer out on the ladder, the second man just scrambling out of the window.

The fact that the detective shot at him settled the main doubt in his mind. They were not pursuing Michael Brent; they were after Sam Steuben. In some way or another his trail had been picked up, some link had been discovered to connect him with the presumably murdered Brent. It was plain enough that his alias had not been penetrated.

Down the passage between the two houses, out into the street, and along the sidewalk the attorney raced. He looked around for some hiding place. Out in the open, capture was inevitable. The brick houses seemed massed in hostility against him.

Near by was a little shop and Brent ran inside just as a heavy figure came plunging out of the passage half a block behind. He caught a glimpse of the white-aproned storekeeper goggling at him and then he was around the counter and out the back door all in a twinkling. The fugitive plunged past a lad burning rubbish in the back yard. He was in an alley littered with refuse. Where now?

He raced down the crooked little lane, where a great pile of empty boxes caught his eye. They formed a defile about a gloomy door. Brent hesitated. It seemed the only refuge in sight.

He heard an uproar back in the shop and this decided him. He dived in between the ranks of beer cases, crossed the threshold and found himself in the back of a tavern.

It would profit him very little to walk right through the place and out by the front door. The detectives would trace him quickly enough, and there was always the chance that he might be stopped before he reached the street. He heard a shot, back in the alley.

Brent slipped in behind the half-open door. There were beer cases in the passage and they partly concealed his hiding place. He waited, breathing heavily.

A moment later he heard running footsteps, a

man's voice, and then some one came thudding into the passage. He caught a glimpse of a man's head and shoulders, above the topmost case; then another man, and a third. A door slammed. A voice was roaring.

No time to lose. The fugitive peeped out, saw that the passage was clear, emerged from behind the door and dived out into the alley again. He knew he was running the risk of colliding with additional pursuers, but had to chance it.

In the alley, he could see the boy by the rubbish fire, the shopkeeper and a few miscellaneous bystanders in a group, all talking at once and gesticulating. A shout went up. He bolted up the alley.

There was an abrupt turn in the narrow lane, immediately ahead, where it twisted back of a brick tenement. Thus it was that he did not discover that the alley had no outlet until he came around this sharp corner and found himself confronted by a stone wall.

He was trapped. The wall was high and solid. Beyond it he could see an old gray building, like a church. On the one side was a steep board fence, even higher than the wall, and on the other was a sheer side of a brick house.

There was no way of escape. The lawyer leaped up, trying to catch the top of the wall, but it was at least a foot beyond his reach. He looked around, hoping to find a box or some support that would enable him to scale the formidable barrier, but could see nothing that would aid him.

Back in the open alley he heard shouts. Some one yelled: "He went in there!"

If Brent retraced his steps he would run into the

arms of pursuers and his masquerade would come to an ignominious end.

He looked for a possible weak spot in the fence, but it was newly built, without sign of a gate or a loose board.

Running footsteps in the alley. So he was caught? Well, he could at least surrender with good grace. His pursuer plunged panting around the corner.

Minton!

Brent almost shouted with relief, for the faithful servant was alone. There, in the cul-de-sac, they faced each other, Brent against the wall, Minton coming to a dead stop and opening his mouth to roar for help.

"Shut up, Minty!"

Minton uttered a strangled squeak instead of a roar. This was not his master, but it was his master's voice.

"Help me over this wall, Minty. Hurry!"

"M-Mr. Brent!"

"Yes. Quit gaping, and give me a hand over the wall. I'm all right, Minty, but don't give me away."

Mechanically, the faithful servant advanced. "Is it really you, Mr. Brent? You're not dead?"

"Over the wall, Minty. Over the wall, before your boy friends come along."

Dazed but obedient, Minton crouched down and braced himself as Brent stepped lightly onto his shoulders, grasped the top of the wall and scrambled up.

"Minty?"

"Y-yes, sir?"

"Keep up the good work. I'm still dead, understand?"

"Yes, Mr. Brent."

There was a great uproar out in the alley.

"No matter what happens, keep your mouth shut!"

"They're coming, Mr. Brent."

The fugitive disappeared beyond the wall.

The uproar in the alley grew louder. The detectives were just beyond the cul-de-sac. Minton looked wildly around and then, although he was more completely upset and bewildered than ever before in his life, displayed rare presence of mind by dropping prone on the ground and lying quite still.

The two detectives, trailed by a squad of small boys and volunteer assistants, came plunging around the corner of the brick building. They had fully expected to find their quarry at bay against the wall, and their revolvers were drawn, but all they found was the apparently unconscious Minton, sprawled in the rubbish.

The small boys and volunteer assistants, who had halted at a respectful distance, surged forward when they saw there was to be no gunplay, and crowded around as one of the detectives hauled Minton to his feet. The other officer ran restlessly about the foot of the wall and the fence, like a disappointed beagle.

"Where am I?" inquired Minton, blinking and looking about, with a dazed air. Not for nothing had he been a member of the Seventh Avenue Amateur Dramatic Club.

"What the hell happened?" growled the detective, giving him a shake. "Where is he?"

"Water," murmured Minton, playing for time.

"Water, my neck! Where is that guy?"

"When you sent me out of the tavern," stammered the faithful servant, "some people shouted to me that he had just run in here—"

"Yeh! Yeh! But where *is* he? Where did he get to? He couldn't get over that wall. What happened?"

"I'm trying to tell you. I followed him in here. He came at me with something in his hand and he struck me over the head. And then," concluded Minton, with a quiet force that would have aroused the admiration of his fellow-members of the dramatic club, "everything went black."

The detectives were too deeply puzzled by the mysterious escape of their quarry to take note of Minton's suspiciously orthodox behavior. While the bystanders solicitously mobbed Minton and jostled him and hurled questions at him and requested permission to see and feel the bump where he got slugged on the dome, the two officers leaped vainly at the stone wall, trying to grasp the top.

"Well, I'll be damned!" the senior officer finally exclaimed. "Nobody saw that guy come back out of the alley, so he must have climbed over that fence or this wall, and there ain't a sign of a box or a board or a ladder to help him, so he must 'a' jumped it."

"What kind of a guy is he? A kangaroo! No matter how high I jump I can't come within six inches of reachin' the top."

"Well, he ain't here now, so he must 'a' done it. Gimme a h'ist. He can't be far away yet."

The junior officer obliged with a "h'ist" and helped his companion over the wall, then requested a h'ist from the volunteer assistants, who rendered this service with such enthusiasm that they almost hoisted the detective directly over the wall into the churchyard beyond.

As for Minton, the chase had lost all charm. Astounded and puzzled beyond measure at the discovery that Michael Brent was not only alive, but was deliberately cultivating the legend of his own death, vastly relieved in knowing that his master had not been foully murdered after all, and highly proud of himself for his part in facilitating the fugitive's escape, Minton went back down the alley, escorted by a bodyguard of admiring urchins right to the nearest trolley line.

The detectives, however, were persistent. They went through the churchyard and picked up the trail again in the street. A youngster reported having seen a man run into a second-hand shop, but interrogation of the proprietor brought fierce denials.

The sleuths prowled about, investigated the cellar and the back yard, bullied the proprietor at some length and finally departed. Elsewhere on the street, they learned nothing.

The youngster had not lied. Brent had taken refuge in the shop.

He knew that the wall would not delay the detectives long and there was no chance that Minton could put them on a false scent. The respite, however, enabled him to gain the street and as he ran panting down the pavement he looked vainly about for some possible hiding place. He had not intended going into the second-hand shop, but when he was in front of the door he heard a voice.

"In here, brother!"

He stopped abruptly. Standing in the doorway was a crippled man, with one hand thrust into a side pocket of his coat. For a moment Brent thought he had made a mistake, that the invitation was not addressed to him, but the cripple gestured with his free hand.

"Snap into it. Come out of the cold."

He went into the dark little shop.

"Can't you shake the dicks?"

"They're right behind me."

"Come along."

The cripple led the way behind the counter. "It's all right, Abe," he said to the proprietor. "This bird is on the lam."

There was a trapdoor leading to the cellar, and the guide descended the stairs. Brent followed.

"I heard the dicks askin' about you up at the tavern," explained the cripple. "I been on the lam myself, so I know what it's like."

He paused in front of a pile of packing cases against the wall. He moved one of them, reached in, tugged, and slowly the boxes swung outward, revealing a black opening. It was an ingenious scheme. There was a door in the wall, with a shelf attached to the bottom, and on this shelf the boxes had been piled so that the door was automatically hidden when closed.

They stepped into the dark chamber beyond and the cripple carefully shut the door behind him. They were in utter blackness.

"We'll wait here awhile."

Silently they stood there. After awhile they heard voices in the shop above.

"Just in time," muttered the cripple.

The voices died away. There were heavy footsteps on the stairs. Some one blundered about the cellar for a few minutes, then went up into the shop again.

"That's that," came the man's voice from the darkness. "It ain't the first time they've been down here, but they've never found the door yet." A pause. "What do they want you for?"

"Plenty."

"I've seen you around. Been layin' low?"

"Yes."

"We'll fix you up. Figgered you was regular."

He did not explain the "we."

They stayed in the secret chamber for about five minutes. Then there was a sharp knocking on the boxes outside the door.

"I guess it's all right. We can go out now."

The cripple groped for the door. It opened slowly and they stepped out into the cellar again. The shopkeeper was waiting for them. "They're gone," he said.

"Where?"

"They went up toward the Main. Some brat said he saw this bird come in here, but I bulled 'em out of it."

They went up into the shop.

"Better come with me," said the cripple. "So long, Abe. And thanks."

He did not go out onto the street. Instead, he turned to the back door and Brent followed him out across a yard heaped with a miscellaneous collection of junk, across a lane, through a passage, across an open street into another passage, down another lane and thus by devious ways to the back door of a lodging house. They went into a dark hall, ascended a flight of stairs and the cripple unlocked a door.

"This is my hangout." He gestured for Brent to enter, then closed the door.

"It's mighty good of you. They'd have nabbed me in another minute," said Brent, sitting down on the bed.

"That's all right. I been on the lam myself, I told

you. If I didn't know you was one of us, it'd have been different. Your name's Steuben, eh?"

"Yes."

"Mine's Burger. What's your racket?"

Brent had picked up some underworld argot in his court room experience.

"Prowler."

Burger nodded.

"I got the office that you was to be looked after."

"I don't get you?"

"I don't get it myself. But the boss will know. It's about that turnip you hocked."

"Yes?"

"The dicks come into Sol's place awhile ago and took a look at it. Then they put in a call for a guy uptown to come down. Sol gave his boy the high sign, for it seems the boss has had his eye on that turnip and wanted to know somepin about it."

"The boss?"

"I'll bring you to him. There's somepin funny about that turnip. Where'd you get it?"

Brent thought quickly.

"I frisked a stiff."

"Uh-huh. Well, he wanted to know. He gave me the word to look after you, but I couldn't find where you was hangin' out. I got wise that you made your getaway, but they was right on your tail and I couldn't connect. I beat it into Abe's place, figgerin' you might come down that way—and here we are."

"How come the boss heard about the turnip?"

"He hears everythin' that goes on around these parts. From what I can dope out, it's about that lawyer guy that was knocked off. The turnip got his initials."

"A guy with a beard?"

Burger nodded. "That's him."

"He was stiff when I got him. Dead as a mackerel. I was down by the river."

"Well, you can tell the boss about it."

"I didn't bump the guy off," declared Brent, with fine defiance. "He was stiff when I got him."

"Sure. Sure. I figger the boss knows somethin' about that caper."

"What's the program now?"

"That's up to the big boy. He's a bad egg, but if you stand in with him he can put you in the way of some good things. If you *don't* stand in with him—" Burger turned down his thumbs.

"It's in the papers about this mouthpiece that got his. I was readin' it and I got scared. When the dicks come after me I doped it out right away that mebbe they'd try to hang the job on me."

"You figured right. And now that you've beat it, instead of stickin' around to tell your story like a little man, they'll hang it on you for sure. Mebbe," said Burger shrewdly, "that was the boss's idea."

"Do you really think he's got the lowdown on it?"

Burger shrugged. "None of my business," he growled. "We'd best talk about somethin' else."

They abandoned the topic. Burger seemed restless. Several times he seemed on the point of saying something, but evidently changed his mind. At last, after a long silence, he said "Say, do you know anythin' about women?"

"Women?"

"Yeah."

"A little."

"How d'you go about makin' 'em fall for you?"

Brent was puzzled. The cripple was scarcely the sort one would suspect of amorous ambitions.

"Well—I don't know. Depends a lot on the dame. Mostly, you just be nice to her and tell her she's a swell looker, and buy her some candy once in awhile, and take her to a show."

"Buy candy?" said Burger.

"Sure. Pay her a lot of attention. They like it."

"Buy candy," the cripple muttered. "I never thought of that."

"I don't mean that just buyin' a dame a box of candy will make her fall for you. But it helps."

"I can't figger it out. I ain't never fell for a jane in my life—that is, not till lately—and none of 'em ever gave me a second look, unless they was just pick-ups, y'know, so I don't know much about 'em. But some guys seem to get any women they want. F'r instance, there's the boss. The big boy. He's had a raft of women. But he don't get 'em the way you say. They fall for him, right and left, but I never heard of him givin' one a box of candy yet. He's more like to give 'em a poke on the jaw. But they fall for him just the same."

"He must have sex appeal," grinned Brent.

"Sex appeal, huh? Yeah—that's what they got in the movies, ain't it? Well, if grabbin' off the molls without half tryin' is sex appeal, he's chock full of it."

"Some guys have it, and the rest of us gotta get along as best as we can. There's plenty of women to go around."

"Yeah, but what if there's just one special one you want, and the rest of 'em don't count?"

"That's love."

"I guess that's what you'd call it. I never took much stock in this mush stuff, but—aw hell—this jane is different. She's a good kid, see? The kind you'd want to marry. And the hell of it is, I ain't got a chance. Not a chance."

"Why?"

Burger laughed. It was a short, harsh, bitter laugh, painful to hear.

"You're lookin' at me," he said. "Ain't that enough?"

"Looks ain't everything," said Brent uncomfortably.

"I wish to God"—the words came slowly—"I wish to God I was twenty years younger."

There was a great depth of tragedy in his voice.

"Why not tell me about her?"

To a less sympathetic man than Brent, the fellow would have been grotesque. It was difficult to imagine this uncouth derelict in love, but—why not? Even beggars can love, although Brent could scarcely conceive this battered hulk as being animated by tender emotions. He was a clod, blindly stumbling along the hopeless road of his destiny, driven sullenly toward an obscure goal.

Burger's bleak eyes regarded Brent suspiciously, as though anticipating a smile. But Brent returned the gaze gravely.

"They like the young fellows," said Burger. "Won't look at a bum like me. Not that I ever gave a damn." A snarl quivered in the reedy voice. "But this girl—by God, I tell you I've never met any one—no, there's no one like her. No one!"

Then he stared at Brent, as though hoping to find in the other man's expression some reflection of his own certainty. But he saw only a vague interest and a disguised pity. When a man is in love, the overwhelming significance of the fact to himself is countered only by its monumental insignificance to his fellows.

"I don't know why I'm tellin' you," he said, dully. "But it's been bottled up inside me for two days now—do you understand?"

He slapped his chest with the flat of his hand.

"I have no one to talk to, see! She—she—well, there ain't no use of me tryin' to explain it. You wouldn't get me. I've never felt this way before about any one. Any woman! But this girl—"

Animated by a great earnestness, he struggled for expression of all the murky emotions that seethed in his soul. His face was desperate. It came to Brent that he was staring at the naked soul of an inarticulate man, helpless in the toils of a terrific passion. There was something horrible about it, and he felt a dull resentment, as though he had been thrust into the presence of something shameful.

The puzzled look died. The tense lines left Burger's mouth. His face was again dead and gray, a forlorn mask. The outrageous flame of which Brent had been given this disturbing glimpse was hidden.

"But you haven't told me about her."

Love-sick men must have an audience of some kind—if not the lady of their passion, then the friend of the moment.

It was some time before Burger spoke.

"I can't tell you much—well—I don't know just how to say it, but she's—she's like a child. So young! Like a child."

He contemplated the floor, with a sad smile.

"Young?"

“About eighteen, I guess.” Burger darted a quick glance, but Brent’s face was expressionless. “Too young for me, you’ll say.” He paused, as though turning this over in his mind. Then—

“But I mean to have her!”

He had raised his voice, and there was a frightened note in it, as though he tried to shout down the conviction that his love was without hope. When he spoke again, it was in a whisper.

“I never felt like this about any woman.”

CHAPTER XXIV
NORAH

"ND you've only known her for two days?"

"She lives here. Right in this house. On this very floor. Just came here." Burger paused.

"Pretty?" Brent prompted him.

Burger groped for words, and then sank back with a sigh, as though the effort had been too much for him. "Pretty! Why, she's—yes—oh, very pretty!"

"You fell for her mighty quick."

"The minute I laid eyes on her," Burger answered, with grave simplicity.

"If she's a good kid, like you say, you won't have much of a chance if you stick around with—with us."

"She don't know my racket. She's not wise to anything. Why, her old man is a crook, right on our mob, and she ain't wise to him, either. Honest, though, I'd even go straight if I thought it would make any difference. But everythin's all mixed up. As long as I stick around here, I gotta play with the boys, and I'm scared to leave because somepin might happen to her. She's so damn innocent. The boss has his eye on her, see? That's who I'm scared of. He's a devil, that guy. A devil! When he gets his eye on a dame he won't stop at nothin'. And, mostly, he gets 'em, too. I gotta stick around. I'd kill that guy before I'd let him get his hands on her."

"Can't her old man look after her?"

"Him! Hell. He'd lick Laboeuf's boots. He's a yellow little snowbird."

"Laboeuf? That thc name of the boss?"

"Yeah. I didn't mean to tell you until you got fixed up and he said everythin' was all right. Listen—if he's at home now, we'll go on over. I been talkin' too much."

"Don't worry about me. I can keep my trap shut."

Burger got up and went to the door. He looked out into the hall.

"Midge!" he shouted.

There was no answer.

"I guess he ain't in yet. We'll go and ask Norah."

Norah!

The name of the girl Brent had met in Chat Noir, the girl who had been in his mind ever since. The dirty old man who had been with her that afternoon had called her Norah, he remembered.

Wondering, he followed Burger down the hall. The cripple tapped at a closed door.

It opened. The girl herself was standing there. This, then, was Norah! Brent was so astonished that he could do little more than stare, idiotically. And Burger, in his turn, was obviously so embarrassed at being face to face with the object of his desperate adoration that he coughed, cleared his throat, blinked very rapidly, and at last managed to mumble:

"Your father ain't been around, has he, miss?"

"Isn't he in his room?" Her voice was childish and sweet.

"I just hollered for him."

"He went out about an hour ago. He said he'd be back soon, Mr. Burger."

"If he comes in, tell him I wanna see him, huh—please."

"All right."

Burger waved helplessly toward Brent. "Friend of mine," he muttered. "Mister—Mister—"

"Steuben," gulped Brent hastily.

"Yeah, Steuben. This is Miss Gray."

"Pleased to meetcha." Brent ducked his head in a bow.

The girl smiled. "I'm glad to know you." Her teeth were small and very white; when she smiled her prettiness was radiant.

"Thanks, miss. You'll tell him, eh?"

"Yes, I'll tell him."

The door closed as they turned away. They went back to Burger's room in silence.

"I wanted you to have a look at her," explained Burger. "Do you blame me, huh?"

"Not a damn bit. She's a knockout." Brent tried to achieve a carelessly emphatic tone.

"Not much chance for me, is there?" Burger asked wistfully.

"Oh, I dunno. Keep tryin'."

"I guess I'll do like you said. I'll buy her some candy."

Burger lapsed into silence, evidently meditating on

a plan of campaign. As for Brent, he was trembling with excitement. In a moment everything had changed. Even the frowzy little room seemed brighter; he tingled with expectancy. He had met the girl called Norah. He had spoken to her. A few minutes previous she had been as remote, as inaccessible as the stars; now she was miraculously within reach, beneath that very roof—

"I can't go back to my old room," he said suddenly. "The dicks will be watchin' for me. D'you think I could get a room in this house. Is it safe?"

"What's that?" asked Burger blankly, looking up.

"I said I can't go back to my old room. Is it safe for me to get a room here?"

"As safe as anywhere else. Better wait and find out what the boss has to say. If you're okay with him you can ask the landlady here."

"The house ain't full up?"

"There's always somebody comin' or goin'. I guess you can get a room all right. You'll want to lay low for a day or so until this blows over." They heard voices down the hall, then the slam of a door, and shuffling footsteps.

"Come in, Midge," said Burger.

Brent looked up. He was scarcely prepared to confront the man who had attacked him in the street back of No. 90, although it had already dawned on him that this man and Norah's father must be one and the same. But when he saw the cringing, apologetic Midge, with red nose, rheumy eyes and stubbled chin, standing there in the doorway, he was so surprised that he almost betrayed himself by an involuntary gasp of recognition.

However, he controlled himself and managed to affect an indifferent attitude as Midge shuffled into the room.

"This," said Burger, "is Steuben."

Brent met the little man's shifty gaze and nodded.

"Been hearin' about you," said Midge.

"Boss wants to see him," Burger explained.

"I just come from there."

"He's in?"

Midge nodded. He licked his lips nervously as he glanced at Brent again. So this, reflected Midge, was the man the police wanted, for the murder of which he himself was guilty!

"I guess it's safe to go over."

"Sure. The dicks went uptown."

Burger got up. "Come on, then," he said to Brent. "We might as well go over now."

They went out. Brent hoped for another glimpse of Norah, but her door was closed. At the top of the stairs he looked back. Midge was standing in the hall, gazing at him, his expression at once apprehensive and mystified. Brent wondered if he had stirred some responsive chord of recognition, for even in his new character he felt unsafe, afraid some one would detect in Sam Steuben, self-confessed crook, the resemblance to Michael Brent.

Burger led him out the back way, through the yard, across a lane and down an alley that led to the rear of a brick house. It was not until the dogs, in their shed, set up a ferocious barking and snarling that he identified the house as No. 90!

This was his third shock within the half hour.

"Don't be scared," said Burger, mistaking his startled expression. "Them mutts are tied up."

He ascended the steps and tapped thrice at the door. Brent took a deep breath. From the moment of his discovery of No. 90 his fortunes had described a circular course, bringing him swiftly back to that sinister house again.

There was no doubt that it was the same place. The clamorous dogs settled that. But before he had time for further reflections on his luck, on this quick and surprising advance of his purpose, the door opened and Burger stepped inside.

The woman had admitted them. Brent's pulses quickened. He was in the enemy's stronghold. This sullen, tragic-eyed woman had already heard his voice. Recognition would be fatal.

But the woman paid them slight attention, and after telling Burger that "he" was busy for a few minutes, she resumed her stirring of some savory mixture that bubbled and simmered in a pot on the kitchen stove.

In the light of day, Brent eyed her curiously. She had undoubtedly been beautiful, but although she was still young her face had a hopeless, discontented expression that had eradicated every trace of the girlish charm that had been evident in her photograph.

In a torn, shapeless house dress and dirty apron she seemed merely a discouraged drudge. Yet this was the woman whose shadow had fallen like a blight on the lives of Paul Gregory and Margaret Hilliard, the woman who rose like a veiled figure of mystery from the fog that shrouded their deaths. And here she was, preparing dinner, like any honest housewife.

A cheaply dapper young man emerged from the next room, nodded to Burger, and departed by the back door. A huge voice boomed: *"Entrez!"*

They entered the presence of the boss of Chat Noir. It was Brent's first glimpse of this despot of the shadowy streets. Laboeuf, coatless, with shirt open at the neck, his hairy arms on the table, a cigar clenched in his white teeth, gazed steadily at him as he came into the room. The black, piercing eyes with their little pinpoints of light seemed to search his very thoughts, as though probing the innermost secrets of his soul.

"This is the guy you was talkin' about," said Burger, obsequiously. "The one that hocked the turnip at Sol's place."

Laboeuf grunted, chewed at the cigar, spat.

"Where you come from?" he barked.

"States," snapped Brent.

"When?"

"Coupla weeks ago."

"Why?"

Brent merely shrugged. He had cross-examined too many men, hoping to betray them into contradictions by a volley of rapid questions, to become flurried now.

"The police want for see you today, eh?"

"Yeah?"

"What for?"

"I guess it's about the turnip."

" Where you get that, hey?"

"Off a stiff."

"A stiff, huh? Whereabouts?"

" In the river."

"What part?"

"Where the sewer comes out."

The cigar waggled. "What he look like, huh?"

Brent passed his hands over his face. "Black

beard."

"You kill him?"

"Didn't have to. He was stiff already."

"How?"

"His dome was caved in."

"What else you take besides his watch?"

"He had three or four bucks."

Laboeuf spat again, and thrust his fingers through his mass of black hair. "Papers? Letters?"

"I chucked 'em away."

"You read his name?"

"The papers was soaked, but I saw his name on one of 'em."

"What was it?"

"Brent. Michael Brent."

A cluck of satisfaction. " ou know why the police want you now, huh?"

"I saw about this Brent guy in the papers. I didn't do it. He was stiff already."

"Anybody see you find him?"

"No."

A shrewd look came into Laboeuf's eyes. It would be convenient to keep this fellow within easy reach, in case police investigation in the affair of the missing lawyer should lead dangerously near No. 90. He had ordered Steuben brought to him because he was curious about certain features of Brent's ultimate fate.

"The police find his coat," said Laboeuf. "It was not near the river."

"He had his coat on when I got him," returned Brent readily. "I took it off so I could look through it later on. I chucked it into a garbage can."

Laboeuf seemed relieved. "So! And now what you

want?"

"Nothin'." Brent was sullen. "I didn't ask nobody to help me. I can take care of myself."

"How you like to work for me, eh?"

"What kind of work?"

"Whatever you do best."

"I've been used to playin' a lone hand."

"Better you come wit' us. We have—what you call it?—a syndicate. Everyt'ing is organize. Some of my men tell me of good jobs where we can make some money, I make all the plan and pick the men who can do that job, and w'en it is done I have more men to look after selling the stuff. Everybody has his own work to do and if you are not lucky we pay for a good lawyer for get you out."

"Sounds all right."

"We have somet'ing on for tonight. How you like to come in wit' us?"

This was a development Brent had not foreseen. He realized too well the danger of refusal. He would be immediately under suspicion, would probably be betrayed to the police at once, and all chance of learning more about No. 90 and the woman in the kitchen would be gone. He sparred for time.

"What kind of job?"

Laboeuf shrugged.

"You will find out. I say not'ing now." He leaned forward, his eyes narrowed. "You want it, or no?"

"Prowlin's been my line, mostly. I never been in no stick-ups."

"We give you the lookout."

This would involve no actual participation in crime. The duty of the lookout is to give warning in case a policeman or watchman should draw near.

"Suits me," said Brent.

Laboeuf nodded. "Be here at ten o'clock," he growled. "And now I have somet'ing to talk over wit' Burger—private. You wait in the kitchen, eh?"

Obediently, Brent retired to the kitchen. The woman was standing with her back to the stove, a somber expression in her eyes. She gazed at him steadily. Then, in a low voice, she said:

"Why do you come here?"

Startled, he did not know what to say. What did she mean?

"When you came in," went on the woman," I said to myself, 'I have seen that man before,' but I did not know where. But when you went in the other room, and I heard your voice I said, 'I have heard that voice before,' and I remembered."

Brent felt as though he had received a violent blow.

"You come here at night and you ask for some Mr.

She gazed at him steadily. "Why do you come here?"

Robinson. That was when I heard your voice."

Brent managed an unconvincing laugh.

"You're all wrong, sister. I've never been here before."

But she nodded her head, slowly.

"You had a beard then. A black beard. Now it is gone. That was why I did not know you at first. But you can change your face and you cannot change your voice."

Her beautiful, sullen face was calm. She stood with her arms folded, a fork in one hand.

"Where do you get that stuff?" demanded Brent, trying to bluff his way through. " I never been here in my life."

"Every time you speak I know you lie. I think I should tell Laboeuf."

A chair scraped. There were footsteps in the other room. Laboeuf and Burger were coming out. Brent was desperate. In another moment this woman would expose him. And then—

"You can tell him," said the woman, her eyes smoldering, "why you came here that night, and why you have no beard now."

CHAPTER XXV
PROGRESS OF A LOVER

RENT grasped at the last fragile straw of hope.

"I'll tell you," he whispered. "It's about Paul Gregory."

What impulse prompted this reckless gamble, he never could define. Perhaps he had only a vague idea that revelation of his errand would startle the woman out of her cold composure and earn him a moment's respite. The effect was astonishing.

Her eyes widened, she gave a little gasp, and the fork dropped from her fingers and clattered on the floor.

"Paul!" she said in a strangled voice.

Laboeuf's voice was booming just outside the door. Abruptly, the woman bent, snatched up the fork, and turned to the stove again. When Burger and Laboeuf came into the kitchen a moment later, she was placidly stirring the stew.

"Well, I'll fix the new guy up with a room," Burger was saying.

"Good. We help you make lots of money, my friend," said Laboeuf, as he turned to Brent. "You be here at ten o'clock. Come by the back door."

Brent nodded, mechanically. The woman bent over the stove. She did not turn around. She did not speak.

Burger opened the door. They went out.

As they crossed the yard, Burger said: "That's that. It's all fixed up. You're lucky. It ain't often Laboeuf lets a new guy in the mob quick like that."

"What's the big idea of doin' me a favor?"

"I dunno. You got a good break, somehow, in knowin' about that stiff you frisked the turnip from. I figger the boss knows somepin about that job and he wants to keep you handy. It's none of my business, but—watch your step."

Brent's mind was in confusion. Why had the woman not informed on him? Why had the name of Paul Gregory been like a *sesame*, a magic password to insure her silence? But would she be silent? Would she tell Laboeuf, after all? Did he dare go back to No. 90?

"Who's the woman?" he managed to ask, casually.

"What woman?"

"The one in the kitchen."

"Oh, her? Blanche! That's Laboeuf's woman."

"Not a bad looker."

"Not bad."

Are they married?"

Burger laughed, shortly.

"Laboeuf doesn't have to marry 'em to get 'em. She's been livin' with him a long time. He's got other women, of course, but she has to put up with that."

Fearing that his curiosity concerning the woman of

No. 90 might arouse suspicion, Brent said no more. When they came back to the lodging house, Burger paused in the kitchen and made arrangements with the blowzy landlady for Brent's room. There was one available, adjacent to the room occupied by Burger, and the new lodger paid for a week's rent out of his dwindling supply of money.

"How are you fixed?" Burger asked.

"Nearly broke."

"You'll be all right when you get your share of the split on to-night's caper."

Brent had almost forgotten about his commitment to take part in a criminal venture that night. There seemed to be no way out of it if he wanted to consolidate his position, but he had to face the grim fact that in definitely allying himself with lawless men he was risking their lawful punishment. There was no alternative.

And yet, how could he, Michael Brent, as an honest man, stain his hands with crime? No matter what motive, in the event of capture he would be just as guilty, in the eyes of the law, as the most hardened criminal of the lot.

What was more, these men with whom he had unwittingly associated himself could rise in any court in the land at any day hence and say: "Michael Brent was one of us. Under the name of Steuben, he took part in a crime." They could hold it over his head; the knowledge would hang like a Damoclean sword until the day of his death.

Burger left the lawyer and he went to his room. "Better stick to the house to-day," the cripple advised. "Them dicks may be on the prowl around these streets."

Norah's door, almost directly opposite his own, was closed, and he could hear no sound from within.

He lay down on the hard bed and stared at the ceiling.

Had it not been for the woman at No. 90 he would have abandoned his new identity, dropped the whole dangerous deception. But that woman, he was convinced, held the secret of the murders. The mere mention of Paul Gregory's name had saved him from exposure to Laboeuf. There was more to be learned, and, as a trusted member of Laboeuf's mob, he would have access to No. 90 and opportunity to talk to her again.

Brent was shrewdly certain that Laboeuf's anxiety to have him join the gang that very night was a test of his good faith. If he failed to appear, if he made excuses, he would be automatically under suspicion.

"This," he said to himself, "is the worst fix I was ever in."

Well, he could take part in no lawbreaking. That much was clear. But there was a possibility that he might be able to bluff his way out of the predicament. He would go as far as he dared, and leave a solution to Providence.

He was aroused by an uproar on the stairs, a heavy thudding of feet, a clamor of voices. He sat up, listening. At first he could distinguish nothing from the babel, for it seemed that three or four people were all talking at once, with a man's bull-like roar predominating; then, clear as a bell above the din, he heard a frightened, appealing, feminine voice:

"Father! Father! Where are they taking you?"

Norah!

Brent leaped to his feet. He was halfway to the door when he heard something that brought him to a sudden stop.

"It's the police, gal. Everythin's all right. It's a mistake they're makin'—" The voice of Midge, thin and whining.

The police!

Brent pressed himself against the closed door, listening.

"It's no mistake, you rat!" came the bull-like roar again. "We got you where we want you, this time. We'll just take a look through this room of yours before we bring you in."

The footsteps were thunderous in the hall.

"But what are you arresting him for? What has he done?" The terror and bewilderment in the girl's voice made Brent clench his hands.

"Who's this jane, Midge?" growled some one.

"She's my gal—my daughter. Leave her alone."

"Never knew you had one." They were crowding into Midge's room now, and through the thin walls Brent could hear every word distinctly. "We're takin' your old man down to the station house, lady."

"Why? He hasn't done anything wrong."

"Hasn't he? Suspicion of murder, young woman."

Her voice soared in a hysterical scream:

"Murder?"

"I never done it, Norah," whined Midge. "Don't you believe 'em. I never done it. It's all a mistake."

"Look through his trunk, Tim. Under the mattress." The two detectives were blundering heavily about the little room; a bureau drawer fell to the floor with a crash.

"What did you bump him off for, Midge?" asked one of the officers.

"I never bumped nobody off."

"Banana oil! If you didn't do the job yourself, you know who did."

"What job?"

"The mouthpiece that got his the other night. Mike Brent. What did you do with him?"

"I don't know nothin' about it."

"How come you were seen walkin' down the street with him the night he disappeared, huh? I knew that would hit you. Look at him, Tim! Guilty as hell! You know what job I'm talkin' about now, don't you? How come you were seen goin' up that street with him—the street where we found his hat? What did you do with him? Dump him into the sewer?"

There was a scuffling sound, and a subdued sob.

"It isn't true, is it?" asked the girl, imploringly.

"It's all a mistake, Norah," insisted Midge stubbornly. "I don't know what they're talkin' about."

"Where are they taking you?"

"We're gonna lock him up," growled one of the detectives.

"In jail?"

"Naw—the Ritz!"

A trunk lid closed with a bang. "Nothin' here, Joe."

"Well, we got the goods on him anyway. Put on your hat, Midge!"

They were leaving the room now. Brent heard a sharp, poignant cry, then Midge's whining voice: "Don't take on like that, gal. I ain't done nothin'."

"But what am I to do? I'll be all alone here."

"Come on!" growled one of Midge's captors. "We

can't stop here chewin' the rag all day."

Their footsteps receded down the hall, then went clumping down the stairs. They became gradually fainter and finally a distant door slammed.

Brent peeped out.

He had not heard a sound. Norah was leaning against the wall. She was infinitely appealing in her distress; her eyes were blurred, her fragile little body drooped like a flower, her delicate hands hung limply at her sides, more expressive of despair than her tortured mouth. She looked dumbly up at him.

"Tough luck, miss."

She tried to speak, but no words came. At last: "I don't understand it at all."

"He'll be back. Don't worry. They won't keep him."

She became transfigured with hope.

"Do you really think so? Those awful men—they seemed so sure he had done something wrong."

"It's about that case in the papers. They're pickin' up whoever they can."

"Why did they arrest him?"

Brent felt an overwhelming desire to comfort her, to take her in his arms and kiss the stricken eyes. He scarcely knew what to say. In the presence of this terrified girl he felt constrained and awkward.

"They—I guess they think he knows somethin' about this guy that disappeared."

"Who was he?"

"Some lawyer from uptown. He was down around here the other night and nobody seen him since."

"And—my stepfather was with him?"

"Aw, you can't believe all the dicks say."

He saw that she was crying. Her face was white and

Norah was leaning against the wall. She was infinitely appealing in her distress

without expression, but two big tears coursed slowly down her cheeks.

"Listen, miss, don't cry. It's nothin'. He'll be back all right. You'll see."

But she shook her head.

"They were so sure. I can't believe he's bad. He's all I have in the world. I don't know what to do."

"Don't cry. Please don't cry. Everything will be all right. Why, I know he didn't kill that guy."

The overpowering necessity of relieving her distress had betrayed him. The thing had been said before he realized it. Her eyes widened.

"You know?"

"Well—I mean—I'm sure he didn't."

"But what makes you so sure?"

He gestured helplessly, realizing that he had blundered.

"I—well, I just can't believe he did—that's what I meant."

"Did—did you know my stepfather?"

"A little."

She said nothing, but he knew that suspicions were forming in her mind. She knew he had come to the lodging house only that afternoon.

"I wouldn't worry about it too much, if I were you," he said swiftly, trying to gloss over his mistake. "In a case like this, the police often pick up anybody they can lay their hands on, but when they question 'em and can't learn anything they let 'em go."

She was obviously relieved.

"I hope that's what has happened this time. I'm all alone, you see."

"He's your stepfather, you said."

"Yes. I just came out from England. My mother is dead."

"I wondered. You don't seem—well, you're not just the sort I'd expect to find living in a place like this."

"I don't like it. My stepfather promised we'd move in a day or so."

"It ain't a very nice place, is it?"

"Horrible. You and Mr. Burger are the only people who have spoken nicely to me since I came here."

Brent was touched. He sensed something of the fear and the loneliness that had beset her in Chat Noir.

"I'll help you all I can, miss," he said humbly.

"It's good of you. Somehow, you seem different."

"You can trust me."

She nodded, as though she took this for granted. "I know. You've made me feel a lot better already. Perhaps it is only an awful mistake."

"Sure. Those dumb cops don't care whose feelin's they hurt. Mebbe he'll be back in an hour or so."

"I hope so."

She began edging away from him, back into her room. He did not want her to go.

"Must be pretty lonely here for you."

"I've had no one to talk to—except Midge," she said, simply.

"I'm lonely, too."

A more sophisticated girl would have caught the implication. But Norah took it merely as a statement of fact.

"But you have friends, haven't you? Don't you know the men around here?"

"I don't know any one very well. I haven't been around here very long."

She looked at him in a puzzled manner.

"Do you know," she said, "sometimes you talk—well, rough, just like the other men, and other times you don't."

This was dangerous, he reflected. He must remember to keep in character.

"I been to school a little more than some of 'em," Brent explained. "When you get kickin' around with other guys, you get to talk like 'em. But I don't know a lotta long words, or nothin', like that. Sometimes, when I remember it, or when I'm talkin' to somebody that talks nice—like you, now—I try not to use slang."

This ingenious explanation apparently convinced her.

"I'm glad you think I talk nicely," she said, smiling.

"I do. I've never met any one that talked so nice."

"You mustn't flatter me," she told him, a little breathlessly.

"It ain't flattering you. It's the truth. I've never met

anybody as nice as you. Around this part of the town, most of the girls are pretty hardboiled."

Shyly, she retreated another step. "I—I guess I'll say good-by now."

"Won't you talk to me some more?"

The door was closing. She shook her head. "You flatter me too much. You'll be making me conceited."

"But you'll let me talk to you again, won't you?"

She was peeping around the half-closed door at him, still smiling. "Perhaps."

"Why are you going away now?"

"I'm going to read for a while."

"Have you any books?"

"A few."

"If I bring you a book, will you read it?"

"Perhaps." The door closed.

This interview, brief as it was, encouraged Michael Brent greatly. He had made a favorable impression on the girl he loved—for he knew now that he loved her—and he felt like turning handsprings. This being undignified, he compromised by setting out immediately to buy her a book. This would certainly give an excuse for further conversation and on the common ground of literature he would advance his cause.

So, completely forgetting Burger's injunction to remain under cover for the rest of the day, he left the lodging house and went as far as St. Catherine Street before he found a book store.

In his enthusiasm he had not considered the fact that his finances were low and the purchase of a novel for two dollars and fifty cents reduced his capital to less than a dollar. He justified this extravagance, however, on the ground that he would have been certainly obliged to get in touch with Minton for more money within the week, and that day might just as well be on the morrow.

So he bought Norah a book that recommended itself to him solely because the jacket portrayed a man and a girl in ardent embrace, and hastened back to Chat Noir, keeping his cap pulled well down on his forehead.

If there were any detectives prowling about, they did not recognize him, and he returned to the lodging house, the book under his arm, quite pleased with himself. He even grinned cheerfully at the landlady, whose baleful glare would certainly cow any one but a light-hearted lover, and ascended the stairs, two steps at a time.

At the top of the second landing, however, he paused.

Norah's door was open, and he could hear a man's voice—a voice he already knew!

CHAPTER XXVI
THREE MEN AND A GIRL

IS heart stood still for a second as Michael Brent stopped on a landing of the stairway leading to Norah's room and listened to the voice of the man whose sinister power he dreaded and hated above all things.

"You must not be 'fraid of me. You think I am rough, maybe, because I scare you the other night. Pooh! That was only a joke!"

Laboeuf!

Brent's light-heartedness disappearcd, like air out of a punctured tire.

"You may have meant it as a joke, but it wasn't very funny to me," Norah was saying. "Was that all you came to tell me?"

"Oh, no! I come because I hear they take Midge away. It is so?"

"Yes."

Laboeuf laughed reassuringly.

"I don't want you to worry 'bout that. He will be back soon. We fix it right away."

Slowly Brent went down the hall. Laboeuf, leaning easily against the wall, his huge bulk dominating Norah's little room, glanced at him when he was in front of the doorway and greeted him with a scowl. Norah was standing in front of the window, her hands upon the sill, her whole attitude significant of nervous constraint.

Laboeuf nodded, insolently. Brent nodded in return.

"Hello," he said huskily.

The girl's face brightened.

"Hello, Mr. Steuben." Her eyes desperately invited him to remain. "Were you out for a walk?"

But Laboeuf was not one to brook interference from one of his own men.

"We talk business," he growled.

"Yes, just out for a little walk," said Brent, as casually as he could. He went into his own room and closed the door. Then he pressed himself against it, listening.

Her eyes desperately invited him to remain

"You know that fellow?" he heard Laboeuf ask.

Norah's reply was inaudible.

"So! You t'ink he's nice, eh?" Brent's heart leaped. "Maybe you not t'ink he's so nice if you know what I know about him."

"What do you know about him?" she asked sharply.

"Never mind. You learn, some time." Then he lowered his voice. Brent could hear only fragments of sentences, odd phrases. ". . . maybe you like me better . . . lots of money . . . when Midge comes back . . . you are pretty . . ."

Then, Norah's voice, clearly: "Don't shut that door!"

Brent stiffened.

"You should not be in my room anyway. I didn't ask you to come in. Leave that door open, please!"

Laboeuf's deep tones again. Brent heard the click of

a latch. He flung open his own door. A furious anger overwhelmed him at the thought of Laboeuf's foul presence even in the same house as Norah.

Her door was shut. There was a scuffle going on in the room. Then he heard her call out in a desperate, terrified voice: "Leave me alone! Take your hands off me!" Her voice rose to a scream. "Mr. Steuben!"

Then, abruptly, it was muffled. There was a sound of some one bumping against the wall.

Brent opened the door. In spite of the rage that consumed him, in spite of a murderous desire to rush in, to fling himself upon Laboeuf and throttle and batter the life out of his evil body, he forced himself to be calm.

Norah was struggling in Laboeuf's arms, in the corner by the window. She was twisting her head frantically from side to side, trying to escape his kisses. When the door opened Laboeuf looked up, a ferocious light in his eyes.

"Did you call me?" asked Brent.

Laboeuf stepped back, releasing the girl.

Brent's fists were clenched, the knuckles white. In the back of his mind hammered the one thought that he must keep himself in control.

They faced one another. Laboeuf's face was flushed dark with rage and passion.

"Why you come in here?" he roared.

Brent scarcely recognized his own voice. "She—she called me, didn't she?"

"If you mind your own business—"

Laboeuf's eyes were murderous.

Antagonism, Brent knew, would only defeat his own purpose. He managed an apologetic tone.

"I guess she's kinda frightened."

Norah crept slowly over to Brent, as though instinctively seeking the refuge of his arms. Shivering, she pressed her face against his shoulder.

"Don't let him touch me. Don't let him look at me like that again."

Her voice was childlike and imploring.

Laboeuf swallowed his defeat. Silently he straightened up, stepped over toward Brent.

"Don't let him touch me!" Her arms tightened around him.

"No, I won't let him touch you," said Brent, soothingly, and his own arms crept around her trembling shoulders.

"You have some t'ings to learn yet, Steuben," growled Laboeuf. "And one of them is—to mind your own business. I teach you."

He strode heavily from the room. His footsteps clumped thunderously on the stairs.

Brent looked down at the silky head against his shoulder. His arms crept closer about her slender body. With a sort of awed wonder he realized that she had made no effort to disengage herself. They clung to one another in silence.

At last she looked up.

Her cheeks were flushed, her eyes bright.

"Is he gone?" Gently she tried to draw away from him, but Brent's arms tightened.

"Norah," he said huskily. "I love you."

She gazed up at him, startled.

"I've loved you since the first time I saw you. I do, Norah. I really do. Maybe you'll think it's strange, when you only met me a little while ago; but I've seen you before, and I've thought of you ever since. I tried to find you again."

He blurted out his confession desperately, swept off his feet by her nearness and by the depth of his emotion.

"Why—why, when I saw that Laboeuf had even touched you, I wanted to kill him. You shouldn't be alone, Norah. You're too young and sweet and pretty. If you'll let me—"

She was not as amazed by this tumultuous declaration as she might have been. She was too honest for that. Almost any woman knows when she has inspired adoration, even the most ingenuous, and from the moment of her meeting with this shabby young man who seemed so strangely different from the others of Chat Noir, she had been aware of a feeling toward him that she could not define.

But when she had crept into the sheltering circle of his arms after her encounter with Laboeuf, it had been with no thought that this man was a comparative stranger to her.

On the contrary, it had been with the instinctive knowledge that she would find safety and security and protection, as though she had known him through all her life. His rough shoulder had been comforting against her burning face, and his arms had been warm and strong about her.

The affair of Laboeuf, however, had been a catalytic agent that threw everything out of normal proportion. Conventionally, she would have withdrawn from Brent's embrace, would have been embarrassed or frightened by his incoherent passion, they would have recovered their composure and masked their feelings behind trite and awkward phrases.

But they were caught up in a flame. She knew she wanted his arms about her; it did not matter that she had known him only a little while, for he did not seem a stranger to her any more.

Everything seemed very far away. There was no lodging house, no mean little room, no past, no future, nothing but the strength of clinging arms and the sweetness of approaching lips, release from all restless longings and loneliness.

A gasp, a startled exclamation shattered the spell.

Brent looked swiftly around. There, in the hall, staring at them in amazement, stood Burger.

The cripple's face was tense with incredulity and despair. Then, as Brent's arms dropped limply to his sides and Norah stepped back in confusion, Burger's mouth worked oddly; he made a futile little gesture and croaked:

"What—what—"

There was nothing to say. Brent felt himself going crimson with embarrassment.

Burger's amazement gave way to anger.

"So this—so this is what you're up to?" he stammered.

And still Brent was silent.

"You're a fast worker, Steuben," the cripple snarled bitterly.

Brent took a step toward the door.

"We'll talk it over outside," he said, anxious to avoid a scene in Norah's presence.

Burger's eyes narrowed. His voice was threatening.

"No, we won't. We'll talk it over right here!"

"It won't do any good to start an argument about

this—”

“Won’t it? Who do you think you are, anyway, you double crossin’ crook’? What do you take me for—?”

“Please, Mr. Burger!” appealed Norah.

But the cripple had been aroused to an ungovernable fury.

“I save you from the dicks, and what do you do? I make a friend of you and tell you things I’ve never told nobody before, because I thought you was decent, and how do you pay me back? You do me dirt!”

“I didn’t ask you to save me from the dicks. I didn’t ask you to tell me anything, did I?” demanded Brent. “I’m grateful for what you’ve done—”

“It looks like it! What a dumb egg I am. I figured I could trust you, and you start right in by gettin’ fresh with her!”

“You’ve got me all wrong, Burger,” Brent protested, wearily. He could understand the cripple’s outburst, fed by jealousy and despair and defeat, his soul tortured by the knowledge that one whom he had befriended and in whom he had confided his deepest secrets had held in his arms the girl for whom he had longed in an agony of hopeless desire. “I’m not as bad as you think—”

“No! You’re worse. You’re lower than a snake! There ain’t nobody could be as rotten as you!” His blue lips were drawn back from his yellow teeth, his eyes blazed; he was like a ferocious animal.

“Mr. Burger! You mustn’t talk like that. What do you mean by saying—?”

“What do I mean?” he stormed, facing Norah. “I’ll tell you what I mean. What do you know about this guy, eh? What do you know about him, outside of the lies he's been tellin' you? I can tell you plenty. Did he tell you why he was livin' here? Did he tell you he's nothin' but a crook?"

Gently she tried to draw away from him

By the expression on Norah's face, Burger saw that this shot had told.

"I'll bet he didn't say nothin' when Midge was pinched. Did he? Did he let the dicks get a look at him? No, I'll bet he didn't. I'll bet he hid in his room until they took Midge away. I'm right, ain't I? And why?"

"Burger!" pleaded Brent, grasping him by the arm.

But the cripple shook him off.

"He's crawlin' now, ain't he? He's afraid I'll spill somepin' that he doesn't want you to know. Well, I'll spill it quick enough. The dicks are huntin' him for the very job Midge got pinched for. Did he tell you that? He's the one that should be in jail not Midge!"

He whirled about, head thrust forward, pointing a trembling forefinger at Brent.

"I dare you to tell her it ain't true. Tell her if it ain't true the dicks are lookin' for you."

"What's the use of talkin'? You know why they're lookin' for me. I told you all I had to do with that job."

"Sure, you told me. They're lookin' for you because you hocked a watch that belonged to that mouthpiece. You told me how you got it. Mebbe you told the truth. But here's Midge in jail now instead of you. Does she know that?"

Norah was beginning to grasp something of what Burger meant. She looked at Brent incredulously.

"It isn't true, is it?" she asked. "You're not in trouble with the police, are you?"

Brent was silent. He dared not look into her clear eyes.

"Tell her! Tell her!" snarled Burger triumphantly.

He was stung to defend himself. "There was some trouble," he admitted. "But it's not serious. I haven't done anything wrong."

Her expression clouded.

"But is it true—what he says? That they made a mistake and arrested my stepfather instead of you?"

"No, it wasn't a mistake—"

"Don't lie!" Burger shouted.

"Norah, I'm telling the truth. There was some trouble about a watch, but I give you my word of honor I came by it honestly."

Burger shouldered him aside.

"Lissen," he said. " I'll tell you what's happened, and then he can deny it if he wants to. There was a lawyer disappeared from down around here the other night. It's been said that he was murdered. This man," and he gestured toward Brent, "pawned that lawyer's watch, and when the police come after him to find out how he got the watch, he beat it, and he's been hidin' from them ever since. If they could lay their hands on him they'd put him in jail, for they think he knows what happened to that lawyer, see! If this guy hadn't got away from the cops they'd never have arrested Midge."

Norah was very white.

"Will you go away, please?" she asked Burger in a stifled voice. "I want to talk this over with—with him, alone."

"He'll tell you lies—"

"Please!"

Her tone was imperative. Burger, muttering to himself, and with a final injunction to Brent to "laugh that off," turned away and went to his room.

Norah looked steadily at Brent for a while. Then:

"When my stepfather was taken away you said something that made me wonder. You said you knew he wasn't guilty. You seemed very sure."

"I meant—"

"Please let me speak. Mr. Burger says the police are looking for you now. Is that true?"

"Yes."

"They think you know something about the murder. Do you?"

"Norah—!"

"I want to know. You said you were sure Midge was innocent. Are you still sure?"

"Yes."

"Why?"

"I can't tell you why, Norah. You must believe in me—"

Her eyes were pitiful.

"Tell me—only one thing. Do you know what happened to that man who disappeared?"

"Don't ask me that, Norah. You don't understand. I can't tell you now—there are reasons—"

"Oh, you do know," she whispered.

He was silent.

"You do know?" she repeated.

At last he said: "Yes, I know."

"And my stepfather is innocent."

"Midge never killed him."

"And yet you will let them keep Midge in jail?"

Her voice was sorrowful.

"You know he is innocent, and you could clear him if you wished, but you'll let him stay in jail. You don't know what it means to me. He is the only person I have in the world. I am all alone now, and I have no money. I don't know what I can do."

"Norah! I can't clear him now. Perhaps to-morrow. Soon. It isn't because I'm afraid of the police. I have reasons. I can't explain them even to you."

But she turned from him.

"Please go away."

"You must believe me, Norah!"

" What are your reasons?"

He was beaten. " I can't tell you just now."

He had one glimpse of her white, tortured face, contempt in her eyes, as she swung around. Then the door slammed with a violent crash.

CHAPTER XXVII
COMRADES IN CRIME

DOZEN times that evening Brent resisted the impulse to return to Norah and tell her everything. The knowledge that she held him in contempt was galling, infinitely more so when he knew that by a few words he could again set himself right in her eyes and prove to her that he was not a criminal lurking in hiding while another man stood accused of his crime.

But he forced himself to wait. He had already clashed with Burger and Laboeuf, and he saw that his sojourn in Chat Noir would be brief. It was possible that these altercations had already cost him everything he had gained.

In any case, Sam Steuben was approaching a crisis, and until this crisis passed, for good or evil, it would be wise to hold his tongue.

He lay on his cot, staring at the ceiling, and smoked numerous cigarettes. When he thought of that moment of ecstasy when he had held Norah in his arms, of the mystic flame that had consumed them both, of their mutual acquiescence to a destiny that seemed to have brought them inevitably to that embrace, he wanted to rush out of the room, fling open the door that separated her from him, and tell her all that he had been forced to hide.

But it wouldn't do. He had guarded his secret well, and he could not risk exposure now, when a few more hours might see victory or defeat.

He picked up the book he had bought for her. It had laid neglected upon his bed. He read a chapter, found he could remember nothing of what he had read, and cast the book aside.

He had decided to go to No. 90 in spite of what had happened. Probably Laboeuf would order him away, but he could not afford to risk losing the chance of a word with the woman who had shielded him that afternoon.

If he could but gain entrance to that house once again; if he could have but five minutes' uninterrupted conversation with that woman he might learn something. Even if it meant swallowing Laboeuf's insults, the opportunity was too valuable to ignore.

So it was that at the appointed time Michael Brent made his way to No. 90. The mastiffs, in their shed, were restless, and raised a hideous clamor. They were half-starved brutes, chained in their dark hovel for days at a time, and they were like wild beasts. Their ferocious baying made Brent's scalp tingle. He could hear the rattling of chains as they flung themselves halfway out of the shed entrance at the sound of his footsteps.

"I'd last about two minutes if one of those maneaters got loose," he muttered.

They sensed that he was a stranger, and went into a veritable frenzy. But their clamor died as quickly as it had risen, when the back door opened and a woman's voice spoke sharply, imperatively, in French. A few low snarls and the animals were still.

Brent ascended the steps. The light streaming through the door shone on him, and the woman, peering down from the threshold, said: "Ah! I hoped it would be you. *Entrez.*"

He stepped insidc. She closed the door quickly.

"You are here first," she told him. "It is good."

Her voice was low and tense.

"Ain't Laboeuf here?"

"Not yet. He come back soon. No matter—I hoped you would come here again. Tell me," she said, coming closer to him, "what you know about Paul?"

"What do I know about him? What do you know?"

She grasped the lapel of his coat impatiently.

"There is no time. Tell me, quick—what has happen to him?"

Brent stared at her, incredulously. "Don't you know?"

She shook her head.

"I know nothing. Tell me!"

"Why, he's dead."

Her face was close to his own, and he saw the shadow of dread that passed over her, the terror that leaped into her eyes. Her grasp on his coat tightened, and she seemed to waver, as though she had received a blow.

"He's dead? Paul? Dead!"

There was no pretense—he saw that in a glance. She was dazed by the shock of what he had told her.

"Sure he's dead. Didn't you know?"

She shook her head wildly. Her voice rose.

"I didn't know! No one tol' me. Oh, *Mon Dieu*—he's dead! And I never know." She was shaken with anguish.

"Why should any one tell you?" demanded Brent. "What was he to you?"

If she heard the question, she paid no heed. Instead she cried out hysterically:

"What happen? How did he die? Tell me quick!"

And just then, out in the yard, one of the great dogs began to howl. It was the weirdest, most melancholy sound imaginable, deep-throated, unwavering, prolonged. On the one mournful note it hung on and on, as though it would never end, and it aroused sinister echoes, charged the very atmosphere with terror.

They listened, almost spellbound.

The howl trailed sadly into silence, and then it rose again. A crash, a curse, a sharp yelp, and the howl abruptly ceased.

The woman stepped back, guilty. She arranged her disordered hair, snatched up a towel from the table, and stepped over to the kitchen sink.

"Laboeuf!"

She picked up a cup and began drying it.

"Quick!" she said in a low voice. "What happen to him?"

Brent sat down in a chair by the table. Heavy footfalls sounded on the steps.

"Murdered."

There was a choked, gasping sound.

"When?" Her voice was scarcely audible.

The footfalls clumped on the landing.

"Tuesday night," whispered Brent. He lounged in the chair, apparently studying his finger nails.

The door opened.

Laboeuf, a cap drawn down over his eyes, a black sweater emphasizing his huge shoulders, strode into the kitchen. When he saw Brent he halted, his swarthy, brutal face set in a scowl. He glanced suspiciously at the woman. In that tense moment Brent could not help but admire her composure. She dried the cup, set it down on the table, picked up another, and said calmly:

"You are late."

Laboeuf slammed the door behind him.

"And what if I am?" he growled.

He took off his cap and flung it aside.

"So!" he remarked, staring insolently at Brent. "You came after all."

Brent returned his gaze coolly.

"Why not?"

Rubbing his hands, because the night was cold, Laboeuf went over to the stove.

"I t'ink maybe you 'fraid to come back."

Brent shrugged.

"You got me all wrong this afternoon. I wasn't tryin' to butt in. I heard some one call me, so I came out. That's all." He rose from his chair. "If you're sore—if you don't want me here—"

Laboeuf laughed shortly and waved him back.

"Sit down! Why should we fight about dat, eh? If you had not come back I would say: 'Good! He has not nerve.' But you come. Fine wit' me. You have nerve. Stay!"

"I need the money," Brent muttered.

"Well, you make some to-night."

"What kind of a caper is it?"

Laboeuf, warming his hands over the stove, laughed again.

"You like to know, eh? You find out soon. We have no trouble."

Then the dog howled again. Deep and full, the melancholy clamor rose solemnly in the night. It was hideous. Laboeuf swung around.

"What's wrong wit' him?" he demanded irritably. "He howl like somebody going to die."

The woman, frightened, made the sign of the cross.

Laboeuf wrenched the door open and bellowed a savage command in French. The howl subsided to a whine. Some one was coming across the yard. Laboeuf stood peering out into the darkness until two men emerged into the stream of light and began to ascend the steps. He gave a grunt of satisfaction. They exchanged greetings in French.

The newcomers entered the kitchen. One was a short, plump youth, scarcely out of his teens, with a bulldog chin and a forehead wrinkled and receding like that of a chimpanzee. His little eyes gleamed shrewdly. His name, it appeared, was Henri.

The other was a thickset, unsavory looking fellow with tawny, uncombed hair that fell down over his brows. He had a cast in one eye, and for neckwear he had a black silk handkerchief knotted about his throat. He was called Rioux.

There were no introductions. They merely nodded casually to Brent and ignored him thereafter.

Laboeuf talked to them in French. In low tones they discussed the approaching venture. The woman,

Blanche, finished drying the dishes and went into the next room.

After a while Laboeuf donned his cap. He went to a cupboard, brought out a bottle of liquor and poured four drinks. They drank the whisky straight, and in silence. Rioux wiped his mouth with the back of his hand.

Laboeuf opened the back door.

"We go now," he told Brent.

They went out into the night. It was pitch black, with a bitter wind. When the door closed, Brent almost stumbled on the steps. Henri was only a vague shadow ahead. Rioux and Laboeuf were behind him.

He felt like a prisoner under guard, on his way to the gallows. He did not know where they were going, what crime they intended to commit; he knew only that their errand was lawless, and that only by defiance, flight or betrayal could he escape becoming involved.

Defiance was impossible. He had gone too far for that. Only by taking to his heels at the first opportunity, or by raising an alarm that would bring the police about their ears, could he avoid being drawn into commission of a crime. He certainly could not go through with it; Sam Steuben's bluff had been called.

Henri led the way down the lane, his boots clattering on the frozen mud. Rioux and Laboeuf plodded behind. They emerged in Chat Noir. An automobile, dark and sinister, was drawn up at the curb. Henri opened the rear door and clambered in. Brent hesitated, but when Laboeuf came up and said impatiently: "Get in. Get in," he obeyed.

He sat back beside Henri. Then Rioux wedged in

beside him, and Laboeuf got in the front seat and slammed the door. The driver was a darkly anonymous shadow.

The car jerked forward and bumped its way down Chat Noir. No one spoke. The side curtains were down, but they afforded no protection against the cold. Brent turned up his coat collar and thrust his hands into his pockets.

The automobile poked its nose tentatively into the Main, then swerved into the thin stream of traffic. It roared on up the Boulevard, speeding between the intersections, slowing down, picking up again. The driver was skillful, the powerful engine ran smoothly.

They left the Boulevard and followed a bewildering course through a maze of streets, as though trying to shake off a pursuer. Finally, in a dark thoroughfare, the car slowed down and slithered to a stop.

The man at the wheel relaxed, groped in his pockets for a cigarette. A match flared.

"You ready, Steuben?" asked Laboeuf in a low voice.

Brent answered huskily: "Sure. But I gotta know what it's all about."

"I tell you," returned the leader. "On this next street is a gambling club. To-night is a lot of money there. One man alone went in a little w'ile ago wit' five t'ousand in his belt. We take this place, see!"

"Yeah. And where do I come in?"

"We try to stick this place up once before, but they are wise. They have a man who watch the street door. He is a tough baby, and he knows us all. He do not know you. He is one of Richer's men, and this club pay Richer so his gang will not bother them, and they hire this guy to watch for stickups. If we go in there now he will shoot—quick. He does not know you. We stop in front of the door. You go in, and w'en you see this guy, tell him Marcoux wants for to see him."

"Who's Marcoux?"

"A friend of his. He look out. He see this car. It belong to Marcoux. We borrow it to-night. He come over—and we take care of him. Henri and Rioux and me will go upstairs and take the joint. You watch outside. If any one try to get out, you stick him up and keep him inside. If policc come, fire one shot and get in the car to cover us w'en we come out."

Brent licked his dry lips.

"I'm to go up to this guy that's watchin' the street door, tell him Marcoux wants to see him, and bring him out to the car. When he's outa the way, you will go in and take the place while I'm on lookout. That right?"

"That's right," growled Rioux. It was the first time he had spoken to Brent that night. "And see that you keep your eyes open when we're workin' inside. If you do see a cop, and he ain't on the run, lay low. He might only be the flattie on the beat and not wise at all."

"Got a rod?" piped Henri in a thin, effeminate voice.

Brent dared not admit that he had entered this escapade unarmed.

"Yeah."

"Away we go, now," said Laboeuf.

The car shot forward.

Brent felt sick at the stomach. There seemed to be no possible avenue of escape. From the moment he left the car he would be engaged in commission of a crime, as an accessory at least. It occurred to him that he might gain a respite if he did not deliver the decoy message to the gangster at the door. He could ask some harmless question, then return to report failure. But if that plan failed, Laboeuf would simply devise another. There seemed to be nothing for it but ignominious flight—and in that event he would not dare show his nose around No. 90 or Chat Noir again.

The car swept around a corner and sped silently down a wide avenue. Laboeuf and Rioux were peering through the side curtains. Brent could see little. The windshield was steamed over, with the exception of a segment left clear by the automatic wiper. The car seemed to be slowing down, but in a moment its speed increased again, and Laboeuf looked back.

"He's not there."

"I didn't see him neither," said Rioux.

"The light is on over the door, but there is nobody."

"If he ain't on the job, let's take it, then," piped Henri.

"He's on the job, don't worry," Rioux said. "He's maybe in one of them shop doorways, or else he's up on the landin'."

At the end of the block their driver pulled the car around and they went back on the other side of the road, Rioux and Laboeuf again peering out at the lighted doorway in the middle of a row of stores.

"It's up to you, Steuben," said Laboeuf. "He is not in sight now. You must go in and find out if he is on the stairs. If he is not, come back and tell us, quick."

The automobile had reached the corner and was swinging around.

"How'll I know him? I've never seen him before," objected Brent, still playing for time.

"You'll know him all right," snarled Rioux. "He's a

"He's dead? Paul? Dead!"

tough baby. There ain't nobody else outside but him, anyway."

The car, keeping close to the curb, was gliding down toward the two-story brick block with the illuminated street entrance. The shops on the ground floor were in darkness.

Brent's heart was thumping. If he made a break for liberty the moment he reached the pavement, he would be shot down in his tracks. If he went into the building and failed to find any means of exit save by the street door, he would be trapped. If the gangster on guard became suspicious and ordered him away, he would be forced to return to the car or run the risk of open flight. It was hardly likely that he would be able to obtain entrance to the club without credentials.

He saw that Henri was turning up his coat collar.

Rioux was pulling the black silk handkerchief up about his chin, in readiness for use as a mask when he should enter the building.

The car came to a stop just a few yards from the entrance.

“Be quick!” whispered Laboeuf. Rioux opened the side door. Brent caught the glint of light on an automatic.

He began to clamber out.

A lean, black shape shot swiftly alongside and pulled in to the curb immediately in front of them with a squeal of brakes. At the same moment Laboeuf gave a shout of alarm. Their driver sprang to life, gears clashed, the car slid back in reverse.

Rioux grabbed Brent’s coat, flung him violently back onto the seat, and slammed the door. The lawyer had a confused glimpse of men tumbling out of the car ahead.

The gears grated again, the engine roared, they shot out toward the middle of the road. Some one was shouting. He heard a shot; the glass of the windshield shattered.

CHAPTER XXVIII
SENTENCE OF DEATH

ENRI and Rioux scrambled to the floor of the car. Laboeuf ducked out of sight. The driver crouched low above the wheel. A bullet ripped its way through the side curtains. Brent flattened himself against the seat.

A whistle trilled madly. Men shouted. A fusillade of revolver shots broke out. Something whacked against a rear fender. The other car was roaring in pursuit. The street that had been so quiet a few moments ago was now clamorous. *Thwack!* The impact of lead on steel. Brent fairly hugged the cushions.

He was hurled to one side as the automobile rounded the corner at reckless speed. It skidded—once—twice—seemed to stagger erratically, then straightened out and went zooming down a side street. The tumult behind was muffled. Then it suddenly broke out afresh as the pursuing car swerved around the turn.

"Somebody tipped 'em off!" yelled Rioux. "They was layin' for us."

Henri was babbling unintelligibly in the darkness.

The heavy car streaked down the road at terrific speed. Whining of the wind mingled with the steady howl of the engine. The slightest error in judgment, the merest loss of control on the part of the man at the wheel, meant disaster and death. Brent could see nothing.

He thought they were already traveling at top speed, but suddenly the howl of the engine changed to a scream, something bore down on them with a hollow roar, a bell clanged in alarm, there were two violent jolts and a speeding trolley shot behind them. Air brakes hissed, but already they were racing on. Death had missed his prey by inches.

Brent was trembling as he rose up from the cushions and took a hasty glance out the rear window. The trolley had stopped. The road was blocked. He saw the street car jolt forward, and then the pursuing automobile shot around the rear end. The respite, however, had given them a lead of another block, and the driver was quick to take advantage of it by turning at the next corner.

The breakneck pace slackened momentarily, the rear wheels slipped sickeningly over the smooth surface of the road in a wide arc; then the car shot forward again and Brent found himself launched on top of Rioux, who cursed him. He was just scrambling back onto the seat again when the car made another hazardous turn, brakes squealing.

Their driver's dexterity at the wheel was amazing, his recklessness bloodchilling. "How about it?" he shouted, without turning his head. Brent looked back. There was no sign of the other car. "can't see 'em!"

The man bore down on the wheel, and they swept around the next corner. Another block and another turn. He made the automobile twist and dodge and race madly from street to street with complete mastery and with utter disregard of the peril that lurked at every intersection.

Finally Laboeuf's head and shoulders appeared.

"We shake 'em, I guess."

Henri and Rioux crawled back on the seat beside Brent. A glance out the rear window showed them that the pursuers evidently had been shaken off. The only car in sight was a small coupé, rolling along slowly.

"We gotta get a new bus, quick," snapped the man at the wheel. "Every bull in town will be watchin' for this one by now. They'd spot us by the windshield alone."

"We look for one," said Laboeuf.

Their speed slackened. They were in a wide avenue, a street of solid residences, and before long they spied a sedan parked by the curb. They passed it slowly, and Laboeuf peered at it as they went by.

"Looks good," he commented.

Their driver pulled in to the side of the road. He left the engine running, then scrambled out, taking a bunch of keys from his pocket. He looked around. The coupé that had been following them clattered past. He ran quickly back to the sedan. In a little while they heard him call out.

Laboeuf shut off the engine and they swiftly abandoned the touring car. The exchange took less than a minute. They sped away in the stolen sedan, and by devious streets returned to Chat Noir. When they turned into the familiar thoroughfare, Henri took a deep breath.

"I'm sure glad to get back here again," he declared.

"We're lucky, that's all I can say," Rioux grumbled. "If it wasn't for Pete's drivin' we'd be in the cooler now—or else in the meat wagon. I tell you, when the windshield went I could hear the lead singin' past my ear."

"I'd like to know how they got wise to us."

"We find that out," Laboeuf said ominously.

The sedan came to a stop at the lane, and they clambered out. Pete, the driver, said he would take the car a few blocks away and abandon it.

"I guess that's all for to-night, eh, chief?" he asked, apparently unruffled by the narrowness of their escape.

"You want more?" grinned Laboeuf.

The sedan glided off. Pete shouted: "It 'll do me for a while," and then the tail light went bobbing down the road.

Laboeuf turned to the others.

"Come wit' me," he said shortly, and moved into the blackness of the lane.

Brent did not follow.

"You won't be needin' me, will you?"

Laboeuf looked back. "Yes."

"Well, everythin's off for to-night, ain't it? After that!"

Laboeuf came to a stop, regarded him truculently.

"You t'ink so, Steuben?"

"I figgered we'd be scatterin' for a while."

"I figure different."

"Come on," snarled Rioux. "Don't stand here chewin' the rag. We gotta talk this over."

Reluctantly Brent followed. He had just been congratulating himself on his successive escapes from the frying pan and the fire. Sam Steuben's bluff had been called by neither gangsters nor police.

This new development was not promising. There was something hostile in Laboeuf's tone, something menacing in the attitude of the other men, but he reflected that perhaps they were merely upset over the disastrous outcome of the night's escapade. He fell into step with them, and they strode in silence down the dark lane.

They were just entering the yard back of No. 90 when one of the dogs, aroused by their approach, suddenly emitted a deep, long-drawn howl.

The sound was so unexpected that Henri gave a squeak of fright, Rioux stood stock-still, and Laboeuf cursed. It was a lonely, chilling howl, prolonged and sad. Laboeuf shouted a savage command, and followed it up by picking a tin can from the ground and hurling it against the side of the shed where the dogs were housed.

Laboeuf strode on toward the house, fuming.

"That dog, I shoot him if he howl like this any more."

"First time I ever heard him beller like that," observed Rioux.

"I t'ink he must be sick."

"Maybe somebody's goin' to croak," volunteered Henri cheerfully.

Brent experienced an uncanny sensation, familiarly known as "a creepy feeling." Laboeuf, too, had recalled the homely superstition earlier that evening when the dog had howled. The quavering, melancholy wail still rang in his ears. The blackness of the night, the chill of the autumn wind, the menacing shadows of his companions, all conspired to invest the evil omen with a quality of dreadful significance.

"Yes," Laboeuf said slowly. "Maybe somebody is going to die."

They went into No. 90 by the back way. The kitchen was in darkness. Laboeuf switched on the light, closed the door and locked it.

Henri, rubbing his fat hands, went over to the stove. But Rioux folded his arms and stood with his back against the door, in an attitude curiously forbidding. Laboeuf, without taking off his cap, sat down beside the table. His heavy feet were planted firmly, his chin was sunk in the folds of the black sweater; beneath the brim of the cap his somber eyes were fixed steadily on Brent.

"Now," he said, "we find out what happen to-night."

Brent was conscious of their hostility. It was as tangible as a wall. They seemed to be waiting for something.

"We got a tough break," he remarked casually.

Laboeuf's eyes were hard. His underlip jutted brutally.

"Yes," he agreed. "We got a tough break. You know where we got that tough break, Steuben?"

"Where?"

"When we let you come in wit' us."

There was a long silence. Then Brent said: "How come?"

"The blame is wit' you."

"You figger I was a jinx?"

Laboeuf shook his head. "It was not a jinx. That is

only bad luck, and it cannot be helped."

"Wasn't this bad luck?"

"Steuben, you make pretend you do not understand me, but you know what I mean. I give you a chance. I take you in wit' us. And the firs' time we go out on a job, somebody tips off the police."

"You mean—you think I snitched?"

"I am *sure!*"

"Who the hell else could 'a' snitched?" broke in Rioux hoarsely.

"How could it have been me?" Brent shouted.

Laboeuf's fist crashed on the table. "Steuben, it was you!"

Desperately Brent tried to brazen it out. "Where do you get that stuff?" he demanded. "Just because I'm a new man, you can't hang that on me. Didn't I need the jack worse'n any of you? Was it my fault the dicks come along just then?"

"Yes!"

"It wasn't. I'm no stoolie. I'm regular, I am."

"*Somebody* tipped off the police," declared Laboeuf relentlessly. "Six people know about this job to-night. There is Burger, who tell us about it firs', and get all the dope for us. He done work like that for me a long time, and if he snitch on me he cut his own throat. There is Pete, who drive the car. If he would snitch he would not drive like he did to get us away tonight. There is Henri and Rioux, here, who have work wit' me often, like Burger. There is me. None of us could snitch, for it would jus' be worse for us in the end. There is you. There is only you left. Somebody snitched. It was not us."

"How could I? Why, I didn't even know where we

were goin' to-night. I come along blind, and you know it. You didn't tell me what kind of a caper it was, where it was, or nothin'. How could I tell the bulls where to go when I didn't know myself?"

Laboeuf considered this.

"Burger told you."

"He didn't."

"You left here wit' Burger. And I always know Burger talk too much. You had lots of time to find out from Burger about this job."

"Sure, Burger told him," interjected Rioux. "Burger always was too gabby."

"Bring him here and ask him."

"There is no need," said Laboeuf heavily. His fingers drummed on the table. "Steuben, I tell you somet'ing. When I heard the dicks were looking for you about that watch, I am puzzle."

"Why?"

"I have my own reason. I want to find where you get that watch. I tell Burger to bring you here. You tell me about the watch, and it sound all right. I t'ink you are regular, and I want to keep you here—"

"Yeah, I know why you wanted to keep me handy. Midge got pinched this afternoon for bumpin' off the guy that owned that watch, didn't he? You were afraid of that, and you figgered that you'd hang onto me and turn me in if there was a chance that it would clear him."

Laboeuf grinned.

"You are very smart," he returned coolly. "However, it is not the point. I wonder if you are as tough as you say, so I give you a chance to show me. But I guess wrong. The police are tipped off. And Midge was pinched this afternoon. Two bad t'ings happen so soon after you come here. It makes me t'ink, Steuben, that you are a dick after all."

Brent laughed scornfully.

"A dick? If the dicks had grabbed us to-night you'd 'a' seen how much of a dick I am. Didn't they chase me all to hell and gone to-day when they got onto that turnip?"

"It looked good," broke in Rioux.

"It was all a plant to put you right with us."

Laboeuf reached beneath his coat and withdrew a heavy automatic. He put it on the table.

"Steuben," he said levelly, a curious glitter in his eyes, "it does not matter if you are a dick or not. It all comes to the same t'ing. If a man snitch, he mus' be punish. You know that, eh?"

"Sure I know it."

"And you know what happens to him, eh, Steuben?"

Brent was silent.

Laboeuf gestured toward the automatic.

"That!" he said significantly.

Henri coughed. Rioux lit a cigarette.

"You mean you're goin' to give me the works?"

Laboeuf did not answer. Instead, he picked up the automatic and tapped its nose gently on the table.

There was no other sound.

Then Laboeuf glanced up at the doorway leading into the next room. An expression of surprise crossed his face. He frowned. Rioux and Henri also looked faintly astonished.

Brent turned around. From the shadows of the other room a figure had appeared, as silently as a ghost. Blanche was standing there, motionless. Her untidy black hair framed a white, haggard face, but in her posture there was a somber dignity. Her stony eyes were fixed on Laboeuf.

Her lips scarcely seemed to move as she said in a hoarse voice: “Leave him alone. He didn’t do it.”

The automatic dropped to the table with a thud.

“What?”

“He didn’t do it.”

Laboeuf leaned forward. He was astounded.

“What do you mean?”

“I say he didn’t do it. It was me.”

Laboeuf stared at her in stupefaction.

“You!”

“It was me. I heard you and Burger talkin’ the job over. I told ’em where to go.”

“You—you tip off the bulls?” Laboeuf demanded incredulously.

“They were here.”

Rioux sprang forward, his mouth agape.

“They were here? When? What brought ’em here?”

“They come just after you left.”

Laboeuf’s big hands were clenched.

“Why do they come here?”

“Midge.”

Laboeuf started halfway out of his chair. His eyes bulged. “Midge? He talked?”

She nodded.

“He spilled everything. They’re after you.”

Rioux whirled about. “They’ll be back. Why didn’t you say somethin’ about this?” His hand was on the doorknob when Laboeuf roared at him: “Stay here!” and snatched up the automatic to emphasize his command. Rioux turned. “But they’ll be comin’ back,” he shouted. “We gotta get out of here!”

“Wait!”

“But lissen, chief—” piped Henri.

Laboeuf silenced him with a snarl: “Shut up!” Then to Blanche: “They tell you this?”

“They said Midge had loosened up. He told ’em he bumped off that lawyer, and you put him up to it. And he told ’em more about other jobs.”

“And you—you snitch on me? You tell them where to find me?”

“Yes, I told them,” she returned defiantly.

“Why?”

Her face suddenly became distorted with passion.

“Because of Paul!” she screamed at him. “It was because of Paul I did it. You thought you could keep that from me, eh?” She advanced toward him, her fingers crooked, like claws. “I wish the police had killed you! I know now what happen to Paul—”

Laboeuf rose so abruptly that the chair toppled over with a crash. He struck the woman savagely across the face. She staggered.

He struck her again and she dropped to the floor. Blood began to trickle from a corner of her mouth. Laboeuf towered over her. He was in a cold fury, his nostrils dilated, his lips drawn back from his teeth.

“So! You double cross me, eh?”

She was half stunned, but she managed to gasp: “Yes, and I’ll do it again! You’ll get yours—”

“Shut up!” Laboeuf whirled on Brent. “Now I see why you two look so strange when I come in to-night. You tell her t’ings, eh? You try to make trouble, you?”

Rioux grasped his arm.

"There ain't time, chief. We gotta be gettin' out of here. The bulls will be in here any minute. You know what it means if Midge has squealed. We gotta run for it."

"We gotta get out of town," clamored Henri. "That's what it means."

"Out of the country!" Rioux said, tugging at Laboeuf's sleeve. "We still got time to make a get-away; chief. For God's sake let's beat it. Gauthier's boat is in the harbor to-night, leavin' in the morning. He'll look after us."

Henri and Rioux were frantic with anxiety, aware that any moment might bring the police swarming about them. They sweated with fear. But Laboeuf shook them off.

"If I have that Midge here I break his neck!" he shouted in a terrible voice. "I send him word to keep his mouth shut and we fix him up—but he squeal." He cursed the luckless Midge foully. "We will go, then, but I take wit' me that girl of his. I take her wit' me—"

"Don't go draggin' any women into this, chief," begged Rioux. "We ain't got no time. The bulls—"

Out in the yard the dogs suddenly broke into a furious uproar. Above their frenzied barking sounded gruff voices, and then a rush of heavy feet on the steps. At the same instant came a heavy knock at the front door.

"They're here!" screeched Henri.

Laboeuf, an insane light in his eyes, flung up his arm and wheeled about on Brent. The automatic blazed.

CHAPTER XXIX
BURGER DOES HIS BEST

LTHOUGH Brent sprang aside when he saw the automatic bearing down on him, he would never have escaped the bullets had it not been for Blanche.

An instant before Laboeuf pressed the trigger she shrieked and flung her arms around her master's knees. The scream startled him, the impact threw him off his balance, his arm joggled and the automatic jerked sidewise. The bullets were buried in the wall. Before he could recover himself, Rioux had seized his wrist.

"Lay off, chief!" Rioux shouted desperately. "They're here. We gotta lam."

The door quivered under a thunderous pounding.

Only then did Laboeuf appear aware of their danger. A gruff voice shouted: "Careful, men! He's using his gat." Some one else commanded in French: "Open up in there!"

At the front sounded the report of a revolver, like the slam of a window.

Her fingers were crooked like claws

Laboeuf kicked viciously at the woman clinging to his knees. She fell back, sprawling on the floor. Henri had disappeared. With a snarl of defiance, Laboeuf plunged into the next room, and Rioux crowded at his heels, panting with fear.

Glass crashed at the front of the house. The kitchen door resounded to thumps and kicks. The knob rattled. "Careful, men. Be careful."

A thud from the next room. Rioux growling: "Down you go, chief." Bang, bang, bang at the door. Shouts. "Watch that side lane, Legris!" Thump, thud. "It's locked— Break it down— Get your guns ready—"

A rush of heavy feet. Wood splintered as the police launched themselves at the door.

"All right!" Brent called out. "I'll open it." He was just reaching for the key in the lock when Blanche screamed: "No, no! There is a way out. I show you. Follow him. Laboeuf!"

She was pointing toward the next room. Brent turned, undecided. Blanche, believing that surrender meant arrest for him, was trying to save him.

"I show you. Quick!"

The house was a little island in a sea of tumult. Dogs were barking, men were shouting, doors thudded under a rain of fists.

"They will arrest you. Go now."

She urged him into the other room. There was sufficient light from the kitchen to reveal an open door that led into a clothes closet. Blanche knelt down, tugged at the boards, and a square section of the flooring came away. A black gap was revealed, with the top steps of a flight of stairs leading to the darkness beneath.

"Hurry! It is to the cellar. There is a way out."

"And you?"

"I will stay."

Brent scrambled through the opening, descended the stairs. A great crackling and snapping told him that the police were battering down the door. He looked up, saw her shadowy figure vaguely defined above the trap. She lowered the door.

He was in utter blackness. Feet thudded on the floor overhead as he blundered down the steps. There was a confused uproar of voices.

Brent was in the cellar of No. 90.

Laboeuf and his companions evidently had escaped by now, for not a sound emanated from the darkness. At the foot of the steps Brent halted, irresolutely. The cellar was cold and damp and clammy. He lit a match. Its feeble glow revealed only beams above, and a dank stone wall.

The thudding on the floor overhead became more pronounced; he heard some one roar: "Where are they? How did they get out?" Then Blanche screaming: "I don't know. I don't know, I tell you."

She was not protecting Laboeuf: it was solely because of her conviction that Brent was a criminal like the others, and in danger of arrest, that she refused to divulge the secret of the trapdoor.

Brent blundered about the dark cellar. It was like a prison. There was an outlet somewhere, but he could not find it. He lit another match, but the stone wall seemed solid, unbroken and impregnable. He was in an agony of haste, for he could still hear Laboeuf's threat concerning Norah: "I will take her with me!"

He stumbled over a heap of earth, got to his feet, collided with the wall. His fingers scrabbled at the hard surface. The police were banging tumultuously about overhead. They would find the trapdoor before long.

It occurred to Brent that he should go back, give himself up, proclaim his real identity, and then lead them on the trail of Laboeuf. But he saw that this was impossible. They would not believe him. Michael Brent was dead. Midge had confessed to his murder. He would be held, and in the meantime Laboeuf would be escaping, carrying Norah with him.

The lawyer floundered about the black cellar. Groping in his pockets again he found one match left. He struck it on the damp wall and it flared up weakly. Just before the yellow glow expired, he caught sight of a gap in the stone a few feet away.

The flame died. Brent stumbled toward the gap. His groping hands found an opening in the wall.

The earth was wet underfoot. Brent made his way through the opening. He found himself in a narrow tunnel, the walls of which were not stone, but clay.

It was unfathomably black.

Step by step he moved blindly ahead. The tunnel sloped gradually upward, became smaller and smaller. Brent slipped once, and sprawled in the mud. He got up and went on.

At last the tunnel became so small that he was forced to crouch in order to avoid striking his head on the roof. And still there was no sign of an opening, no glimmer of light.

He stumbled against a step hewn out of the ground. Groping, he found that he had encountered a little stairway in the hard earth. There were only a few steps, and then he collided with a solid object that barred the way above.

The lawyer reached toward this. It was a wooden door. He pushed at it; the door yielded. The cold night air fanned his face.

The police would be watching the yard. He must be cautious.

Very slowly Brent raised the door. He could hear the dogs barking and howling furiously a short distance away. From the sounds he judged that the tunnel outlet was just behind the shed.

Inch by inch he thrust back the barrier. The air was good. He could see a faint patch of sky and the silhouette of a distant roof above the black mass of the nearby fence. He waited and listened. There was a great hubbub in No. 90; the dogs were in a frenzy.

He peeped out. There was no one in sight. The lane was but a few yards away.

Gently he pushed back the door and and scrambled from the tunnel. The shed where the dogs were imprisoned reared its black mass to his left. He stole cautiously toward the lane.

Brent had taken no more than three steps before he heard a sound that sent him plunging silently into the shadow of a rubbish heap. It was a voice, sharp and clear, and it seemed directly behind him. It was followed by the noise of crunching footfalls.

"If they're not in the house yet, they must be hiding in the yard somewhere, Beauchamp. Keep an eye on that lane."

Brent tried to efface himself against the rubbish heap. He heard an earnest, respectful young voice say: "Yes, sir."

The dogs barked ferociously. Their chains rattled as they flung themselves about their little prison in fury.

"What a racket those hounds are making! I'll shoot the devils if they don't quit."

The footsteps drew nearer.

Crunch—crunch—crunch—steadily, through the half frozen mud. A man was coming around the corner of the shed. Brent crouched in the gloom.

The constable spied neither the fugitive nor the dark opening in the ground. He went on out to the lane, stood there for a while and finally returned.

"Anybody in sight?" called out his superior.

"Can't see any one, sir." Brent held his breath. But the constable investigated the deep shadows at the base of the fence before he returned to the front of the shed. "I was thinking—about them dogs."

"What about them?"

"Just an idea, sir. If these men have cleared out somehow, it mightn't be a bad stunt to let one of these dogs loose. Maybe it 'd pick up the trail."

"Not a bad thought, Beauchamp. I'll suggest it to the captain."

Brent turned his head slowly. He could just see their bulky figures beyond the corner of the building.

"We'll all get hell if they slip through our fingers," the officer grumbled.

"I don't see how they did it. We had the house surrounded."

"This guy Laboeuf is a slippery bird."

"He won't get away, sir."

"You never can tell. We should have had him. Damn funny thing. The woman gave us the tip off on that job he was on to-night, in the first place, and now she won't loosen up and tell how he got out."

"If we hadn't got into that smashup when we were chasin' them, we'd have got back here quicker."

"Lucky we weren't all killed. Whoever was handling Laboeuf's car was a drivin' fool."

Brent dared not stir. Would they never go away? His only concern was the necessity of overtaking Laboeuf before Norah came to harm. Every second was precious.

He saw an arc of radiance from a flashlight. The constable was moving back toward him again. The light came closer. It crept along the ground, nearer and nearer. Another moment and he would be exposed in that brilliant circle. Then the light stopped.

"Here! What's this? Look!"

"What have you found?"

"A hole! See! And steps."

The officer came running over. The two men peered down into the tunnel, playing the flash light on the steps.

"It leads into the cellar. That's it. The cellar. Down you go, Beauchamp. Get your gun ready. They may be in there yet."

Muttering with excitement, they scrambled down into the opening.

Brent waited until the second head and shoulders had disappeared. He sprang to his feet, skirted the rubbish heap and raced out into the lane.

There was no one on guard. He bolted across into the deeper shadows on the other side. He ran panting down the lane, crossed a vacant lot, vaulted a fence and made his way to the yard back of his lodging house.

Stumbling over tin cans and rubbish, Brent crossed the yard. The back door was wide open. He was suddenly assailed by a feeling of dread.

He ran through to the front hall and pounded up the stairs to the first landing. There he could hear a gabble of voices from the floor above.

Down the corridor a lodger was standing in the doorway of his room, gazing toward the stairs with an expression of stupefied amazement. Another lodger, who had evidently dressed himself in haste, for there were no shoes on his feet, was bounding up the second flight.

Terror clawed at Brent's heart. Something was wrong. He hurried up the steps.

In front of the open doorway of Norah's room he saw a group of people. The landlady, in a torn wrapper, was gesturing helplessly with her fat hands, and saying: *"Mon Dieu! Mon Dieu!"* over and over again in a husky voice. The others were lodgers, in various stages of attire. They were all talking at once, their tones hushed. One of them was saying: "Somebody had better get the police."

Brent pushed his way through the group. They were crowded in a semicircle about a figure sprawled on the floor at their feet.

It was Burger!

He lay on his back, clad only in trousers and undershirt. One knee was drawn up in a grotesque manner; the crippled arm was stiffly outflung. The front of his undershirt was black with blood.

He was dying, and the lodgers gaped at him and gabbled in awed voices while the landlady groaned: *"Mon Dieu! Mon Dieu!"*

Norah was not in the group. Through the open door Brent saw that her room was empty.

Brent knelt down by the dying man. "Can't you get a doctor for him?" he asked the landlady sharply.

"I phone for one," she babbled. "He's not come yet. *Mon Dieu!* A murder in my house!"

"We can't let him lie on the floor. Here, help me put him on a bed."

Two of the lodgers moved forward, but Burger shook his head.

"Don't move me!" he said in a cold, thin voice. "It hurts too much."

The effort exhausted him. He gasped.

"Burger! Burger! What happened?"

The eyelids flickered.

There was recognition in the filmy gaze, an anguished appeal. His lips moved soundlessly. Then one word seemed torn from the depths of his shattered chest.

"Laboeuf!"

"He shot you?"

His whisper of assent was inaudible, but his lips

formed the word: "Yes."

"Tell me, Burger. Did he take her?"

A flame of implacable hatred blazed suddenly in the dull eyes.

"Laboeuf came."

Burger's fist beat the floor in the agony of his struggle for breath. By a supreme effort he gasped: "He rap at her door. Said Midge was out of jail, had to see her."

"Yes?"

Burger twisted his head wearily from side to side. He was very weak now.

"I heard him. Knew he was lying."

"You tried to stop her?"

"Came out. Told her not to go." The voice died away, and although the lips still moved, there was only an unintelligible murmur. Then, with startling clearness: "—and he shot me."

"What about Norah? What about her, Burger?"

The fist beat impotently at the floor. "She fight," whispered Burger. "He carry her away."

The landlady broke in tumultuously: "She near scratched his eyes out. I hear that gun go off, and when I come out of my room he's just dragging her out in the lane. *Mon Dieu!* It is terrible."

Burger clutched at his throat.

"Guess I'm goin' to kick off," he muttered.

The landlady moaned: "We should get the priest."

Burger shook his head, weakly.

"Wouldn't do me no good." His eyes were closed. He spoke as though in a dream. "I wouldn't mind croakin' so much—if only—I could 'a' kept him—from gettin' his hands on her."

“Don’t worry, Burger,” Brent said reassuringly. “They’ll get him. The bulls are after him now.”

The blue lips quirked in a smile. “ Ah! The bulls!”

“They’re huntin’ him this minute.”

“First time,” whispered Burger, “they ever did me a good turn.” He sighed. “She—she knows I did my best, anyway.”

Death was near. Brent got to his feet. The movement, slight as it was, brought an imploring cry.

“Steuben!”

“What is it, Burger?”

“Don’t—don’t let him get her!” Burger seemed to summon all his ebbing strength, and he cried out huskily: “There is no one like her. No one. She is so kind—and—so pretty!”

He turned his face to one side, as though falling asleep. They heard him whisper: “So pretty!” Then he shivered, as if from cold. His clenched fingers relaxed. He was dead.

CHAPTER XXX
THE MASTIFF

EAUCHAMP, the young constable who had suggested turning one of the dogs loose on the trail of Laboeuf, saw his plan adopted. The discovery of the cellar passage indicated only too clearly the method of the fugitive's escape, and the harassed captain who had taken personal charge of the raid seized at this last straw.

But when it came to actually releasing one of the infuriated mastiffs, the police found themselves facing a difficulty not easily overcome. The first constable who entered the shed was almost bowled over when one of the huge animals launched itself upon him. He retreated hastily.

The next volunteer, advancing bravely enough, found his courage oozing when he saw the flaming eyes and gleaming teeth, and heard the clamor that greeted him as he ventured as far as the doorway.

He stepped back, mumbling that the only way to get the dogs out of the shed would be to shoot them first and then drag them out.

Matters were thus at a deadlock when the captain thought of the woman.

"Maybe she can handle 'em," he said, and ordered Blanche brought out of the house.

She came sullenly, a constable grasping her arm. She had obstinately refused to tell the police how Laboeuf had escaped, she had been stubborn in her insistence that she would give them no help whatever, and the captain had slight hope that she would aid them now. But, to his astonishment, when their purpose was explained to her, she consented eagerly.

"If it is to catch Laboeuf, I let him loose."

She wrenched her arm free of the constable's grasp, and advanced boldly toward the little shed.

As she entered the door she spoke rapidly, soothingly, in French. Almost instantly the animals ceased their furious plunging and frantic barking under the spell of her voice. They whined and crept toward her, bellies on the ground, tails lashing. The police could hear her talking to them in the gloom.

A chain jangled. In a few moments she emerged, one of the great dogs by her side, the leash wrapped about her wrist.

The police gave ground, for the mastiff bared its teeth at them and growled menacingly. A sharp word from the woman, however, and the brute was submissive, fawning on her. It was a gigantic, evil-looking beast with murderous jaws; it had the savage, sullen ferocity of a captive who refuses to admit defeat. But toward the woman its attitude was unmistakably gentle.

"Laboeuf keep him hungry. I feed him sometime when I can, so he like me," she explained simply.

"We'll need something to give him the scent," declared the captain. "Something Laboeuf has worn. Some old clothes—"

Blanche shook her head.

"He understand me."

She led the mastiff back of the shed, back to the entrance of the secret tunnel. There she spoke to it shrilly, waving her arms, stamping her foot. She repeated the name: "Laboeuf! Laboeuf!" over and over.

The animal circled around, its nose to the earth, whining with excitement, plunging so that she could hardly retain her grip on the leash.

Then, abruptly, it found the scent of its master. A deep-throated howl and the dog sprang violently away, the leash dangling behind. The animal sped toward the lane, baying. In a moment the gaunt shadow had disappeared in the gloom.

The captain had not been prepared for this. His men bolted in pursuit, but the house would have been left unguarded, so he bellowed orders. Everything was in confusion. Hurriedly he detailed two constables to remain behind, then dispatched the others to follow the dog.

By that time the brute was far down the lane, his frightful baying awakening clamorous echoes.

Beauchamp, however, had ignored his captain's shout. He did not turn back like the others. He wanted to be in at the death. The success or failure of the mastiff to run Laboeuf to earth became an intensely personal matter with him; after all, it had been his own idea. He raced down the lane in pursuit of the fleeing animal, his greatcoat flapping about his legs.

He gained ground when the brute left the lane and

plunged into a yard back of a lodging house, circled about for a moment, clamoring, then raced out into the lane again and away. When he came even with the yard he was astonished to see a dark figure stumble out of the gloom, just a short distance ahead of him, and also take up the chase.

This dark figure was Michael Brent. The lawyer had just emerged from the lodging house, frantic with anxiety for Norah's safety, almost sick with the knowledge that there was slender hope of picking up Laboeuf's trail now.

Then he saw the mastiff come plunging out of the shadows. He remembered the conversation he had overheard between the two policemen, and when he saw the animal circle about and go loping back toward the lane again, he sprang down from the steps and raced across the yard. Hope blazed in his heart.

His great fear was lest Laboeuf should have reached an automobile and thus made his escape with the girl he had abducted. No mastiff could trail him then. He knew that it was the man's intention to take refuge on one of the boats in the harbor. In the maze of shipping how could he hope to hunt out the fugitive?

But the great dog still held the scent. His gaunt body streaked through a patch of light that fell across the lane from a near-by window. Then he vanished.

Brent heard the pounding of feet behind him. He looked back and saw the constable, but he did not slacken his pace. They were on the same errand—with the difference that the constable sought Laboeuf as a cold matter of duty, while Brent sought him with rage and hatred in his soul.

The mastiff was howling and barking insanely now.

Brent saw the animal flinging itself at the door of a little house set in a short distance from the lane. At the same moment Beauchamp came up beside him, and they were abreast of one another as they ran into the yard.

The mastiff whirled about, its teeth bared, snarling. The constable shouldered Brent aside and plunged toward the door. He was just wrenching his revolver from its holster to shoot down the animal when it sprang. A great body surged through the air. The mastiff had launched itself full at Beauchamp's throat!

The terrific force of the onslaught was too much for the constable. He staggered and fell. His revolver spun from his grasp into the mud. They went rolling over and over in a desperate struggle.

Brent flung the door open.

In the dimly lighted room he saw Laboeuf. Norah was in his arms, fighting vainly for release, and one heavy hand was over her mouth, preventing outcry. Beyond the table crouched an old woman, an evil, hook-nosed crone, her seamed face a mask of terror.

As Brent sprang through the doorway, Laboeuf hurled the girl to one side with such force that she fell against the wall and crumpled slowly to the floor. Laboeuf's automatic was out. He pressed the trigger, but there was only a metallic clatter. The clip was exhausted.

Brent sprang at the bigger man. Disconcerted by the failure of his weapon, Laboeuf was caught off his guard. A swinging blow struck him on the side of the face.

The boss of Chat Noir stumbled, brought the barrel of the automatic down viciously, but missed, lost his balance and fell.

As he crashed to the floor, Brent pounding at his face, he gave a hoarse cry. It was not a cry for help, it was a purely involuntary shout, but the mastiff heard it.

Beauchamp had been unable to fight the animal off, and had it not been for the heavy collar of his greatcoat the teeth of the infuriated dog would have torn at his throat. As it was, the shout saved him. The mastiff swung around through the doorway to Laboeuf.

But the big man had no need of assistance just then. Tightening his grip on the automatic, he brought it down with crashing force on Brent's head.

Again and again he hammered mercilessly. The stunning blows weakened Brent, trying to defend himself. Then the mastiff pounced on him. Its sharp teeth tore at his coat collar.

Laboeuf struggled out from beneath the animal. He was just getting to his feet when a revolver barked explosively from the darkness beyond the door. Beauchamp had recovered his weapon.

A dazed expression came into Laboeuf's face. His mouth opened. His knees buckled. He sank slowly to the floor, his teeth bared in a defiant leer. The automatic fell from his hand.

There was a second shot. The mastiff gave a strangled howl, flung up its head, twisted violently to one side and sank down in a heap. It writhed a little, snarling, and then lay still.

Beauchamp strode into the room, his revolver raised. He saw that Laboeuf was still alive, and he covered him swiftly, but Laboeuf's only defiance was a curse.

Feet thudded out in the little yard. Uniforms appeared in the doorway. Revolvers gleamed in the light. There was an uproar of voices. Beauchamp snapped handcuffs on his prisoner.

The dog had fallen across Brent's body. Weakly he thrust aside its inert form. His face was torn and bleeding, his coat and shirt were in shreds, he was still half stunned from the blows of the automatic.

With a little cry Norah hastened to his side. Her face was deep with concern, and although the tumult about them was growing in volume as policemen crowded into the room, he heard only her anxious voice.

"Oh, are you hurt? Are you hurt?" she was saying. "Please—"

Her cool hands caressed his bloodstained face. He smiled at her, and with a sob she crept into his arms.

CHAPTER XXXI
OFFICIAL DOCUMENTS

ICHAEL BRENT, smartly attired in a new suit that had been delivered to his apartment that morning from the best tailoring establishment in Montreal, immaculately uncomfortable in a stiff linen collar, polka-dot cravat and starched shirt, sat back in the swivel chair and put his feet on the desk. His new shoes glistened.

Across from him sat Minton in all the somber glory of his Sunday clothes, looking and feeling a trifle naked because of a hair cut to which he had submitted only on the insistence of his wife.

Brent held a number of typewritten sheets in his hand.

"I have here," he said, "copies of a couple of documents that the Crown Prosecutor was good enough to send me this morning. They are very interesting, Minton."

"No doubt, sir."

"The substance of them has already appeared in the newspapers. Oh, those newspapers! Ever since I got out of that mess I've been interviewed and photographed so often that I feel like a—like a—"

"Like a transatlantic flyer, sir?"

"That's very good, Minton. Yes, like a transatlantic flyer. Although I must say the vaudeville and movie people have been very backward. And I haven't yet been asked to indorse any popular brand of cigarettes. There's that to be thankful for, at any rate. However, these papers make rather good reading. Want to hear them?"

"Certainly, Mr. Brent."

The lawyer glanced at his watch—the precious watch with his initials on the case. "We have lots of time." He turned to the first document. "This is the woman's statement."

Minton permitted himself a small chew of gum and settled back to listen. Brent read aloud:

" 'My name is Blanche Gregory. My age is twenty-eight years.' "

"Is that all?" exclaimed Minton in astonishment. "Why, she looks considerably older, sir."

"No wonder! Her life with that man—but here's the rest of it. And, Minty, please don't interrupt."

"No. sir."

" 'I am the sister of Paul Gregory, who is now dead. My parents are Pierre and Celinie Gregory, who live in the village of St. Rosarie, County of Pontiac, Province of Quebec. I came to Montreal seven years ago, and worked in a factory for several months. It closed down, and I was out of work.

" 'My money gave out. I was lonely and hungry. A man came up and spoke to me on the street one day. This man was Raoul Laboeuf. He persuaded me to go to a restaurant with him. He said he could get me a job. He took me to his house. He wanted me to live with him. I liked him, and I had no place to go. I remained at his house. I have lived with him since that time.

" 'He was not a good man, and when I spoke of leaving him he took my shoes and stockings from me and locked them up. After a while I knew there was no use going away from him, because I was a bad woman, and I knew that if any one employed me he would tell them about me. I did not write to my parents, because I did not want them to know.

" 'At first I did not know much about Laboeuf, but from the people who came to the house I found out that he was at the head of a gang of thieves and holdup men, and that he also owned two gambling houses. One night I saw him shoot and kill a man named Casavant, who had been in his gang and had given information to the police!' "

"Gracious!" exclaimed the horrified Minton.

" 'Laboeuf was a strange man, and I think sometimes he was insane. He used to keep the dogs locked up, and would only let them out when he would take them for a walk through the streets. He liked to make people stare at him, and he would laugh when the dogs snapped at them. He had a power over the dogs, and although he starved them, they would always obey him. He said he had a power over women, too. Sometimes I would give the dogs something to eat, when they were very hungry, if Laboeuf was not around. He found out about this and beat me very hard.

" 'He knew that I had seen him shoot Casavant, and he said that if I ever went away he would follow me and kill me, because I might tell on him. I went down into the cellar one day and found that some earth had been dug up at the back. It looked like a grave. I think Casavant is buried there. I can take you to that place.' "

"And, as you know, Minty," Brent interpolated, "she did take them to the place, and Casavant was buried there."

He resumed:

" 'One day a woman came to the house when Laboeuf was out, and told me that a young man had been searching in the streets and in the dance halls for me. This woman knew my name. She described the man, and I knew it was my brother, Paul. I told her to tell him where to find me, and to come to the house at a certain hour next day. I was to leave the front window blind up if Laboeuf was not at home. I thought Laboeuf would be out, but he stayed in the house, and I was not able to see my brother. I looked out the upper window, however, and saw him pass by, and I recognized him.

" 'I sent word to him again, and this time I was able to talk with him. He said my parents were greatly worried about me, and thought I might be dead, because they had not heard from me for so long. He wanted me to go home to them, and said they would forgive me.

" 'I told him about Laboeuf. I even told him about Laboeuf being a murderer. My brother wanted to tell the police and have Laboeuf arrested, but I made him promise not to do this, because I was afraid. He asked me to leave No. 90, but I knew it would not do any good. I was ashamed to go home, and I was afraid Laboeuf would follow me and kill me as he had threatened to do.

" 'Paul came back to the house twice to persuade me. The last time he was at the house Laboeuf returned early, and Paul did not get out without being seen. Laboeuf made Midge Tapley follow Paul to find out where he lived. Then he beat me and made me tell him who Paul was.

" 'That night Laboeuf went out. When he came back he acted very strange. I did not hear from my brother any more. I asked Laboeuf, and he said he had told Paul to leave me alone, and Paul had said he was through with me, because I was a bad woman, and not fit to be his sister. I felt very sad because of this.

" 'It was not until the man named Steuben came to No. 90 that I learned Paul had been murdered. I knew then that Laboeuf had killed him. I was angry, and when the police came to the house that night and said Midge had confessed to killing the lawyer, and had said that Laboeuf made him do it and helped him, I told them where to find Laboeuf.

" 'He escaped from them, and would have shot Steuben, but the police came to the house. The reason I did not help them at first was because I did not want to see Steuben arrested. That is all. Laboeuf was an evil man, and I am glad he is dead. I am going back to my parents.' "

There was a long silence. Brent put the document aside.

"What a life that poor creature must have led!" Minton exclaimed pityingly.

Brent turned to the next sheet.

"But it doesn't clear up the mystery of the Hilliard girl's death," Minton continued. "Of course she didn't know anything about that—"

"This paper," interrupted Brent, "is the antemortem statement of Laboeuf. The worthy Beauchamp deserves congratulations for killing him, but I'm glad Laboeuf lived long enough to blurt out this much. If ever there was a colossal scoundrel—oh, well, Blanche was right. He was certainly insane. Listen:

" 'My name is Raoul Laboeuf. I killed Paul Gregory in his apartment. I did this because he was trying to persuade his sister, Blanche Gregory, to leave me, and because he threatened to inform the police on me. I found that she had told him I killed Casavant. To protect myself, I killed him. I struck him down with my automatic.

" 'On the table I found a letter from a woman, warning Gregory not to go back to No. 90, because she was afraid he was in danger. From the letter I found that she knew about Blanche. I saw that the letter was from Gregory's sweetheart, and I knew that when Gregory's body was found, she would tell the police. I tore up the letter.

" 'While I was in the apartment the telephone rang. I answered it, and a girl asked for Gregory. I asked if her name was Margaret, the name signed on the letter. I told her I was a friend of Mr. Gregory, and that there had been some trouble about Blanche. I said Gregory had left word that she was to meet him in Mount Royal Park. I told her a certain place, and said it was very important. She said she would go.

" 'I went to the park and waited for her. I hid in the bushes. I had to wait a while after she arrived, because there was a policeman near. When he went away I shot her. I make this statement of my own free will, because I know I am dying.' "

Brent tossed the paper back on the table.

"That," he said, "clears our charming client, Hinky Lewis."

Minton shuddered.

"To think of it! The cold-blooded rogue!"

"He was in a trap, Minty. One crime inevitably led to the next."

"What will happen to Midge?" Brent grinned amiably.

"When a man like Midge starts to talk, he does the job very thoroughly. He has already coughed up the details of a dozen minor offenses, but he is so relieved to learn that I'm alive, and that he won't be arraigned for murder after all, that the prospect of five or ten years isn't worrying him very much. If he can live long enough without his dope to see the end of his sentence, he will be deported. Exit our friend Midge."

He looked at his watch again.

"I guess we'd better go. Norah is waiting at the hotel."

Minton straightened his black necktie with nervous fingers.

"I—I wish you all possible happiness, of course, Mr. Brent, but—but I do wish you could have found somebody else. I'm not used to it. I've only been at one wedding in my life, and that was my own. It was bad enough, goodness knows. I—I'd rather be there just as a spectator."

"Go on with you," said Brent, pushing him out of the office. "Somebody has to give the bride away."

He closed the door and they went down the dusty stairway into the sunlit street.

TO THE READER

If you enjoyed this book, you will be glad to know that there are many others just as well written, just as interesting, to be had in the Fiction House Press Library.

You will find the Fiction House Press Library online at

www.FictionHousePress.com

www.ingramcontent.com/pod-product-compliance
Lightning Source LLC
Chambersburg PA
CBHW021954010726
47494CB00003B/730

9781947964327